PRAISE FOR
WHICH BRINGS ME TO YOU

"Sexy, funny, and touching…provides keen insights
into sex, love, and coming to terms with one's own
unruly imperfections. A winner."
— KIRKUS REVIEWS, starred review

"The writing is piercing, funny, and emotional. Baggott…
and Almond's…collaboration makes for a delightful
and robust work that readers will not be able to pu
down as they savor every messy confession."
— LIBRARY JOURNAL, starred review

"Sharp humor and insights into the modern
psyche pervade the book."
— PUBLISHERS WEEKLY

"Coauthored by pop culture darlings Baggott and Almor.
this is a surprisingly poignant and meaningful read…
a no-baloney, no-holds-barred, show-me-your-soul roll in
the emotional hay. No gimmick here, just a great story."
— BOOKLIST

"Enormously satisfying…coauthors Steve Almond and
Julianna Baggott expertly capture the swooning optimism
hiding in letters that are often arch or even glib…it is the
bright and funny writing, even in the telling of sad stories,
that makes the book great reading."
— MSNBC

WHICH BRINGS ME to YOU

BOOKS BY STEVE ALMOND

BOOKS BY JULIANNA BAGGOTT

First edition: 2023
ISBN 979-8-212-41724-2
Fiction / Romance / Contemporary

Version 1

Blackstone Publishing
31 Mistletoe Rd.
Ashland, OR 97520

www.BlackstonePublishing.com

STEVE ALMOND &
JULIANNA BAGGOTT

WHICH BRINGS ME to YOU

BLACK
STONE
PUBLISHING

"And what was it that delighted me? Only this—to love and be loved."

The Confessions of Saint Augustine (JB)

"The world is full of love that don't come true."

R. B. Morris (SA)

Portions of the following have appeared in the magazine and/or anthologies:
Lit Riffs
Sex and Sensibility
Sixteen
Glamour Magazine
Ninth Letter

PRELUDE

know my own kind. We're obvious to each other. I suppose this is true of other kinds, too: military brats, for example, anarchists, mattress salesmen, women who once got ponies as birthday gifts.

And so I see this guy standing under a white crepe paper wedding bell (so sad, this dopey bell, so exhausted and ghastly, even it wants to be someplace else.) He looks embattled. It was a long service in a stuffy, sour church. All the men have sweated through their suits. The photographer has just told him to smile. The smile is beyond him, but he musters something instinctively boyish then gets hit by the flash.

He's a few people in front of me in line, signing the wedding book. I recognize him as one of my people. Without knowing him at all, I'm already convinced his jacket's too big because it's somebody else's. (My own kind doesn't plan well.) And the cheery boutonniere, already crumpled (Did he bump into something? Did he get hugged by somebody's overzealous mother?) was pinned to his lapel against his will by somebody—his sister? His do-gooder friend who loves him out of a sense of charity, like donating to a nonprofit without the tax deduction? And while pinning it, this sister, this do-gooder said things like: *This isn't supposed to be agony, you know. They didn't invite you as a form of torture.* Still he can't help but take the new couple's abundant joy a little personally, like they're just doing all this to rub his nose in it. The paper wedding bell, really, was that called for? I watch him sign and shuffle off to look for a seat at the edge of things (our kind can't get enough of edges) never mind that he's been given a slip of paper to indicate he's supposed to sit at table seven. (I'm at fifteen.)

My own kind. I'm not sure there's a name for us. I suspect we're born this way: our hearts screwed in tight, already a little broken. We hate sentimentality and yet we're deeply sentimental. Low-grade Romantics. Tough but susceptible. Afflicted by parking lots, empty courtyards, nostalgic pop music. When we cried for no reason as babies, just hauled off and wailed, our parents seemed to know, instinctively, that it wasn't diaper rash or colic. It was something deeper that they couldn't find a comfort for, though the good ones tried mightily, shaking rattles like maniacs and singing *Happy Birthday* a little louder than called for. We weren't morose little kids. We could be really happy.

Once there may have been an early tribe of us. We'd have done alright at cave wall art, less so at hunting. We'd have only started a war if traumatically bored. (Boredom is our most dangerous mood.) But most likely we broke up and scattered. The number one cause: overwhelming distraction.

A wedding is the worst scenario. We're usually single—surprising, I know—and least comfortable when socially required to say *Awww*, about kittens, sure, or greeting cards, and, in the present case, horrible toasts where weepy accountants say things like: *To the happy couple. Reach for the stars!* Weddings are riddled with socially enforced *Awwwing*. And so I'm pretty sure that I'll meet up with this guy at the bar where we'll amuse the bartender, and we'll wander the golf course, talk pop culture, play the good game of cynicism. I'm fairly certain that we'll have sex awkwardly, like in his car or in the coat check once it's abandoned midway through "YMCA" and "Shout!" (though I might regret missing the opportunity of seeing middle-aged men rip their pant seams singing *A little bit softer now, a little bit softer now*), and later one of us will call the other one or not or we'll both think about it and we won't. It's a little exhausting.

I reach the registry and I wonder who I should sign in as, just thinking associatively: Miss Pacman, Miss Jackson-if-you're-nasty, Miss Led, Miss Taken, Miss Understood. I choose Miss Chubby Petunia because there's something awful about the hug of this dress.

I slide my finger up a few names and there he is: Ted Nugent, address: The Kingdom of Rock and Roll. Under the comments section, he's added what I take to be a seminal Nugent tenet: "I test drive all meat." A nice choice, really, in the grand scheme. Nicely done.

It's a wedding. I refuse to describe it in detail. I don't know why I'm here. I'm suddenly blurry on particulars. Am I related? Is this a work thing? It doesn't matter. The groom hovers around shaking hands. When there's a lull, a hand shortage, he goes out and finds more and pumps away. The bride's face is deep red, almost purple. She's gasping for breath because her gown is too tight. It makes her look like a giant fishbelly.

They've long since wilted under the strain of all this honeyed adoration, but the photographer keeps shooting them and they keep smiling and the guests keep saying *Awww*. The band ("Fast Train") radiates an indentured pitifulness. Their sound quality sucks, but they make up for it with jacked amps, and a lead singer who wants to be Carol King or Queen Latifah. She can't decide.

I avoid the guy in the crumpled boutonniere during the dancing and the cake cutting and the throwing of stuff. I also avoid the cousin of the groom who seems to think he's the Marquis de Sade of his junior college. When I go out the back door to walk around the grounds, I'm not thinking about my own kind at all. I'm touring my love life, the Madam Tussaud version that exists in my head. It's plain that there was a dogleg turn I missed, the one that would have landed me in the wedding dress. It doesn't matter how much I hate the dress, of course, or this grand affair. It's only that love—something pure and less groping for glamour—still holds a certain promise, and I've done bad by it.

It's dusk. The golf course grass is clipped to an inch. I walk down a bit of a slope. There's a pond, a green, a pole, and an abandoned golf cart. And down a little ways to the left there's a figure, staring at the ground.

I walk downhill a little farther until I'm a few yards away. Now I see that he's staring at a white lump on the ground. I say, "Have you heard that Ted Nugent is supposedly at this wedding?"

He looks up and nods, as if he half expected me. "I can't comment on that," he says. "Just not ready to release any kind of statement."

He smiles a little. He's pretty. He has full lips and wet blue eyes. He's tall and hunched and rumpled. He points to the white lump on the ground. "Dead cat. Caucasian. Cause of death unknown."

"Maybe he was an older white republican cat," I say. "I hear golf courses are where most of them come to die." And here I am doing all of these things I can't quite stop. I lick my lips and rub them together, squint in this way that I think makes me look more exotic or at least more interesting, but now, upon reflection, probably makes me look like I'm near-sighted. I look at his shoes and then work my way up, slowly. "Have you poked at it?" I ask.

"What?"

"The cat. You should always poke at a dead thing you find. Didn't your mom ever teach you that?"

"I was raised by nuns," he says. "Hot, horny nuns."

It's gotten darker by now and he's looking a little softer, a little more toothsome, against the yawning green of the fairway. I can feel the wine I downed through dinner, warm under the ribs. He is standing over the cat, glancing down in a way that makes me want to gnaw (softly) on his jawbone. Three thoughts flash through my mind, in quick succession:

1. The coat closet
2. My failed record
3. The total irrelevance of my failed record

I'm a grown woman, after all, at a bad wedding. I should be allowed to fuck Gandhi. "When I first saw you," I say, "I thought we should probably have sex in the coat closet."

He cocks his head, grins, tries to pretend that he hasn't been caught off guard. "You too?"

"I'm not sure now. It seems unfair to the coats."

"My sense is that they'd be able to handle it, the coats. We could do some follow-up counseling." Meaning: he's up for sex. He is, after all, a man. I think I went over this.

This is the part where something's supposed to happen, something convincingly carnal. He's supposed to step toward me and set his hands on the merchandise and let out the long, pleased breath. He's supposed to palpate my shoulders in that way men always think women enjoy. He's supposed to brush my hair back and press his mouth against my ear and murmur, in true Nugent style, Wang Dang Sweet Poontang. Isn't that what we're after here?

But he doesn't make his move. Instead, he stares at the glow from the wedding tent. A reggae version of "My Cheri Amour" is pouring out over the lawn. For a second I think he might be drifting off, toward that exquisite loneliness our kind favors. Then he turns and looks directly at me and I can feel the jolt of it, this strange little half-concession to what might be happening here.

His eyes drift down the front of my dress, a long, appraising gaze that makes me swallow.

"I've taken a wrong turn," I say quickly, "made some sort of error in judgment. In general. I've suffered a prolonged lack of clear thinking."

"Clear thinking is kind of overrated," he says. His eyes have settled on the neckline of my dress.

"It wouldn't end well."

"How'd we get to the end already?" He steps toward me, close enough for me to smell a little, aftershave, something not too sweet, almost smoky. "What about the start? I'm awfully good at starting."

"And finishing?"

"Finishing? Hmmm. Not so good on finishing."

"What's with us?" I say.

"Could be the alternator. Or the timing chain."

"We should probably cut our losses," I say.

"Probably."

He steps back and swings an invisible golf club, an action which nearly dislodges his boutonniere and the prospect of this, for no good reason I can name, brings me to the brink of tears.

We don't say anything for a while. We stand there and look at each other and the dead cat and back at each other. Finally, he reaches down gives the cat a nudge with his finger and then stands up and shoves his hands in his pockets.

And then, with only a moment's hesitation, a little tremor of white fur, the dead cat rolls over. It licks itself indiscreetly, eyes us with disdain, and cautiously walks away across the lawn.

"Or . . ." he says.

"Yes, or."

———

The coat closet is dark. Earlier there had been a hefty woman shoving hangers into sleeves, handing out tickets. But she's gone now. The entrance hall is empty.

The coats breathe as we move through them. They sway like underwater things. I don't know his name, I realize. But it's too late now, we're kissing. His mouth tastes like gin and pesto. There's a wall somewhere. We find it, inch down until we're on the floor between two coat racks. Coats—how simple and soulless they are. They hang like old skins, but, I imagine how, soon, people will stuff their bodies inside of them, and the bodies will warm the coats with their ardent blood, the dogged pulse of working hearts. And here we are below, the grope and tussle of two people engaged in polite sexual mayhem.

"I love the dress," he says, ruffling its fluted skirt through his hands, up over my ass. I work his coat off, set to undoing the buttons of his shirt. We're still trying to kiss, but it's turned a bit frantic, getting all the fabrics cleared away.

He's fumbling with the zipper on my dress, whispering "nice, nice," half to himself it seems like, and I'm working my way down his shirtfront until all at once the shirt and the dress slip out of view and there's all this skin to consider, his skin, my skin, and our shoulders are blazing.

Then we hear a sharp rapping noise, like the distant report of a rifle (are we being shot at?) and both of us freeze. A voice calls out, "Hello? Hello? Anyone back there? I need my coat."

The voice is deep, baronial, a little wobbly, some Main Line uncle three gimlets over his limit. "Anyone?"

"Just us coats," he whispers.

We wait for what's going to happen next. Will this gentleman stumble back and find us instead, two of a kind, unzipped and panting with dread? ("Oh, I see, excuse me, yes, I see...")

No, he merely calls out once more, disconsolately, and we listen to his shoes clacking away.

This is certainly a good time to gather my wits, and I very much mean to do so. (Wit! Wits! Get over here!) But. But this long, blue-eyed stranger is above me and the ball of his left shoulder is exposed, and before I can stop myself, I take the flesh into my mouth, warm, salted with sweat, and let my teeth sink in a little.

His eyes startle, and this makes him look unbearably cute, and I bite harder and he lowers himself gently down onto me, until I feel all of him. Then his hand is working its way up my thigh, under this hideous blooming flower of a dress, and he's taking his time, thank you, tracing the curves and hollows like velvet. I'm so relieved that I decided to shave, just in case (God bless the endless sexual optimism of our kind!). His fingers slip inside my panties and he touches me, very slowly. This goes on for a number of minutes (three or four or maybe sixty-seven). His tongue is on my neck and I feel myself unreeling.

When I've recovered my breath enough to speak (more or less) I look up at him. "Did the nuns teach you that?"

"The monks," he says.

I pull him down onto the carpet and climb aboard. Giddy up! My hand slips down to his thigh and I can feel him tense up, a thin band of muscle rising to my touch. I fumble with his belt, fling it over my shoulder, while he reaches up. It's no longer enough. Despite the fact that all I have to offer is a blueberry-flavored condom (long story), despite common sense and a decent playing surface, I want the whole enchilada, the flushed and sticky geometry of the act.

He pulls a nifty reverse and before I know it I'm on my back, wriggling out of my panties, and he's shucked his pants and boxers and he's ready (yep!) and I'm ready, too. I've taken a hold of him and we're pressed together, just at the boundary of the act. I place my hands on his ass—a nifty little property, as these things go—and I press down. I can feel him there, pressing, too, and that gorgeous, familiar feeling just before it's too late.

He's braced his knees on the carpet and I'm sure he's being coy, prolonging the moment (which I no longer want prolonged) but then he pulls back and there's a horribly earnest look on his face, which, I'm sorry to report, I've seen before in these circumstances. It's that sneaky modern chivalry in effect, oil the lady up but force her to decide, so there's no question of blame or guilt in the court of regret to come.

"It's okay," I say, a little impatiently. "I want to."

He shakes his head. "I don't think I can."

I glance down at the full flush of him, which is sending the basic message: *But I can! I can, boss!*

"I beg to differ," I say. I angle my hips up, slide myself along the length of him, and he lets out a whimper. "Do I need to explain the rules? I'll be the woman and you be the man."

"Please," he says. His tone is pleading. He rolls away from me, hoping to exclude his boner from the debate, then leans toward me again and sets his hand on my cheek.

"You're serious, aren't you?" I say.

"I'm afraid so." He looks at me glumly. "I'm sorry. I'm acting like a real jerk, aren't I?"

I'm not sure what to say. He's even prettier now. Have I mentioned his teeth, one pushed up in front of the other? He rubs his knuckles against his chin and stares at me and my heart catches. "It's okay," I tell him.

"I've hurt your feelings," he says. "I'm sorry. I want to do this. I'd love to do this." He lets his eyes swim over my body, which suddenly feels conspicuously naked. I fold my arms over my chest. I think of a line from an old movie—Myrna Loy says, "I've hurt your ego," and Cary Grant says, "No, no, I was just going to go take my ego for a walk." But it's all wrong. I'm Cary Grant? I should at least have a pocket to casually slip my hand into. "Of course not," I say. "The only thing I like more than having sex in a coat closet is not having sex in a coat closet. Really. It's been grand. Don't worry about it." I look at his jacket, marooned beside us, his ruined boutonniere.

I try to slide away from him, but he rolls after me, so that we're actually under a rack of coats, the hems brushing our shoulders. He brings his lips close to my ear. "This is going to sound crazy," he says, "but I think I like you." He sighs, warmly, and the shiver travels across my back. "I don't feel like this too often, and I'm scared that doing this, like this, before we even know each other might, you know, mess things up."

"Are you breaking up with me?" I say. I give him a smile, to let him know that I'm joking, though, the truth is I don't especially like where we're at, the spell of desire broken, and all this meaningful talking he's doing. Am I looking at another conflicted schmuck, another set of dodgy shoulders?

"Listen," he says, "I've got an idea. I'm staying at this really swanky Motel 8 just down the road."

"I don't even know your name," I say.

"John," he says, holding out his hand.

"Jane."

This is the first confession, our ordinariness. It's incredible how ordinary we seem now, reduced by the sex, the almost-sex.

"Why don't you come back to my hotel with me?"

"Nah."

"Why not? Give me a chance to explain. Pick up a free bar of soap."

"I don't think so," I say.

"Why?"

"Because."

"Because? Because is pretty hard to argue with."

I stand up first. He follows. We pivot in the small space, fixing ourselves up, though it's little use. The wedding is almost over. He zips up. I find my stray shoe.

"The cat was a small miracle," he says.

"The cat changed everything."

He's looking at me. I love the way his shirt sticks to him and reveals the outline of his collar bone. There's a rise of lonesomeness. I suddenly remember my parents eating from their stewed plates, the cleft of silence. I think of what lies ahead, the long drive back to my apartment, through the ass-end of the city, with its prim retail avenues and cracked bell.

"Look," I say, "my past is littered with regret, and I'd rather not add you to it. I'd rather not have to fit you into an overcrowded memory." Ah, the past, that swollen tide, Asbury Park's unending rot, a boy galloping across a green campus lawn in the driving rain, a woman staggering around a yard with rocks in her fists. Why am I here in a coat closet with this man? "I'd rather unload memories, frankly."

"So do," he says, nodding. "Seriously. Tell me everything. I'll do the same thing. Let's tell each other everything." He looks like a soldier or something. He could be standing near a bus with an Army-issue duffle bag. "It would be like handing over a dossier."

I run my hand down the line of coats. Empty hangers at the end of the rack chime.

"Confessions," I say.

"Full disclosure."

"A fair warning."

He grabs my hand and kisses the palm. "I'm serious. Let's do this thing."

But I'm not ready to forgive him yet. I turn away and start looking at the coats. I like the pale blue ladies' raincoat. I slip my hand in its pocket, idly. Empty. "I had a fine childhood," I tell him. "I mean it wasn't war-torn. I've got no real excuse for myself."

"Me neither."

The beige coat's pocket holds two mints. The chalky kind.

"Where do you live?" he asks.

"South Philly," I say. "Just down the road."

He tells me he lives in New York.

"An equidistant confessional booth might be hard to find," I say.

"We can write letters."

It feels like a lark now. "Okay," I say, and I'm wondering if we mean any of it. It's hard to tell. In the pocket of a man's beige overcoat, there's a money clip pinching twenties. It seems a stupid thing to do—who would leave a wad of cash in an overcoat? I slip it back. "No email."

"Absolutely," he says. "Real letters. Ink. Paper. The whole deal. We'll be like the pioneers, waiting by our windows for the Pony Express. In bonnets."

"But we can't be honest and woo each other at the same time."

"No seduction." He isn't a soldier now. He's more like a cub scout. Finger combed. Dutiful. "I'll be on my best behavior. I'll stick to confessions, to the past. And then we'll see each other again, if we want to, after we've said everything we need to."

"You might not want to," I say.

"You might not want to either."

"Aye, there's the rub."

"I thought we already did the rub," he says.

There's an awful rim shot moment, and I stare at John. His eyes are wet, the lashes heavy. "You aren't an ax murderer, are you?" I ask.

"No. Are you?"

"Not yet."

The heavy-set coat check girl is walking back behind the counter. She's laughing and talking to someone in the distance. "That'll be the day!" she says. She twists an earring, sits with a huff on the stool, picks at her skirt.

"Well, I can't find it," I say loudly.

Her head snaps to us. She peers through the row of coats. "Can I help you?"

"We had to forage for ourselves. You weren't here," John says, as we pass by her. "But no luck."

"Oh, well," I say.

"Don't leave your coats here!" the girl says, as if she's left with so many coats every night—little orphans—and she doesn't know what to do with them all.

But we're already walking out through the glass front doors. We can still hear the cicadic trill of someone ringing a fork against a wine glass, and then another and another, until, finally, the bride and groom have found each other and handed over their obligatory affection.

The night air feels good. In fact, the night itself kind of humbly admits its perfect clarity. We wander together out into the parking lot. I say, "We should use words in our confessions that people don't use . . . Why do people say, You will rue the day, but refuse to use rue for other things?"

"I rue this boutonniere," he says.

"You don't think I rue buying this dress?" I say.

"I love the dress."

"Why always disheveled and never sheveled?" I ask.

"Why discombobulated and never combobulated or, better yet, bobulated?"

We're standing by my car now. I fiddle with my bracelet clasp. He jerks his tie loose, pulls it out through the collar, and, for no good reason, buttons his cuffs. It's gorgeous, really, the way a man buttons his shirt sleeves. It requires a certain delicacy.

"We shouldn't comment on the other's failings," I say. "This isn't therapy."

"God no. Just the sins."

The lights spilling out on the broad lawn go dim. There are waiters collecting glasses off the patio tables. Guests have started trickling out of the front doors behind us. They meander through the lot, fold themselves into cars. The band hasn't yet called it quits though. They're staggering through a Chicago ballad, something about destiny. It dawns on me that we don't know each other at all.

"I'm pretty sure this is a mistake," I say.

"Maybe," he says.

But we exchange addresses in my car. I tell him, "Look, you don't have to write a letter."

"But I will."

"But you don't have to."

"Neither do you."

I squint up into the parking lot's streetlights. Knowing I'll never hear from John, knowing I'll shove the card in my ashtray and never look at it again, I say, "But if it works out . . ."

"We'll tell our kids about the cat," he says.

"That it was a dead cat."

"Yeah," he says. "It was dead alright, and then it came back to life."

JODI DUNNE

October 9

Dear Jane,

I was sixteen when I started dating Jodi Dunne. It astounds me now to think of myself at sixteen. It astounds me to think of sixteen. I see these kids in my neighborhood, scuffing along in giant boots, their hair all sculpted with gunk, like they'll never take one on the chin. Sad.

Jodi was a year behind me. We sat across from each other in second-period art. The class was taught by this old guy, Mr. Park, who was famous at our school for being a flamer. He wore a beret and called us children. "Children," he would say, "who on earth is going to pull down those shades?" We were all totally terrified of him. The whole class was us looking at slides of paintings, while Mr. Parks walked around and talked about how delicious they were. There was a kind of intimacy to that class, is what I'm saying. You can't put a bunch of teenagers in a dark room and show them Gauguin's nudes and not expect the sap to rise.

Jodi sat pretty near the screen. The colored lights from the paintings revealed the subtler aspects of her beauty: the articulation of her nostrils, the pink swell of her lips. She had a small, exceptionally expressive mouth. And her hair. She had the greatest hair I'd ever seen, a pale orange that turned blond in summer and if you examined each individual hair (as I later did) what you saw that was the color went from rust, at the roots, to a burnished gold. If I close my eyes I can still see those things.

The one thing about Jodi, she was a pretty big girl. Not fat. Not even close to fat. But wide-bottomed and fleshy. In high school, as you'll recall, you were either thin or fat. There was no real in-between category. Also, she played volleyball and hung out with the girls who played volleyball, many of whom were dorks (or whatever the female equivalent of dork is). She sometimes wore sweat pants to school. She wasn't interested in trying to doll herself up, which suggested some kind of inner strength, which, of course, most of us boys wanted nothing to do with. We wanted the pliant ones, who wore makeup and flipped their hair and chewed gum at all times so their breath wouldn't stink. The main thing, the thing I'm most ashamed to mention, is that Jodi's family didn't have much money. I knew this because I'd asked Sean Linden about her one time and he told me she lived over by Los Robles, which was this crappy part of town with one-story ranch houses.

None of this should have mattered, especially her finances. But it did. You should know this: from the beginning, I was making certain kinds of judgments about Jodi, holding myself above her a little. It was a kind of disease in our family, a way of casting out weakness by assuming superiority.

I knew I was attracted to Jodi the first week of class. But I put off asking her out. I started to second guess myself. I can't imagine this comes as a terrible shock to you, given my conduct in the coat check, for which I apologize, again, profusely, and not just to you but to myself, as I can assure you I have been beating myself over the head for the crap-headed sensitive routine I pulled, when I should have been diving into that totally adorable ocean of yours. And, if I may add, at the risk of derailing my little tram down memory lane, I can still feel the shape of you in my palms, in particular the curve of your hips, but also the dimples at the small of your back, which I did not see, only felt and imagined, and, while we're on the subject: I spent the entire flight home sniffing at my shirt, which still smelled of you, and going stiff in my window seat. But okay, enough. We promised no seduction. No tawdry fluffing.

So.

Most afternoons I'd see Jodi and her friends camped in front of the gym in kneepads and think: she is kind of heavy, her friends are sort of lame. Four months of this nonsense. All I could manage was to stare at her every day. And she stared back. So that was our courtship. We sat in that darkened room staring at each other. There was even kind of a language that developed between us, an initial stare that was like, Hello, good morning! then another one, with a little more smolder, which meant Lookin' good! and some eyebrow work if Park said something especially swishy, or, if one of us made a comment in class, a respectful little nod, like *Nice going!* The whole thing was so Hello Kitty. I remember one day I got caught cheating in my math class and I was so ashamed that all I could do was glare at Jodi, which of course confused the hell out of her, and she looked back at me with such tenderness, Are you okay? What's wrong? which made me even madder, so I did this silent scoff, and she got fed up and turned her eyes away, then I panicked and tried to stare an apology at her (Oh hey, I'm sorry, just having a rough day) but she wouldn't look at me. So then I didn't look at her. Fine. We had this whole week-long spat, a really dramatic little emotional event I mean, without having actually spoken a word.

Lord knows this episode should have goaded me to ask her out. It did not. What happened was this: Brent Nickerson pulled me aside one day after class.

"Your girl's got herself a new ride," he said. "A Ford Mustang."

"She's not my girl," I said.

"Check it out," Nickerson said. "Some very cherry shit." Then he punched me in the shoulder.

Nickerson was a popular kid, one of those guys who finds himself in the pursuit of girls. He had fucked Melissa Camby and Holly Kringle, allegedly at the same party. That he had taken notice of Jodi placed her on a different level in my mind. And the Mustang. These things suggested that she wasn't just what she seemed, that she existed outside the little box I'd placed her in and puzzled over day after day.

I can't remember how it all started, how I finally broke through my own doubt, only that at some point we were in the parking lot behind Swensen's with our shirts off.

We spent a lot of time in parking lots, kissing, touching each other. We weren't experienced, but we were eager to learn. We understood that sex was our surest path to intimacy, to being able to feel more sure of ourselves in the world. And we were kind to one another. That's what I remember most vividly.

One night, a few months into our relationship, we snuck into the room where my dad kept his grand piano and lay on the thick, antique rug and Jodi took me into her mouth. This was something new between us. We had both tired of the upstairs groping. But I was too embarrassed to complete the act. I handed her a tissue instead. I assumed this was the chivalrous thing to do. Coming was messy and strange. It made me feel ashamed to think of squirting myself onto Jodi's lovely teeth. (I think Clinton, incidentally, experienced this same feeling with Monica. If you read the Starr Report—guilty as charged—It becomes clear that the reason he keeps holding off isn't fear of incrimination. It's that he doesn't want to degrade her, or further degrade her, and there's a tenderness to this restraint that's always made me feel a weird allegiance to the dude.)

Anyway, I reached for a tissue and gently touched Jodi's naked shoulder. She looked up at me, in the blue light, and smiled. There was nothing dirty to that smile. She might have been a nurse. "It's okay," she whispered. "I want to."

There was also a good deal of erotic incompetence. The incident that leaps to mind, rather unpleasantly, took place a few months after we started having sex. I'd gone down to Mexico play soccer, so we hadn't seen one another for a couple of weeks. I mention this because I'd like it to serve as some sort of excuse for my premature ejaculation, though, in point of fact, I was a veritable baron of premature ejaculation (perhaps *The* Baron of Premature Ejaculation) in those days. I would have to pretend that I hadn't actually come. I did this by murmuring something about being "too excited" and then going down on Jodi. Or I would say that I had to go to the bathroom. My only saving grace was that I could reload relatively quickly and get back in the saddle, though often I would prematurely ejaculate again.

Well.

On this night I'm thinking of, after the Mexico trip, we went about our usual rubbing, and of course Jodi needed this prep time; it was the way her body prepared for sex, whereas I was a walking boner. Jodi stripped her clothes off and there was her big curvy body, with her warm tits standing out against her tan. She lay down and pulled me onto her and told me how much she'd missed me and named all the various body parts she'd missed.

"Let me put something on," I said.

She shook her head. "You don't have to. I took care of it."

And this gesture, just how ready she was for me to have sex with her, her wetness, the prospect of riding into that wetness bareback, the inside of her. Jodi placed her hands on my ass and she pushed down. She murmured exhortations. I had this idea that I could buy myself some time. But what happened, she reached out and took hold of me and just that one gentle touch—not even a full stroke mind you, a half stroke, a *stro*—set me off. I didn't want her to know what was happening, that I was ruining our reunion, so I tried to slide down her body and I sort of brought my knees up and bowed my head so she could see what I intended to do and I even started to explain myself, said, "Honey, I want to taste you first," but by then it was too late, I had started, and the result of all this twisting around was that I came in my own mouth. There's no need to labor the physics of the thing, the angles and so forth, though I do feel compelled to add that I squirted a bit into my eye, a maneuver that I'm told, by reliable sources, is known in porn circles as the Pirate Eye. So this was me: Cap'n Spunk!

I hope it will not come as a shock that Jodi was less forthcoming in the orgasm department. We spent a lot of time *In Search of . . . Jodi's Orgasm*. I read books. I consulted friends. I purchased a gel intended to numb the end of my equipment. I portrayed these measures as princely consideration when they were, in fact, a kind of desperate vanity. ("Whatsamatter, Nuge, can't bring your girl off?") I confused Jodi's sexual apparatus with an AP exam I hoped to ace. It had not occurred to me that the chief determinant of the female orgasm was a state of relaxation.

And so, weirdly, maddeningly, the few times that Jodi did reach the Promised Land were always random and unexpected. The best example I can provide took place at a Berlin concert (the band, not the city) during which I slipped my hand down the front of her pants. She was into a pronounced panting mode by the end of "Like Flames," and signed, sealed, and delivered in the midst of "Take My Breath Away."

I realize I'm placing a lot of emphasis on the sex. But this was the terrain of our time together. We had things to talk about—friends, classes, plans for college—but we were too young to talk about what really mattered, the secret miseries our families inflicted on us, our half-realized plans for escape.

We loved our families, after all. Jodi loved that my dad had once sung opera, that my mom wrote books for a living, that my beloved older sister Lisa was in the Peace Corps. I couldn't explain to her that there was something merciless in their achievement; I was only dimly aware of this myself.

The Dunnes were a joyride by comparison. Jodi was their youngest child by ten years, a happy mistake. You got the feeling that raising the other three had worn them out. They seemed delighted to have this sweet young woman around to keep them company. Bill spent most of his time in his workshop, designing the boat he hoped to build when he retired from Ford, where he was an engineer. (This explained the Mustang—he leased a new one every year). He'd served in the Navy long ago and he moved like a sailor, with a wide, rolling gait. He was missing certain teeth. He had big rough hands, stained yellow from his Newports and a sardonic way of dealing with the world that obscured the fact that he was actually terribly shy. I guess the word crusty applies. Jodi's mom, May, watched her evening soaps and laughed a lot and hugged me whenever I came over.

They were both alcoholics. I didn't see this, of course. They just seemed more relaxed and affectionate than my parents, a little more sentimental when they got going, Bill with his tumbler of whiskey next to the cigarettes on his workbench, May with her glass of red wine. Happy drunks. So what? Most of the world is happy drunks.

Jodi's older brothers and sister were considerably less happy. They were all divorced; they had money problems. Sometimes, later on at night, when I was sneaking out of Jodi's room through the little courtyard next to the Dunne's bedroom, I would hear May on the phone, singing out in her blurred alto: "I know, honey. I know. It's hard."

Her older sister Sue spent a few months at home, with her two boys. Jodi and her mom loved fussing over the kids, at first. But these guys were out of control. They draw stuff on the walls, pooped in the bath. Sue took one of those multi-level marketing jobs, selling health products made from apricots and seaweed. She was desperately happy for about a week. She'd bought $600 worth of the stuff and was going to make ten times that. I can still remember her sitting at the dining room table with a bottle of sherry, stabbing at her list of debts. She had the same beautiful hair as Jodi, though her face had gone doughy with chardonnay.

Jodi had another brother, Dave, but I didn't hear too much about him. He'd gone to Europe with a Belgian woman and her son. They were street entertainers, jugglers or something. Billy, the eldest kid, lived on a houseboat up around Half Moon Bay. He invited the family for lunch one time and we trolled to this little lagoon near the harbor, so Sue's kids could angle for sunfish. Billy was a handsome guy, a charmer, but he had that same agitated quality as his dad. After lunch, those two went down into the galley. He wanted Mr. Dunne to go in on a charter boat with him. That had been the whole point of the invite, it turned out. We could hear Billy setting out the plan, his voice rising through the registers of imploration. But his dad wasn't sure. Billy'd had some scrapes with the law, some problems with drugs, whatever it was.

Billy reappeared, surly and squinting and everyone gave him a wide berth. One of the kids, Devin, complained about the fruit plate Billy had set out. He didn't like pineapple. Billy walked over and picked up the platter—it was one of those plastic deals you get from the grocery store—and hurled it over the side of the boat.

"No more pineapple," he said.

Devin pitched a fit and Mr. Dunne started to holler at Billy to settle down and Billy snapped back at him, then Sue got in on it and Jodi's mom, who was in her cups by this time, went below decks to cry. Jodi and I, meanwhile, paddled the dinghy out into the tullies, where we screwed incompetently. It was what we did when the family traffic got too thick.

This was the life of the Dunnes, besotted and needy, tumultuous. At their parties, people got drunk and sang songs and flung the dip around. They flirted with each other. I secretly loved the mess of their lives, the brazen displays, the emotion flowing sloppily from one human to the next. When my parents had friends over it was for intellectual discourse, little concerts, linzer torte. They were people of the mind, not the flesh, and incredibly boring to a teenager.

The Dunnes liked me. They understood I was poking their daughter, but they also understood that somebody was going to be poking their daughter eventually, and they could have done a lot worse than me. I was from a good family. They could smell the ambition on me, though, and it sometimes made them stiffen a little when I showed up.

My family really wasn't so much richer than hers, by the way. But I guess it's important to know a little bit about the town I grew up in, how much attention was paid to the subtle gradations. There was a rich part of town, and a super rich part of town, and a big, prosperous university where my mother worked. There were a set of kids who had their own cars and others who were destined for the Ivy League. There were mansions with lawns so green I wanted to eat them. Some afternoons, I peddled through these neighborhoods on my way to work and felt that old American itch to pull a Gatsby.

I didn't want to be rich. (It's not what Gatsby wanted either.) What I wanted was the sense of ease I imagined the rich kids possessed, of being able to relax, not having to try so hard all the time. I wanted to be loved, of course, but more than that I wanted to be able to receive love.

Jodi did what she could to help. She rescued me from what might have been a terrible misery. All around us, we could see the cruel theatrics of our classmates, the breakups and minor betrayals, the public humiliations of unsteady love. One night Jodi and I hung out with Sean Linden and his girlfriend Tess and it was awful to see what he did to her, how he tore her down a little bit at each turn. She'd gotten a new perm that hadn't set quite right and he kept calling her Shirley (as in Temple) pretending it was affection. He stroked the soft flesh of her stomach and made a blubbery noise. She drank a bit too much and wound up spilling Chex Mix on the fancy new rug and Sean made her pick up every piece. Or, actually, as I remember now, it was worse than that, because Tess did this herself, without his prodding. I can still see her down there, on her hands and knees, a pretty girl in loose curls, digging around my feet for pretzel sticks.

One of the reasons I hate Hollywood so much is that they portray the travails of teen life as so innocuous and fun-loving, some kind of idyll before the mean business of adulthood. People forget how much it all hurts back then. Someone pinches you and you feel it in your bones. They don't want to face what a bunch of sadists teenagers are, wounded narcissists, killers. All these folks who acted all shocked and outraged when those kids in Columbine went off—where the hell did they go to high school?

My point is that Jodi and I protected each other from a lot of that. We were in that dinghy, floating away from tribulation. We were the bodies in that dinghy, streaked in sweat, tender from the sun, braced against the gunwales, taken up by the awkward contortions of love.

I can remember Jodi walking into the music room one night, as my father was rehearsing his lieder. It was something I would never have done. To intrude on such a moment of vulnerability; that was not how we did business. My father had failed as an opera singer, after all. That was why he sold sheet music. But Jodi didn't see him as a failure. She sat primly on the piano bench as my father released the somber notes that lived within him. He was a baritone, though he often sang in the low tenor ranges, and when he did his face tilted up and his eyes took on an almost unbearable yearning (my sister called this his Figaro Face). His nostrils flared, as if he could smell his lover racing toward him through the Schwartzwald.

My father finished the song, and looked up. He hadn't realized Jodi was there.

"It's so beautiful," she said. "Your voice."

My father smiled shyly. He smoothed the wisps of hair onto his brow. "I was just warming up."

"What's he saying?"

"That he loves too well and not enough, something like that."

"He's singing to his lover?"

"Yes."

"Beautiful," she said. "Thank you."

"Well," my father said, "I didn't write it."

Jodi leaned forward on the bench. She looked as if she might want to touch his arm. "John told me you used to sing, in New York."

There was a moment when I thought my father might relent, might open his chest of shy memories and lay them before Jodi. But he seemed to catch himself. He took a step backward and leaned against the piano and inhaled through his nose. "You're sweet," he murmured. "A sweet young lady." (He must have been thinking of his own daughter, just off to college, whom he missed terribly. We both did.)

But Jodi had this effect on people, an optimism that struck me as close to magic. And there were moments when I felt ready to receive the full weight of her love, when I believed that we could live quite happily together, one of those lucky couples who find the cure early. We breezed through junior year and into senior year and when it came time to apply to college, I chose five schools, four schools back east, plus UC Santa Cruz, Jodi's first choice.

In our town, among the bright young sires and sirettes of the landed gentry, where you *got in* carried the weight of a life sentence. Several years earlier, a kid had tried to kill himself when he got wait listed at Harvard. I myself tried to affect an air of nonchalance about the whole thing. Or maybe it would be more accurate to say that I was simply avoidant. Whatever the case, I took it harder than expected when, on a single afternoon in early May, I got rejected by three of the East Coast schools.

My mother, who had gone to great pains not to appear overly concerned about where I applied, called me into her study that evening.

"I hope you're not going to take this personally," she said.

"Oh no," I said. "It's not like they rejected me personally."

"I've sat on these admissions committees, Johnny. It's all a formula. I don't mean to denigrate the process, but it's riddled with quotas. Diversity is the new mantra."

"I guess Lisa was more diverse than me."

This was a somewhat self-pitying reference to the fact that my sister had been accepted by every school on the Eastern Seaboard, including the ones she didn't apply to.

"Your sister—" my mother said. Then she stopped herself. "It's gotten more competitive, significantly so. I see the application figures, kiddo. I know about this stuff."

"I'd like for it to have been my choice, that's all."

"You've still got a chance."

"Plus Santa Cruz," I said. "Jodi would be pretty happy if I wound up there."

"Yes, I imagine she would." My mother sighed. She took off her glasses and fixed me with a sober look. "Now listen, Johnny. You know how fond we are of Jodi. She's a wonderful girl. This isn't about her."

"What isn't?"

"We would love it if you went to Santa Cruz, to have you nearby, your father and me. We want you to be happy. But you need to make sure you're thinking about what you want to do. Do you understand me? You and Jodi, you're both very young."

I could feel something squeezing in my chest. "So you're saying to disregard Jodi?"

"That's not what I'm saying at all," my mother said. "I'm saying to regard yourself. You make the decision that's best for you. It's as simple as that."

I looked at my mother, at the massive bookshelf above

her, the volumes of Marx and Freud and Spinoza, all those big-ticket Jews in worn bindings.

"She's a wonderful girl," she said again. "You know how fond we are of her."

I don't remember the exact chronology on the rest of the college shit. I got into that last school back east, and Santa Cruz, of course. That's all you need to know.

What I should tell you about is this one night in particular, a week after the talk with my mother. It was a Friday and my parents were away at a conference. Jodi and I were going to spend the weekend playing house, cooking ourselves meals and screwing wherever we pleased. Jodi was supposed to swing by after volleyball practice, but by eight she still hadn't appeared.

When she did finally call, I could hear loud voices in the background. "Hey baby," she said. "Can you come over and pick me?"

I figured she and her pals had started the weekend early, that she was maybe drunk, and this excited me. Then I heard someone scream, an angry male voice, and the sound of something slamming.

"Where are you?"

"Home," she said. "My house."

"What's happening over there?"

"Nothing. No big deal. But it's better if I don't use the car "

"Are you okay?"

"I'm fine." She laughed her patient laugh. "Just a little family drama."

"Is this a bad time?"

"No, I want you to come by. Just honk. I'll be ready."

So I got in my dad's car and drove over to her house. I figured either her mom or dad, maybe both of them, had hit the sauce a little too hard. When I pulled up to her house, I could see the new Mustang in the driveway and a car I didn't recognize, right up on its bumper. The Mustang looked a little off-kilter and when I passed by I could see why: the left rear tire had been slashed.

The front door was flung open. The frosted glass window next to the door was busted and the shards were scattered on the pebbled cement of the courtyard. I walked over to the sliding glass door. I could see right through the kitchen and living room to the backyard, where there was a little pool. Billy Dunne swung into view. A little string of blood was dripping off his hand onto the flagstone. He had a glass in his other hand and he was glaring down at his father, who was perched on the edge of a chaise lounge. These faint blue ripples kept washing across them, from the light in the pool.

Billy was screaming all kinds of crap. "Get up! Get up! Fucking sailor! Fucking phony-ass sailor!"

Mr. Dunne had his jaw set, but I could see, from the smoke coiling off his Newport, that his hands were trembling.

Then I heard another voice, an imploring, female voice and I thought: Jodi, it's my Jodi! She's back there! I felt I should do something, rush into the backyard and make sure Jodi was okay. I could step between the men and get them to cool off, make the peace. The adrenaline kicked in and I reached for the door. Billy Dunne raised his highball glass and smashed it on the flagstone and the sound was like the report of a rifle.

I stepped back. There was another shriek. A woman lurched into view, her blond hair up in a ponytail. "You're ruining it," she screamed. "You're ruining everything." Then May appeared and pulled her away from the two men. Mr. Dunne dropped his cigarette and started to get to his feet, but his son struck him, a soft quick blow above the eye and Mr.

Dunne slumped back down onto the chaise lounge. He looked stunned and helpless, like a child.

Something turned in me, just then. I lost my nerve. Rather than leaping forward, into the fray, I turned and hurried back to my car and leaned on the horn. I told myself that if Jodi didn't appear in a minute or so, I'd head back inside. When I've thought about this moment in the past, taken it apart, I've made the kind assumption that I knew the woman with the ponytail was Sue, not Jodi. The truth is I wasn't sure.

And then Jodi did appear, a big, sweet dumpling of a girl hurrying toward me. Her hair was wet and loose across her shoulders.

"Hey," she said.

"Is everything cool?" I said. "I heard some screaming."

"Oh, it's so stupid. Let's just go, baby. Okay?"

"I don't know," I said. "Should I—"

"Please." She looked at me and took me in her arms and hugged me, hard. "I love you," she whispered. "I love you so much."

We had ourselves a fabulous weekend of fucking and sucking and frying and slurping. Jodi was grateful for these pleasures. We both were. I managed to convince myself that I'd shown admirable restraint in the matter. It wasn't my place to interfere in family politics. And so on. I wasn't ready to face the truth, which was that you reach a point in every intimate relationship where you have to be brave, to move forward into the dangerous territory. Because if you don't, there is nothing left to you but retreat.

My own retreat came in a familiar form: I started making judgments. The Dunnes were drunks, failures, makers of shabby scenes. Their poor breeding had finally revealed itself. And how long would it be before Jodi met the same fate? Here was my bigotry rising again to rescue me, the idea that I was above Jodi, that my family had more money and more sophistication, that our minds were more refined, our blood a little purer.

So this isn't some kind of after-school special where the booze is the culprit. My family was just as sick as hers, beset by envy and guilt and a need to withhold, all the silent violence of the modern suburb.

There were some other things I could mention, minor acts of infidelity, but I'm not sure they matter so much. They were more effect than cause. By summer I'd decided to head back east for school and started to pursue other girls who were going east, thinner models who doled out the abuse I was seeking.

The worse part, of course, is that Jodi didn't hold any of this against me. She was totally, maddeningly forgiving. She understood that I wasn't ready for the happiness she was offering, that I needed to get away from my family.

The last time I saw her, the last memorable occasion, was the next summer. Mr. Dunne had built his boat. He'd even agreed to let Billy—back from rehab and looking contrite—to take it out for charters. They threw a party at the dinky little public marina near the marshlands and Jodi sent me an invite, with a note informing me that her father insisted I be there. It was rousing affair, with margaritas and platters of salty salami and dancing. Jodi came and embraced me. I felt the solid warmth of her flanks against me. The breeze moved through her hair, golden with summer. It was strange to see her again only because it didn't feel strange at all. It felt perfectly natural, as if we'd never missed a beat. Then May came along and gave me a hug and Bill threw his giant straw hat on the dock and gestured for me to dance around it. I didn't get it. Couldn't these people see me for the heel I was?

Later, at dusk, Jodi slipped from my side and went down

to the launch. She and her mother smashed a bottle of Mott's against the hull and they climbed aboard for the maiden voyage of the Jodi May. Everyone let out a cheer and May hugged Bill and the rest of the Dunnes waved like mad. I felt the oddest sensation then, as they puttered out under the high, distant streaks of colored clouds—as if I were the one drifting away from land, from the happy crowd on the dock, from the wine and song, from the simple human pleasures of fellowship. And it's true, I was.

That is all for now.

Yours in relentless rue,
Nuge

Oct. 20

Dear Cap'n Spunk,

Well, I'll be damned. You've restored some of my tiny faith in humanity; you wrote me a confession! I didn't think you would. I would have bet against it. I'd have bet against you, honestly. But here you are. And I really mean here you are. I love the body's memory, how the cells hold on, deep within them—my hips in your palms, wasn't that what you were getting at? I have it too, when I close my eyes and concentrate, your weight, the full length of you. I think of you each time I put on my coat, each time someone else puts on a coat. You'd be surprised how very many coats there are in the world and how often people put them on.

Even though I wasn't expecting a confession, I was still preparing one, mentally. I was trying to figure out how to cast my love life—failed, doomed?—into some kind of luxurious epic in which I was at one point, maybe, blinded, and then miraculously regained my sight on, say, an ocean liner or in a small Italian villa. But then I got your confession, the first shock, and it was honest, the second. Did you really come in your own mouth? My God! Now that could have easily been omitted. But, no, you seemed bent on this honesty thing, and so, inspired (and a little dumbfounded—by God, let's ponder the physics of it at some point, okay?) I owe you something honest.

As it turns out, I'm no fan of honesty. I prefer well-told lies. So, I'm in a bind. There is no ocean liner or small Italian villa in my past. And I've only got a small stigmatism in my right eye which seems permanent.

All of this fluff means, I've frozen up. I don't know if I can tell you about my life—not like you just did yours. I mean, it's one thing to suggest having sex in a coat closet with someone, and quite another to talk about the truth of your past. Me. Jane. That girl who was drawn to Asbury Park boys, who lived with her sad parents. Was I a sad girl? Did I hate my youth?

And, no offense, but what little I know of you indicates that you might start off hot and heavy, but, when it comes right down to it, you're likely to call in the troops and retreat. Is this true? Is this confession just more foreplay? And, at the last minute, are you going to take off your blueberry-flavored condom and just go home, Johnnie?

Sensefully yours,

Jane

Rocktober 23, 2003

Dear Calamity Jane,

Oh no you don't. A deal's a deal, ladyfriend. The contract called for one confession, heavy on the lurid disclosure, with the option of one (1) gratuitous money shot. We both signed.

Legal obligations aside, I'm disappointed. The Nuge is disappointed. He gets the envelope. He's sees the handwriting. He's, well, the Nuge is very wowza at this point. The Nuge has developed *hopes*. And then he opens the letter, the Nuge does, and, you know, he's not expecting Pride and Prejudice or nuthing, but all he gets is this little scaredy burp of a note. Takes maybe a minute to read, an extremely confusing minute.

Now help the Nuge here, cuz he's still trying to get it straight: he restrains himself from making sweet wang dang in the coat check and confesses that he broke up with his high school sweetie and suddenly . . . he's a flight risk?

Huh?

No.

No no no.

The Nuge knows a decoy when he sees one. And this business about honesty—you're no fan of honesty. You prefer the well-told lie? Boy, you really know how to butter a Nuge up.

Or, wait, let me put it this way: I've felt some of that secret skin. I know a little about your mouth. Isn't there something you *want* to tell me, something filthy and lovely and true?

> Don't make me fetch
> the cross bow,
> Nudge

MICHAEL HANRAHAN

Depraved Robin Hood,

Well, now I've imagined you with a crossbow, wearing green tights. I know that Robin Hood didn't use a crossbow, but the image, though unfortunate, can't be undone. I'm pretty sure that you're on a good deed mission, forcing me—suddenly a Jane Austen type fritting around a small room with my quill pen—to spill it already. I give. A promise is a promise.

I loved boys—how's that? A simple start. I loved their lean hips, their hairless, muscled chests, their necklaces—a lot of Italian horns bobbing in the dips of collarbones—their loping gaits, their swelling pricks, their soft wet lips, and teary eyes—some were already deeply sentimental. I loved them with primal biology; I loved them because of an internal bent, a moist yearning imprinted heavily on my genes, perhaps passed down through my mother, stunted (and highly polished, too) by her need for romance. I loved them like we were a country at war, like I was a nurse (and not some Jodi Dunne nurse with a tissue, no!), a heart-sore, bullet-wounded nurse.

And sometimes, I admit, I was compelled by a sweeping

maternal drive. I had no choice. Boys, they're the home of my youth. Not a nice grassy yard and a little blue house in suburbia by the Jersey shore, not the ghetto of Asbury Park where I spent too much time. No, the home of my youth is the bodies of boys, sprawled out, adoring, that's the place I was raised.

And so your body in the coat check was a kind of homecoming. Can you see how that would be true? I confuse men with home, and neither—my men, my home—share the Saturday Evening Post's versions of the pure American Dream. There won't be anything too Norman Rockwellian going on in these pages.

I'll start with musty classrooms with crank open windows, spring, mud and the lusty pollen of apple tree blossoms. You're right. It's as good a place as any. Although basements are a close second. The remodeled wood-paneled finished basement—was it solely designed for groping? I'd had boyfriends, so-called, before neighborhood boys, chubby, lanky, and polite. But Michael Hanrahan is the true beginning, because it was also an ending of something else.

I liked the same five boys that every girl in our school liked—Kevin, Joe, Mark, Mark, and Eric. But my tastes eventually became my own. And more and more I turned to the sweet, tough types. I don't have to go over it. I think you know—half pimp, half little league. This one—Michael Hanrahan, mohawk, black eye, a feathery mustache, a practiced sulk—had shown up, fully grown (without a history of braces or having thrown up in gym or having been dumped by a famous cheerleader), a transfer from somewhere exotic: Ohio.

We attended the vastly overrated Immaculate Conception High School (don't snicker; it's so unbecoming.) It was a huge modern building inspired by a folksy Jesus-of-the-sixties where we mixed in the buzzing halls amid modern-style nuns who dressed as civilians. We languished helplessly clamped into desks and prayed before every class. (There was something to this praying, though, this languishing and praying that was good for me. Some of it did drift settle in my soul, maybe. A fine sediment down there somewhere.) The bad news: our uniforms were not even plaid and pleated like a stripper's school-girl costume. My apologies. It was green herringbone A-line skirts with polyester blazers. In such a place, one would think that a fine young woman from a mediocre household would flourish or at least not take up with the likes of Michael Hanrahan. I should have been with an off-to-college boy, more like myself, or better than myself—a dentist's son. Now that would have shown some real ambition. I should have dated someone more like you, I guess, though my family would have surely come off like the Dunnes. No, worse. They aren't drinkers, but there is the undeniable issue of class and money and a lack my mother was especially aware of.

But I wasn't on the list of the top five girls that every high school boy got nauseous and sweaty around. I wasn't pretty yet—I would have a few particularly good years there early to midtwenties—but that wasn't too much of an issue. Boys in my high school, as far as I could tell, were after one thing. Consistency. It wasn't the prettiest girls they necessarily seemed to be all ape-ish about or the sluttiest, really, but the girls who looked the same day in and day out, who always said exactly what you thought they were going to say.

Mostly, I was bored. I would risk embarrassment for the possibility of something actually happening, hence my mouthiness. I was stunned by the sheer stupidity of the world as I was coming to understand it, the aw-shucks-they're-growing-up-before-our-very-eyes, the bubble tests, hall passes, the hold-hands-and-sing expectations of the choral director. At every turn there was more of it—vote for homecoming court, really? Cutest couple? Are you kidding me?

Michael Hanrahan was something that I hoped would happen. In fact, I hoped he'd go off like a bomb in my life, obliterating most everything except me, still standing, albeit charred and dizzy.

I was seventeen, a senior, and just beginning to have an inkling that things were wrong. I'd started musing about what I'd eventually label in an overzealous, clunky college treatise for an undergrad class in feminist studies: Self-Esteem Warfare. (I apologize in advance for the ardent, high-minded phase that's still to come. If it's any consolation, the ardent, high-minded phase is necessary for the ménage à trois scenario that follows it. And so I'll try to go short on philosophy and promise—in a future confession; if we keep at this, I mean—girl-on-girl action, poetically rendered.) I would eventually define it as a plot hatched by the mediocre minds of desperate, well-intentioned high school administrators. See, teenagers were, once upon a time, allowed to be sexual. They were good marrying age. When time was up on that notion, the natural urge to get sweaty still had natural consequences—pregnancy. The Pill came along so they had to invent something else. For a while, there was much bawling and shrugging in the face of calamity: the deterioration of society via the loose morals of high school girls wearing frosty lipstick and mini-uniform skirts. Sex ed at the likes of Immaculate Conception High School, was, at this point, taught by a Danny Devito–sized priest who smelled goaty. It was a mixed with lectures on sin—whore/Madonna peer pressure singing du-wop. Sin was failing by the time I came along, high school administrators took over with a new message: girls have sex with boys because girls lack self-esteem and are seeking approval and love that is insufficient in their lives.

Self-Esteem Warfare was dirty pool. It allowed judgment not just on a girl's abilities at self-restraint. No, it gave the girls sticks and asked them to poke at each other's souls. *Are you insecure?* It asked. *Do you like yourself? Are you some sad lost thing we should all feel so very sorry for?*

I remember folks like Mrs. Glee, my ethics teacher, an ex-nun, and the eggy Mr. Flint picking at the dismal sour creep of his boxer shorts. They patrolled the halls; the breathless tenacity of the administration, charging to catch us, electrified by their own urges, really, for each other, for us, our then-beautiful bodies, rubbery and buoyant, and their own filing cabinets full of sorrowful regrets.

I was a virgin, but not impressed by it. I wasn't interested in the whole idea of purity. (Not a big surprise, huh. I think of myself in the coat check and I wonder how I must have seemed. Was I being a bully? Did I really say something about going over the rules: I'll be the woman and you be the man? I'd like to blame some of it on the dress. It was this horrible Venus Flytrap number bent on devouring you. Of course, I'm above blaming my behavior on my clothes. Just barely.)

My friends were a mix—loners who clung together. Tula was gorgeous, but Greek so not allowed to do anything about it. Amy was extremely tall and quiet and just simply showed up and followed us around, which was fine. Jillian was wild, but lived two towns away so I never saw her except in school.

I'll say this about my friends in high school: I wasn't very good friends with them. Mainly, they were girls and I find it hard to be friends with a group of girls. I don't know what my friends wanted, but I wanted to have a filled out, messy life. My parents' home was tidy and claustrophobic. I have the impression from photographs that my mother had once been loud and rowdy, but by the time of my earliest memories, she'd retreated.

She had a nervous, frustrated energy, and easily lost her patience with lids she couldn't unscrew. My mother claims that she was once a debate team champion, but it never seemed plausible. Though, if so, it was because her nervousness set everyone else— bent on being steady and rational—into squirrelly fits. Maybe she asked obvious, yet dumbfounding questions, loudly, with an irate tenacity, the kind that they mistook for undeniable conviction. She could have made her points with a certain menacing I'll-pinch-your-leg-under-the-table-and   the-judges-won't-see-it kind of way. Her life was not designed for intellectual discourse, little concerts, and linzer torte so present in your youth. I don't know how my mother would have done with the first two—she might not have really been up for too much mini-opera or Marx/ Freud/Spinoza, but, my, my, she'd have liked the linzer torte! And she knew that linzer torte existed elsewhere, and it burned her. (Not to reduce your childhood to discourse, opera, and rich desserts. I'm just using that line for the sake of comparison. Reduction isn't what I'm after and it isn't what you handed over, not at all. Not in the very least.)

My father, a saintly man (in fact, maybe the Patron Saint of Exact Change for Toll Booths?) knocked her up, forcing the marriage. She'd come from money and he'd never really do. She had this glowing rounded bulb look and my father beat around her like an exhausted moth.

We were taught that boys have sex because it feels good. There's no stopping them. And here we have the most logical example. Who could have stopped Michael Hanrahan? It would have been un-American to try. The administration set out to cure girls of their tragic flaw, this weakness not for pleasure or even an inevitable biological yearning, but for acceptance. I only had a dim idea, a feeling of being unjustly accused, even though I was still grudgingly a virgin.

Mrs. Glee and Mr. Flint, deflated by another ball-busting school year, hunched over their ledgers. It was late spring, and there I was, daisy-eyed with ringing hips and a punching heart, ready to be strung-out on screaming guitar and growling motors, aching. I'd prayed for Michael Hanrahan, for a release from this excruciating on and on of things. And God answered my prayers.

His parents moved from Ohio back to their hometown of Asbury Park for reasons unknown. He wound up sitting in front of me in Mrs. Glee's painful ethics class. I touched his mohawk, the soft fuzz, then said sorry as if I'd bumped into him in the halls.

He turned around and said, "That's okay. It's fine with me."

That afternoon he offered to give me a ride, but he didn't take me straight home. We drove around Asbury Park—the Adriatic with its old regulars in fishing caps, listening to lounge music under leaky skylights, the mini golf course overgrown except for patches of indoor/outdoor carpet, hotels looking like Eastern Bloc old age homes, the boarded-up casino, the old tilt a whirl, the abandoned fun house, auto body shops, auto parts, paint shops and detailing, signs like: New Jersey's hottest night spot: closed, the old Greek statue: the Patriarch of Eternal Graces or is it Infinite Love? All I know is the adult movie theater was thriving and the ocean was the ocean, big wide blue, the widest eye. It was gorgeous decay. It was how I felt about things.

He took me out driving the next day and the next it was a set plan. We'd meet up with his friends from the public high school. They were boys who called each other pussy and motherfucker, endearingly. I liked them and they got used to me. They called me BB. I'm not sure why.

When we were alone, I conducted an ongoing interview. I

wanted to know what his life was like. I had this Connie Chung undercover investigative feeling about all of it, which was wrong, which may have been the worst thing. I was trying to be there, but I was pretending or trying to pretend that this wasn't real. I was in it as an observer. The problem was that Michael made it difficult. He didn't like questions, didn't talk about his parents. He had a little brother who liked Debbie Gibson and so he derided him mercilessly whenever family came up. If I complained about my folks, he'd just say, "Yeah, uh-huh. I know how it is." We sometimes drove by his house. He pointed it out. It was a tucked into a sloppy row. "We're renting," he told me.

"Are you moving back to Ohio?"

He shrugged. "One day, maybe."

His father didn't work. His mother had a job at a deli. I met her by accident. Michael needed something from his bedroom—money, a rubber, a roach, I don't know. And she was walking home from work, her apron hung over one arm.

She stopped at the car. "You must be Michael's girlfriend," she said. She dipped her head down close to the open window. She smelled like honey ham and pepperoni. We shook hands and hers held the oiliness of cheese. I assumed he was ashamed of her. But then he appeared and walked up to her. He said, "You two meet?"

We nodded.

"We're gonna take off," he said. "I'll help out tomorrow morning." And then he kissed her on the cheek. It was the most shocking thing I'd ever seen. He kissed his mother, right there in front of me, on the street, for anyone to see. I almost started crying. I was already sure that I would probably have sex with him, but this kind of sealed it for me. As soon as he got in the car, he dodged questions, turned up the radio, and drove too fast.

That night, we parked by a line of trees down a solitary road. I remember our radio-lit bones, how the car, sealed shut, filled with steam so like a bathroom pumped with hot shower water I could only think of my mother, her puffy body, sausage taut, rocking me on the tub's edge. It's what you do with a child suffering midnight croup. The car was hot like that. I cried out urgently. It wasn't an orgasm. I was crying out because I needed to. (In fact, I'd trade in an orgasm now—so easy to come by, really, at this point in my life—for that other unnamable release.)

This was, I guess, the most pure sex of my life. Michael didn't care about my orgasm, and I didn't care about his or my own. And I wasn't fronting and maxing. I wasn't yet aware of myself enough to put on a show or, at least, not a showy show. His dick, for example, was just that. It wasn't odd or typical. It just was, by God. And isn't that nice? What I'm saying is that Michael and I were two bodies, uneducated, unrehearsed, free from the notions of what sex should be. We hadn't earned each other or won each other. Our bodies were beautiful, slick, warm, and the wetness and the warmth alone were a shock, a sweet, stunning shock.

Afterward, I rested my hand on his tan chest. It began to rain, and he drove me home past unwashed churches, seam-rusted silos, a man shoveling a raccoon from the roadside.

I stood in front of my house after he pulled off. My mother often sat staring out at the street. During the day she could look out on the kids playing four square, and in the evening the red-fringed windows of the Chinoiserie on the corner couples leaned together in the dull glow. (I absorbed my mother's desire.)

Tonight she was still there, waiting for me, her pale, dimpled arms perched in the open window. But when I arrived, her face slid inside. To talk to me, she would have had to talk about herself, and she was unwilling to do that. Her life was flimsy—I could already see that.

The basement's bare bulb shined through the window wells; and the dark house, belly-lit, seemed to hover just above earth like a space ship. My father lingered underground, fingers running over the gears of other people's clocks and toaster ovens, a side job. Through the open upstairs windows, my mother whispered urgently, "What's wrong with you?" This, in retrospect, is how she often prefaced a question. "What's wrong with you? Standing out there like that."

"I'm taking my time."

I didn't want to go inside. I was somebody else now. I felt like everything had changed. It seemed possible for the house to heave from earth in a whir of chewed screens and shingles, dust-ruffles and dust. It didn't. My father pulled the chain on the basement bulb, and turned on the front porch light. It burned like a golden pear, like fruit on fire.

And so that spring of my senior year, I became the girl you see in a pack of boys. High, windblown from riding in the backseat. (A mercenary, a tender nurse, a mother, angel. My father once said, "Be kind to boys. They're not as tough as they seem. Don't break their hearts." He was drunk, confused. He'd cut his finger with a paring knife. I was twelve. I promised.) Some people develop a split personality; I developed a split landscape, shrugging off timed sprinklers and newly painted gutters, mailboxes with little erect red flags, for the boardwalk, worn and rotting, held together by rusty nails, the roller coaster's click, click, click and its labored whining motor, its seatbelts frayed and busted, the gray, sickened ocean and wheezing gulls, and what that meant to me: the terrain of boys.

Michael brought me along wherever he and his friends were headed. The guys accepted me—Tony, Victor, Marty. To them, I was the exotic one, bound for college. Michael Hanrahan, didn't I even know then that he was bound to become, I don't know, an Atlantic City Bus Driver? I offered some small condolence of the body. I did backbends out car windows on the highway, flashing my tits.

Now that I was Michael Hanrahan's girlfriend, I had this new air about me. My herringbone mini-skirt was too short to be regulation, but fuck it, and that polyester blazer—I refused to wear it in the halls even when it meant detention. People now whispered about me—a small battle in Self-Esteem Warfare. The Greek girl was the only one who stuck by me, mainly because she starved for facts that I became her sexual CNN. I assume that most of the good girls felt sorry for me. Did I lack self-esteem or did they, sitting in their bedrooms, damp and listless? The answer is we all lacked. The administration was partially right. Love was insufficient. But this is always true. It's the human condition. I don't regret my decisions. My ass remembers the hot hood of a car, and it was time well spent.

The high school administration kept trying, though. They'd developed an arsenal of filmstrips. They were losing the battle, I wasn't the only piece of evidence. What had once been the uplifting story of an armless woman (she could trim her sons' bangs, bake a cake, stir batter, swat a fly, all with her toes) was replaced with stories like *Cathy, Cathy!* about a promiscuous girl who needed love and a virgin football player talked into having sex with her in a van. You were looking at Gauguin's nudes while projectors were wheeled into our stuffy, chalk-dusted classrooms. Lights off, the room took on a backseat feeling, the expectation of fondling. The filmstrips did no good.

Afterward Mrs. Glee dogged me all the way to the door. "I want to talk to you." But she had nothing to say. She kept things vague. "Is there something wrong? Do you need help?"

I stared at her. An underbite and stitched eyebrows, concern knotting at her nose. "No," I said. "I'm as fine as you are. We're all fucked up."

"Don't speak that way to me! I'm reaching out."

"Was there a teacher memo on that?"

"I should give you detention."

"Okay, but in your professional opinion, do you really think that would help?"

I'm proud of this now—you can tell. I didn't have a vocabulary for any of it then, but I was calling bullshit on the whole thing.

I don't think Michael Hanrahan loved me. I bewildered him. He looked surprised to see me every time I walked out of my house and jumped in his car. I was going to go to a small Catholic college a couple hours south come fall, and Michael knew there was no point in falling in love with me. But we did fall in love our bodies together, with blind physicality, which some would claim isn't love, but I'm sure that at seventeen it is.

One afternoon, he was supposed to show up but didn't. I waited an hour then called his house. An old woman answered, not a voice I recognized. I asked if Michael was there.

The old woman backed away from the receiver. There was whispering. Then she asked me, "Which one? Older Michael or younger Michael?"

"The younger one, I guess." I hadn't know there were two.

The old woman muffled the receiver this time. There was a long silence, and then she came back. "His father passed away this morning, dear. It's been a long battle, may he rest in peace."

I had no idea, of course, that his father had been dying. I was stunned. "His father passed away?"

"Yes, dear." She stopped a minute, someone was talking to her again.

"Are you there?" It was his mother.

"Yes."

"Oh, it's you." Did she know it was me? We'd only met once, and I rarely called their house. "Oh, it's been awful." Her voice cracked. She was crying now into the receiver. "I loved him. I loved him."

"I'm so sorry," I said.

But it sounded as if she'd dropped the receiver and then someone hung it up.

I hung up, too, and was standing by the rotary phone, my mother moving around the kitchen, talking about my Uncle Jack's collection of calypso albums. My face was coming apart, unstitched, my chin loose.

Michael's father was dead, and I didn't even know he'd been sick. One time, after having sex in his car, he'd made a strange sound, a choked bark. I'd assumed it was something sexy or meant to be. But now I knew it was a sob, choked off. During all of it, the long drives and the radio and the desperate sweatiness, his father had been dying. I wanted to tell her.

She turned to me, chewing her lipstick. "What?" she asked.

I shrugged. "Nothing." And I left her in the kitchen.

Michael called that night. He asked me to come to the funeral. He sounded different, altered by grief, or maybe it was only my perception, maybe he'd always had some measure of grief in his voice. I just hadn't ever noticed it before.

I didn't want to go to the funeral. I'd only been to the funeral of an ancient aunt—the happy send-off reserved for the extremely old and not especially well loved—more reunion than funeral. Still it had made me uncomfortable. The dead body, dolled-up. But I had to go. "Sure," I told him. "I'll do whatever you want me to."

The funeral was a small gathering, mostly family. Michael

was in the receiving line. His mohawk had grown in, and he'd shaved down to a sturdy crew cut. He looked skinny in his stiff-shouldered suit, brave, attentive, at the ready. I barely recognized him.

At first, he didn't see me. I sat in a chair in the back and watched his mother who stood by the casket. Her twin—he'd never told me this either—her identical twin, came up behind her and they held each other, swaying. They stayed like that for a very long time.

Michael finally saw me. I waved and he nodded me over. I cut across a row, ignoring the line. "Stand next to me," he said.

I shook my head. "I think it's for family. I'm not supposed to."

"I want you to," he said. " Just stand here." It was a whisper, but it labored in his throat. I was afraid he might cry. I did what he said.

It was at this point that I realized how much I looked like Michael Hanrahan. We were both lanky with big green eyes. We had round faces and small noses. It was confusing. The friends and family wanted to place me. I could see them shuffling through lineages, searching for Michael's sister. No, no, he doesn't have a sister, only a little brother who was lying down in the back row, humming loudly. I had to explain myself a few times, but it was surprising how many just wanted to hug me. They wrapped me up in their arms. They smelled sweet, their breath minty with gum. They told me that they were sorry, so sorry for my loss. They smiled at me with great pain and radiance. They said, "Time will heal this wound." They said, "It's hard when you're so young."

And I took it all. I knew that I was stealing, but I took it anyway. I said, "Thank you. Yes, yes. Time." I said, "It's hard. Loss." And all of it was true. Here, we agree, Mr. Motor City Madman.

These years are hard. They aren't sweet. They are bruising and lonesome and urgent, and I was understanding loss. Things were falling away.

Michael and I saw the summer through, but we seemed tragic now. Once we were drinking bad wine, stolen from someone's basement. It was a going-away party, I think, for me. This was toward the end of it, summer, yes, and the end of all of it for me. There was a fight. A bloodied face. A boy ran into the woods. Arms outstretched. One staggering on shore, calling him back. (See, they loved each other. They howled for each other.) One passed out. And Michael was with me under a tree on a flannel blanket. I was riding him. So pretty, and when we were done, he sang "Amazing Grace." I'd heard him scream lyrics, drowned out by pumping bass but I'd never heard him sing. His voice was rough, but nice. "Were you a choir boy?"

"No, you know that. You know everything about me."

But I didn't. For all of my interviewing, I'd come up pretty blank. I didn't say anything. I was breathing softly on his neck.

"Why don't you stay here?" he asked. "Why don't you forget about that college?"

As soon as he asked the question, I realized I'd been waiting for it. I know he wanted me to say, *How would I survive without you? What we've got is so good. It's hard to come by, something this good.* But although I lacked experience and although my parents offered no great example or much of the world, I had the idea that what we had was pretty easy to come by. I sat up, topless, skirt bunched at my waist, and saw the other boys, and I couldn't keep them all safe forever. The boys were dangerous. Each one was shining, lit from within; their souls were torches. I had to let them go, let all of it go, and it was hard to do. And maybe even then I knew it was wrong to let it go, despite rhetoric to the contrary. I loved it: the dirt, the bad wine, the skin, the cars, squealing tires, the radio pitched and reeling. But I was already seeing it through a certain head-tilted gaze. I knew it was something else. That there was a larger swirling, what? Import? Implication? I was reading it. I couldn't stay in the body even though I tried. I told him the truth. "I'll miss you."

Michael looked at me with vacant hurt. He pushed me off of him, zipped up and ran to his car. He drove off, kicking up gravel. One of his friends drove me home, and I left for college two days later.

A month later, maybe two, my mother told me that she'd just heard about the Hanrahan boy's car accident at bridge party. Radio-cranked, he skidded across a scrim of water at an intersection and ran into a telephone pole. He didn't die. He emerged from the car and walked home, in shock. He appeared at his front door, covered in blood, missing his thumb. My mother said, "That's where his mother found him. How awful! What a thing for a mother to see!"

I don't know how he lost his thumb. Now I'm not even sure that it was the same night that I told him we wouldn't stay together. It could have been a week later or more. But still I was sure it was my fault—which is part vanity, isn't it?

Did his mother look at him and know that love was the cause? That I had done this to him? That is what I learned: Sex is destructive. Love is nothing to be fooled with. I learned that I was dangerous, not to be trusted. I wondered if my parents weren't right, with all of their stiff lovelessness. Maybe they knew better. My parents don't dole out love for the deserving or the undeserving. I was learning that love could cost me.

I would like to admit to nothing short of perfection about my growing up: our cheeks were pink, our knees like wax fruit never bruised. Our mothers made sure our toilet water stayed fresh and blue, and our fathers kept map-folded handkerchiefs in their back pockets. But you're right about the silent violence of the modern suburb. My nice little neighborhood wasn't short on grim reality—affairs, neighborly rape, a poisoned dog, once an abduction, the girl found dead. And Asbury Park was fat on it. That's why I liked it there, I suppose, and why I spent so much time with Michael Hanrahan that summer, and the buddies he took up with. When I think of Michael Hanrahan's black eye and mohawk, I know that I recognized myself in him. I felt bruised and there was something comforting about someone who was willing to wear his bruises like that. I found the black eye and the mohawk, too, as some outward sign of having gotten his ass whooped by the world, by taking it, and enduring. And this bloodied version of him? I walked away convinced that I'd nearly killed someone, and that I'd nearly died myself.

And I'm thinking of you as a boy on a dock, feeling unworthy of love, banged up inside, dying a little bit there, some small part of yourself cordoned off and shot. I understand. I am confessing that my first love went wrong. I walked away from my hometown and my bloodied boyfriend, feeling wrecked, lost, already ruined and dangerous. I was unsteady. (I may still be unsteady.)

When boys grow into men, their boyishness is still apparent each time they abandon themselves a little. I stretch against them sometimes—lovesickness, it is the same ache as homesickness for me—and I marvel. The length of their bodies, it's where I find my house, my old street, Asbury Park and all of its yowling—men, they walk around carrying my country, my motherland, and they don't even know. They don't have the tiniest idea.

A little scathed,
Jersey Girl

EVE

November 5

Dear Freeway Flasher,

I was beginning to worry that you weren't going to write back. But I guess you were just taking your time. It's quite a thing, your letter. Reading it (then re-reading it) I felt like I finally got what Bruce was singing about all those years ago, before he came out to California and misplaced his soul. Not some romantic, run-down vision of Jersey, the dying amusement park that becomes another, more perverse, amusement, but the actual desperation of being young and restless and a little too smart for your prospects, revving up on sex and dying hope. I couldn't help but to think of that song, "Janey, Don't You Lose Heart" (a lesser ballad, but terribly on point). And "Sad Eyes." I thought of that one, too, the way his voice rises so gently into mourning. And, though I tried not to, I also thought of you at the wedding, still prowling for danger, for the chance to unpeel your dress and become real. It was a beautiful letter.

I have about a thousand and one questions, but we're supposed to be fessing, not messing, so here goes.

This was the summer I met an older woman. How sophisticated that sounds. How I yearned to feel sophisticated! I was nineteen years old. She was twenty-four. She lived in Hoboken, New Jersey—another Jersey girl—and went to art school in the Village. She was an artist. She dressed in torn oxfords and black tights. She knew the subway system. She had tried heroin. She had friends who were junkies and friends who played rock music and friends who were gay. All that comes later.

The beginning went like this: I took a job as a camp counselor. My original plan was to work at the sleep-away camp where I'd gone for years, and where my sister had been a counselor. I chunked the interview, though, and had to take a job at a day camp near my college. On the first day, we had a staff meeting. The room was filled with young men and women like me: college students at loose ends. This was kind of our first chance to case out the romantic prospects for the summer. I'd worn a tank top for the occasion, and gone down to the little gym they had, to buff myself up. Marnie, the director of the camp, made everyone introduce themselves. We went around the room, the usual thing. All I remember about Eve, the Arts and Crafts counselor, is that she was a friend of Marnie's, obviously older, an adult woman with poise. This put her in a separate category from the college girls, with their eager sympathy and ponytails.

I would like to report that I was an exemplary counselor, wise, compassionate, even-handed and so on. Nope. I tended toward strategies of threat and bribery. I was not beyond setting one child against another, if this decreased the amount of oversight required by me. Perhaps the most unfortunate example was a game of Capture the Flag, during which two of my charges (Corey Gregg and Nicky Slocum) slipped into the graveyard adjoining the campgrounds and urinated on the Pell family crypt. I know this only because the groundskeeper returned the children to my custody, with all due assurances that they would be punished. I cut a deal with them in which I agreed not to tell their parents, if they didn't tell Marnie.

Nicky Slocum. Pudgy, hyperactive Nicky. Nicky with his yellow tube of Ritalin and his grubby windbreaker and his truculent little snout. Like any kid with an insatiable need for attention, he quickly established himself as a pariah. On our first day as a troop, I took my boys to Foothill Park for a nature hike and asked them to close their eyes and tell me what sounds they heard. A hush came over the group. Someone said a bird. Someone else said the wind. A third said, The leaves are rustling. And then Nicky let out a staggering fart, a true vibrato of the butt cheeks.

I mention Nicky because he was the proximate cause of my first encounter with Eve. One day, after lunch, he simply disappeared. I was relieved, initially. But by swim time it seemed important that I take some kind of action. I went to the main office, which was empty. On the way back, I peeked into the Art Studio, and there was Nicky, hunched over a giant sheet of butcher paper.

"Whatcha working on there?" I said.

I could see perfectly well what he was working on: an elaborate painting depicting a giant squid ripping apart several innocent bystanders. The artist had apportioned each victim a bright splash of red. Many of them, even those torn jaggedly in half, appeared to be howling. The squid had an *N* on its chest.

Nicky ignored me.

"Listen," I said, "you can't just disappear. I'm responsible for you. If something happened, like someone abducted you, I'd be held responsible. Do you understand?" I tried briefly to imagine what sort of character would abduct Nicky Slocum.

"I had a stomachache and Marnie said I could come here."

"Okay," I said, in my bogus hard-ass counselor voice. "Just stay put."

I walked into the next room and there was Eve, rinsing her brushes at the sink. She was wearing a spattered smock and cutoffs. Her hair was in pigtails. She looked younger than I remembered.

"Howdy," she said. "You're John, right?"

"Right." I felt embarrassed because none of my kids ever did arts and crafts, because I let them play dodge ball instead, because this tired them out and made them easier to manage. "Here's the thing," I said. "Nicky's supposed to be at the pool. You know, the activity grid, and he didn't say anything about leaving, so obviously, as his counselor, I was concerned, because the other kids, if they get the idea . . ."

Eve smiled. She had these big brown eyes that were slightly pulled down at the corners, and unusually thick eyebrows. Her look was sultry and a little mournful, like a spaniel. We were standing there, amid jars of colored water and tubes of paint and construction paper hearts ringed with macaroni.

"Okay," she said.

"Okay?"

"Sure."

"Because I wasn't sure, Nicky said he talked to Marnie."

She smiled again and slipped past me and squatted next to Nicky, who pretended not to notice. She took his painting in, every criminal slash. "This is great," she said. "You want me to save this?"

"I don't care," Nicky said.

"I think we should save this," she said. "Why don't you go wash up in back."

Nicky, grimacing so as not to be caught smiling, slouched off.

"Sweet," Eve said. "A sweet kid." She set the painting across a desk to dry.

"You don't find his work a little disturbing?" I said.

"In what way?"

"Just, well, in the sense that there's some violence there, like, a desire to rip people apart for instance."

"Huh," she said. "I hadn't thought of it that way."

I stood there, glancing at the smooth white skin of her legs, perplexed. There was some kind of heat rising up between us. I could smell a sweet lotion on the back of her neck. It's really not so complicated most of the time, in terms of chemistry. The body always knows. (You have your own Exhibit A on this one, don't you?)

Eve elbowed me softly in the ribs and grinned. Kidding. She was kidding.

"Oh, I see."

I was trying so hard, even then, not to seem the rube. And Eve was trying, too. Nicky's picture was violent and angry. But there was something bold and hopeful there, as well, in the energy of the lines, in the use of color. The two couldn't be distinguished—that's what made it art.

After that, I started taking my kids to Arts and Crafts. They complained at first, but Eve basically let them do what they wanted. She didn't give them anything to buck against. She supplied them with finger paints and Flair pens and glitter and said: have at it, boys! This was life, this colorful disarray. And Eve hurrying across the room in her cutoffs, answering their urgent pleas. *Miss Eve! Miss Eve! Lookit! Lookit!* Kids can sniff a fake a mile off and they knew she wasn't faking. She was totally unselfconsciously fascinated by what they created. Watching her helped relieve me of the cloak of duty I wore so clumsily. I became, if not a better counselor, a little less wretchedly phony.

You know how it goes from here: the fluttery stomach, the excuses to be near her, the little things you might say. Still, I took the crush to be one-way, even after Eve invited me over to Marnie's house, where she was staying. I expected Marnie to be there, along with her unctuous husband, Dolf, some kind of adult type party thing.

But they had gone to Napa for the weekend.

We drank a bottle of wine and ate some apples and cheese. We talked about whatever we talked about. Eve had a bump in her nose I wanted to kiss. She smoked with a nonchalance I found unbearably sexy. "Do you want to take a hot tub?" she said.

"I didn't bring a suit."

"That's okay," she said.

I still didn't get it.

I couldn't quite convince myself that an adult woman with poise would take much interest in me. When you grow up in the shadow of an older sister spun from gold, when you spend your pubescent years in the orbit of all her golden friends, you tend to think of yourself as invisible to older women. Or maybe not invisible exactly, but off-the-map sexually. It's not true. I remember all too well the way Lisa's friends handled me, mussed my hair, stroked my cheeks, brushed against me, how, only half meaning to, they fed a confusion of lewd and the motherly gestures into the bubbling cauldron of my hormones and watched them boil up into a terrified desire—it was all perfectly vicious and sweet. And, if we're going to lay it all out there, I should confess that I was deeply in love with Lisa herself, and that this love was brotherly admiration mainly, but also contained germs of a less wholesome variety. More about that later. I need to stay on point here. It's all that keeps me from chaos when the memories start popping.

Eve opened the back door and stepped into the backyard. There was a wooden deck and a hot tub. A soft light was shining somewhere out of view. Eve unhooked her overalls and let them drop to the ground. She pulled off her T-shirt. She stepped out of her little white panties. There was nothing showy in these actions. She was utterly relaxed in her body. She went to take the cover off the hot tub. Steam rose from surface of the water and clung to her body.

"Are you coming in?"

I nodded.

The rim caught a little as Eve slid herself down into the tub, and the pale swell of her bottom caught the light.

I stepped back into the shadows and removed my clothing very slowly and folded my underwear and my pants and my shirt and my sweater and rolled my belt up (I had overdressed) and waited for my goddamn boner to relent.

Eve made a sound of pleasure. "It's nice."

"Should I get some towels?" I said.

"Oh shit," she said. "Towels."

She got out of the tub and walked toward me. I was in, what, a minor panic? I hopped from one foot to the other, gave my boner a stern little whack, which my boner, bless its stupid Cro-Magnon soul, actually enjoyed. This was not something I'd done before, to get naked in front of a woman in such a casual way. I didn't know the rules. Getting a boner seemed, well, gauche. What was happening here? Were we going to have sex? In the tub? Were there neighbors at issue?

I had eased myself onto this little brick path near the back door. Eve came and stood in front of me. "Are you okay?" she said. "Is this making you feel uncomfortable?"

"No," I said.

"I don't want you to feel uncomfortable."

"Not at all."

I had been sort of hunched over, in a bogus, just-checking-the-ground-for-change pose. To prove just how comfortable the whole situation was making me I straightened up. I had, back then, the body of a nineteen-year-old. I was lean and muscled and terribly insecure. If a girl was within fifty feet of me, I flexed everything. Eve examined my body in the same concerted way she'd taken in Nicky's painting, a gaze that might be mistaken for adoration, but was really more like ravenous perception. And I felt the same excruciating pleasure Nicky had. A part of me wanted to run away, another part wanted leap forward.

Eve's gaze scrolled down my torso, then stopped.

"I see," she said huskily.

I began shivering a little.

"You're cold," Eve said. "You need to get warm."

So we climbed into the tub and floated slowly toward one another and her tongue tasted of wine and Parliaments. I will spare you the details of our further aquatic exertions. I don't really remember them. I do remember the smell of that first time which took place later, inside—the musty redwood of Marnie's attic guest room—and I remember Eve looking up at me and whispering, "I'm on the pill." The magic of those three little words! On the pill. No ardent fumbling. No stopping and starting. No stinky condom smell to foul our congress. It was all so adult. Eve didn't need any excuses; she certainly wasn't worried about Self-Esteem Warfare. She was perfectly at home with her pleasure, gallant, unashamed. To reiterate: an adult woman.

I don't expect I was much of a lover, but Eve wasn't interested in skill. "When I saw you at that first meeting," she told me, "I wanted to jump over the table and just attack you." We were lying on the musty bed in Marnie's little condo and Eve was running her fingers down my chest.

I don't know that I can convey how happy this statement

made me. Eve was the first woman who had ever made her
desire for me so explicit. What she was saying: she noticed me;
she took notice of me, and not because of my frantic efforts
to be noticed—though those were, of course, perpetual—
but because my body, just my body, my still-mostly-hairless
post-adolescent body, lit something inside her.

And one other thing from that first night: in the morning,
when I woke up, I felt a warm, steady breath on the back of my
neck and a soft body curled around mine and for a moment (as
sometimes happens when you awaken in a strange bed) I lost
track of where I was, how old I was; I believed I might be much
younger than nineteen, a boy again, and that the body curled
around mine belonged to my sister Lisa, who had allowed me
to climb into bed with her in the months after my parents built
an addition to the house and moved upstairs.

It was the briefest moment, but I felt my heart flushed with
a terrifying impermanent joy, the kind you feel in a dream, because those months had been the closest I would come to Lisa
again, before she cast me out of her bed, out her life, become
a complicated and remote teenager engaged in some wordless
battle with my mother that I didn't understand and wasn't allowed to speak about.

I promised not to skip ahead, so I won't here. But it's important to know that Lisa, in her twenty-fourth year, was living
in Nicaragua, where she'd met and secretly married an amiable
Sandinista named Daniel. I would get a letter every six months
or so, filled with chilling domestic details (scorpions skittering
across her skin at night, open latrines) and what I can now
see as factually accurate but emotionally disturbed polemics
against the evils of the Reagan administration. I was to tell
none of this to my mother.

But my disappointment, there in the bed in Marnie's

attic, was momentary. I was delighted to be in bed with Eve, shocked, drowsy, almost immediately horny.

I'm sure I spent the next few days tormented about what all this meant, whether Eve had just taken me to bed on a lark, as an older woman might, or whether she was interested in something more. But it couldn't have been too bad, because Eve was, from the beginning, forthright in her affections.

We picnicked in the golden hills above my college town and snuck in overnights when my roommate agreed to vacate our one-bedroom dump. We slipped off during various dreary staff parties and dry-humped in the kitchen. One night Eve took me to a sushi restaurant—sushi was all the rage in New York—but I was too frightened to try raw fish and ordered chicken teriyaki instead. More successful was her introduction of the Violent Femmes. I became an insufferable fan. I must have listened to the first album a thousand times, those dark, catchy anthems of the yodeling unlaid, the gospel music of the anguished suburban white boy.

And though it will no doubt seal my reputation for disturbing sexual associations, I should mention one August episode, as it was typical of our covert enthusiasms. This took place on the last overnight of the summer, to Moony Lake. The kids went to sleep and I snuck over to where Eve was and we zipped our sleeping bags together and went to town. It was sexy, going at it with a bunch of eight-year-olds dreaming all around us. Before we could get to the main event, though, Eve told me to hold on. "I'm just at the end of my period," she said. "It may be a little messy."

"Messy's okay," I said.

Eve reached down and took off her panties. Then she turned away from me and sat up and tossed something into the woods.

"What are you doing?"

"Nothing," she said, and climbed on top of me.

I awoke, just after dawn, to the sound of excited whispers. Nicky Slocum and half a dozen younger boys were gathered at the edge of the woods.

"What is it?" one of the younger kids said.

"I told you, it's a dead mouse."

"How did it die?"

"Bubonic plague," Nicky said scientifically. "That's what happens when you get bubonic plague. Your guts turn inside out."

It's probably true that children should not be examining dead rodents. But it was typical of my managerial style that summer to ignore them. It was Eve who leaped up from her sleeping bag and hurried toward them. I thought, absurdly, she might be worried about the plague. Then she looked down at the object of their gleeful inspection and her face froze. She calmly told the boys to get back to bed, immediately. I needn't elaborate.

Well.

Somewhere in there, Eve informed me that she had a boyfriend back east. I'm sure I was hurt, but I realized Eve was an older woman and this implied certain prerogatives. I might even have felt proud that I tempted her to stray.

What happened next? She took a bus back to New York City. The students returned to campus. We wrote one another. I mucked around with a sociology major who bored me to smithereens. Eve called. She came to visit. She brought a bottle of champagne and an advance copy of the new Violent Femmes. We spent all of our time in my room. It felt ridiculous to be with her on campus, like: Uh, here's the dorms, here's the cafeteria. Eve wasn't so much older than me, and she was in art school herself. But the life she led—the Italian restaurant where she waitressed, the clubs where she drank and

smoked till morning, the run-down studios and galleries—
struck me as dangerous and authentic, a world apart from the
neat lawns of my semi-elite college. We didn't talk about her
boyfriend, either. He was a musician of some kind, a few years
older than Eve.

We settled into a sort of routine. Every two weeks. I sat
in classrooms and scratched out notes under the humming
florescent lights. Significant ideas floated around me like dust
motes. I went to parties and held plastic cups of beer. I returned to my room and cranked the Femmes. The skies outside my window turned a pointless gray. I pawed at the hours
until Eve appeared.

Eve was changing, though. She seemed diminished by
winter. Dark patches bloomed under her eyes. She lost weight.
She seemed restless. One night, I woke to find that she had
slipped out of bed and seated herself by the window, naked and
blue in the moonlight. She was smoking a cigarette; the fallen
ash was on her thigh.

I got up and stood behind her and she slumped against me
and stifled a sob.

"What is it?" I said.

She wept for a long time.

The story slowly emerged. Her boyfriend had gotten himself addicted to heroin. He was doing more and more of the
stuff. He owed money. He'd moved in with her. She'd kicked
him out, but she was worried he would kill himself.

I didn't know what the hell to say. They hadn't covered this
in any of my psych classes. And yet, I felt weirdly honored to
be taken up in such a drama. Here was something worthy of
my emerging passion, a cause.

Later, I asked Eve if she'd ever tried heroin.

"Yeah."

"What it's like?" I said.

She paused. "It feels like life should feel."

"Sounds dangerous," I said.

"We're not together anymore," she said. "I want you to come down and visit me, John. Will you do that?"

So I began taking the bus down to New York City, the Path train over to Hoboken, to Eve's railroad apartment, which was littered with tubes of paint and papier–mâché masks, wine bottles and kitty litter. And all those weekends are a kind of golden blur to me now, mixed up with the myth of New York City which infects the minds of all us kids from California towns, of avenues so wide and frantic as to obliterate doubt and buildings as tall as gods, and with the memory of Eve herself, who smelled luxurious from the shower, smoothed down in amaretto lotion, who went off to work in the city and returned with wads of grubby dollar bills and cabernet on her breath, who smoked on the window sill and wore her floppy breasts in scented bras and who took me up to her rooftop to make love on the hot tar and eat Chinese from white boxes and gaze across the Hudson at the city's sylvan blocks and to eat French toast in the Irish bars along Channing Avenue on Sunday mornings, the smell of coffee beans a thick, descending plume from the Chock Full O'nuts factory and the empty lots full of Puerto Rican kids playing stickball and spitting proudly and her hand in mine as I claimed the sunny sidewalks and inhaled the green scent of adulthood.

We drank cheap vodka from paper cups on her fire escape with her homely gay roommate, Raphael, who told us about all the boys he had fucked and sucked and what it was like to burp up sperm and rim another man and laughed like a maniac because he was so lonely and didn't know what else to do.

Later we retired to her room, where we lay on her wide bed,

under the cracked plaster rosettes, and listened to the patter of the streetwalkers floating up from the street. *You got enough for this, Romeo? How much, twenty? That'll get you a ticket to Newark, babydoll.* Her room was full of art, paintings of shadowy figures, bright plastic daggers of color, driftwood-and-wax sculptures. Eve and her friends traded pieces incessantly. Her own work was stunning. She created giant creatures made of plaster, eight feet tall, with elongated limbs and heads made of crankshafts or subwoofers. I found these figures unsettling at first, and then, as they became familiar, oddly soothing, like benign uncles. I didn't really see it then, but Eve was, in her own unobtrusive way, leading me toward my own love of art.

You spoke, in your letter, of a desire to transport yourself. You wanted to escape the safety of your hometown, the needy delusions of your mother. You were desperate for emotional honesty, or maybe you wanted the emotional honesty of desperation. Whatever the case, you threw yourself into a second life, tragic and bracing, the funeral, the boys, your body, their blood. But, if I'm reading you right, this was only a temporary thing. And that's what I should confess about Eve. I can see now how much she protected me from the darker aspects of her life, the long hours of humiliating servitude, the struggle to create, the vicious hopeless envy of the New York art scene, the drugs done to numb all of the above. She made it easy for me to be a tourist. And it's probably true that she needed my innocence, as well. I was young and pretty and amazed by all of it. She was protecting herself by proxy, I guess.

Why, then, did I decide to take a semester abroad? Because I couldn't stand the thought of returning to school and I was afraid to drop out. I also believed a foreign country might make me more worldly. Eve, who had spent a year drifting in Europe after dropping out of college, encouraged this belief. The other reason (one I was only remotely aware of back then) had to do with Lisa, who was, after all, offering me her own bleak vision of the world from a dirty pueblo outside San Salvador. I chose Mexico City because it was the only city on earth larger than New York and because I knew its poverty would please Lisa, and would infuriate my mother, and thereby strengthen the allegiance that might bring my sister back to me.

But that's not the way it went at all.

Instead, a month into my stay, I received a phone call from my father, who told me that Lisa was missing. Word filtered back that she may have been in an accident, the bus she was (maybe) traveling on had plunged into a ravine. And later, to make a very long story short, dental records confirmed that she was on that bus, that *cuerpo numero dies y ocho* was, as we feared, Lisa Janis _____.

Lisa used to joke about those bus rides in her letters. She talked about the careless drivers, the narrow roads, the blind curves, the young boys charged with crowding people onto these buses, prodding at them with steel-tipped canes. This was part of her posturing. She knew that I would convey some of this to my mother, and that my mother would fume and fret and sprout more gray hairs.

I know we promised not to get into all the family shit, but I can't fairly withhold this information. I hope it doesn't reduce me to some pitiable category, *the guy whose sister died*. The real tragedy, after all, wasn't her death, but whatever forces turned her away from our family, caused her to flee into another culture, to abandon even me, who worshipped her with the fierce, doomed loyalty of a younger sibling.

Eve, of course, was mixed up in all of this. It's too simple suggest she was the sister I wished to reclaim. She was more like the sister I wished to invent, older and wiser, but not embittered by this wisdom, a gentle guide into the hardness of the world. Most of all, she found something in me to desire. She kissed me. She held me. She held on.

When she found out about Lisa's death, she offered to come down to Mexico. And later she wrote to invite me to stay with her over the summer. I refused both offers. I was too guilty to permit myself these comforts, not just because Lisa had died but because I had been angry at her when she died, and therefore, in some deeply fucked up way, I had killed her, and now that she was dead and I was the murderer, Eve was the last person I deserved. Or maybe Eve became Lisa and, in my rage, I killed her off again.

"You're no savage, right?" That's what you asked me. But you know as well as I do that we're all savages at some point. Our love gets hammered into something sharp and we stab the people around us, for the unpardonable crime of refusing to abandon us.

As I say, a lot of this is retrospect, guess work, pieced together in offices with muted lighting and bearded doctors. I had no idea what was happening at the time. I just bailed. Eve wrote letters of concern. She called. She pleaded with my answering machine. Then she stopped writing. Then she wrote a letter informing me she had started to see the guitar player again, he was clean and sober, she loved him and wished me well.

When I got back to the States I called her, and hung up until she answered. I begged her to meet me somewhere. This was senior year. I was stumbling toward a degree in Who Gives A Shit, sleepless, vacant, surly, not-very-nice-smelling. She did come to meet me and we sat over plates of seafood in a Spanish restaurant in Chelsea, while I tried to explain that I loved her, had made a mistake, my mind was a little cloudy, couldn't we go back to how it was. I started crying. The waitress and the other patrons glanced over. Eve looked at me helplessly.

I went to the bathroom and when I returned I told her: "It's okay. I'm fine."

Outside, on the sidewalk, I began crying again. I couldn't stand the idea that she was going to leave me. She let me fall against her and took me back to her apartment. I'm not sure how she did this. The rocker must have been out of town. But there were signs of him everywhere: guitars, amps, mic stands, a brisk cologne type smell, and no Raphael.

She even slept with me that night. "What did you want me to do?" she said afterward. "You broke my heart, John."

I woke up at dawn with Eve curled around me. But it was too late, the dread was surging inside me again and I slipped out of her apartment a few minutes later and ran down the half-lit streets of Hoboken, past the pawnshops and bodegas, the butchers and the laundromats, toward the Path train.

It's too easy for people to blame their bad behavior on misfortune. My sister Lisa could have told you something about that. She had the sort of mind that could have rescued whole countries. But her heart made her stupid with revenge.

And she passed some of that on to me.

You want a confession? How's this:

Eve let me back in and I killed her off again.

> Putting the blood in bloodlust,
> Ted

Nov. 13

Dear John,

I should admit that I'm clumsy and awkward with loss, even small ordinary goodbyes. I can't imagine having a sister. I can't imagine then losing her. I know you don't want my sympathy. But it's irreversible. Your last confession made me miss you, not the version from the coat check, but this other new version that is being revealed in such a way that I was almost too superstitious to even comment on it—too afraid it might stop.

I wouldn't be honest if I didn't tell you that I've played this letter out a number of ways. In one version, I stick by the rules. I hand over my confession the way you probably want me to—without all of this cloying sympathy. I begin: *Dear the guy whose sister died.* But I can't bring myself to send it.

I've also worried out a soft version where I begin by bending the rules, veering from the past enough to say it's snowing here too early in the season—the lightest kind of moth-like snow that seems to blow upward as much as it does down, and then I confess that the rules we've designed—confession for confession, no present-day life, no commentary, no therapy— they all seem too restrictive now, too contrived. Why? Because we can suddenly die.

Since I read your last confession, I've found myself eyeing people—the way we bustle from place to place, squint at streetlights. We scoot around in our office chairs and point to things and explain. We sip our drinks and fuss at our plates and dig for our cell phones. We preen and huff and gaze. I'd be more impressed by orangutans, frankly. At least they are sometimes in love enough to pick each other's ticks or furious enough to throw their own shit.

All of this waiting, is it a waste? Should we rethink this? Shouldn't we dole out our compassion in person? Shouldn't I be allowed to whisper some sorrow about your lost sister? Shouldn't you be allowed to whisper back?

J.

November 19

Jane,

I'm not sure what to tell you. This is a weirdo scenario we've gotten ourselves into. Utterly. There's no present-tense relationship to pad the wreckage of the past, no body language to read, no domestic clues to inspect (from me, it goes: CD collection, bookshelf, refrigerator, mattress, not necessarily in that order). No first awkward meal with friends. No first night together, no first morning, no first fight, or reconciliation. I have no idea how you spend your days, or where you live, and, most important, no clear sense of what you'd order at my favorite taqueria, or whether the menu (a field of faded Polaroids taped to the front window) would enthrall you as it does me.

What's even weirder: I can't bring myself to disclose this thing—whatever it is, a written audition, an extended power-flirt—to the appropriate confidants. It feels too intimate and fragile, maybe even desperate. And yet I find myself working on these letters at all hours, skipping brunches and movies. (Already, I'm blowing off my friends for you.) The mail has become this major event. I count the days between letters. It's like I'm in prison.

I should mention that the storm you guys got last night is, at the moment, swirling down the lower avenues, whiting out the awnings. I'm just back from an errand—yes, reading to the orphans again—and pleased to report that the fresh dog poop in Saint Christopher Park is steaming, the homeless vets are knuckling for grate space, the Chrysler Building has dandruff.

And beneath all this fancy throat-clearing, here's what I

really want to say (as much to myself as to you): Don't stop. I mean it, Jane. Every famous case of love boils down to reckless honesty. And that's what's happening here, I think. We're both smart enough to know this might not work, probably won't. But that the chance to tell the truth, the whole truth, doesn't come along too often.

[Insert sound of tin cup
dragged across prison bars],
Inmate #102766

ELTON BIRCH

November 27

Dear #102766,

Here, let me break the rules, because this seems crucial, make-or-break. If looking at the menu at your favorite taqueria—that plate glass store front of pale Polaroids—maybe I would find one that the photographer took a little impatiently, and there in the corner is the arranger's hand, part of the sleeve—the owner's wife? Cousin? Did they fight about it? — and I would wonder out loud whether they noticed and decided to let that picture stay—out of laziness or maybe because, at your favorite taqueria, they aren't afraid of some humanity. In either case, that's the dish I would choose. That or the enchilada supreme.

(I'm not stopping. See me, here, not stopping?)

Elton Birch. The El. L-tone.

The last time I saw him he was crazy—fierce but trapped, like the lion forced to wear the strap-on bowler who used to ride in a motorcycle sidecar at the Casino Arcade Motordome on the old Wildwood boardwalk.

But that wasn't the real Elton. Not absolutely. He will be hard to explain.

He was rich. He drove a beaten Saab. He set up bar tabs under secret code names that got whispered around till he was buying drinks for everyone. His father, Ned, was crazy. He'd say, "The old bastard's crazy." And he meant it. Institutionalized off and on. His mother was a rudder, though. He called her Gloria as in "Gloria wants me to go into plastics." (He loved the movie *The Graduate.*) Sometimes Elton wanted to be called Madden, because he'd learned that Owney Madden had owned the Cotton Club and was eventually given the state of Arkansas as his illegal fiefdom. He liked the name Blaze, too. And people would call him whatever he wanted, because he was wearing a cowboy hat, shorts, and flip-flops, which demands a cockiness hard to deny, and because everyone was drinking on his tab . . . sometimes Owney Madden's tab or Blaze's, sometimes Mr. and Mrs. Misterandmissus's tab, which was code for the two of us. He called people "Old boy," because he'd read *Gatsby*, and "old bastard" because he'd read *Catcher in the Rye*. He was, of course, as crazy as his father Ned, but I didn't know crazy at the time. So I thought it was all astonishingly cool.

Elton saved me from college. He'd dropped out of a few top-notch institutions. He'd say, "I'm doing the Eastern Seaboard. I'm gauging educational experiences. I'm running my own private survey-says!" And then he'd say *bing!* as if we were on that game show. He was very Tourette's associative.

Also gorgeous, in a banged up way. He had a broken nose, a crooked jaw, but beautiful teeth, an undying smile. His blond hair was permanently windswept—the Saab was a convertible. He would pick me up off the ground right in the middle of talking to me. Just pick me up. It's hard to explain. He was unstoppably loveable and unstoppably unpredictable. I once saw an old man in a bar slip him twenty bucks, saying, "You, fella, are going places. Here, just a little something." And

Elton said, "Why, thank you mightily." And after the old man shuffled off, Elton rolled it up and tried to smoke it.

Before I found Elton, I was desperately disappointed with college. My parents—neither of whom had gone—had billed it as otherworldly. A pair of art professors lived on our street. My parents treated them like they were giraffes. If they didn't mow their lawn or take their garbage around back, my parents forgave them with a kind of shrug that seemed to say: *Can't blame them. They're giraffes after all. God bless 'em, they only have hooves.* And my own notions of college weren't very solid. *Paper Chase, Animal House.*

But this college was cheerless with only one swatch of grassy lawn and a chime every hour that lacked a commanding gong; it seemed to be announcing that it was kind of ten-ish, sorry to interrupt. The faculty in their cardigans showed up late for classes, catatonic, sometimes with tubercular coughs and mustard-crusted stains. They were deluded, often confusing themselves with the historical figures they were teaching. Every once in a while one of the professors seemed to try to muster a Rah-rah for Descartes—maybe because he suddenly thought he might be Descartes—or the Great War, but it was drowned out by the overwhelming drone of boredom and echoing clatter of someone with a bucket swabbing down a hallway.

What made things worse—I'd been hit with an unexpected wallop of guilty. I'd left my parents behind. I'd served for years as a necessary distraction. Hunkered down over roasts and pudding desserts, my parents would sometimes have to break their fixed, atrophied attention and regard me. Now I imagined catastrophe, as if they could wander into their own private despairs and die of hypothermia or heart failure.

There was nothing I could do for them. I was living with

Kelly from Perth Amboy—a chalky girl with long mousy hair that smoothed to nothingness down her back because it had never been cut. She called home often.

I worked my ass off to get her stoned. (One of the boys had given me a parting gift in a plastic baggy.) I told her that rebellion was a patriotic duty, citing the Revolutionary War. I followed her around the dingy room lined with milk crates and her posters (colorized black and whites of children in top hats holding flowers and such) while humming the national anthem. I played on her thorough education in being nice. She finally relented.

We blared pop radio while I cut her bangs with tiny nail scissors. We got busted by a pair of overly officious security guards. The RA, a knock-kneed young republican, held up our charts.

"You're off the field hockey team," the republican told me.

"Really?" I said. I wasn't on the field hockey team, but was still stung by the injustice. (It's my nature to be stung by injustice.)

"And look at that poor girl's hair!" He shook his head. "Well, well, Kelly, you've made your own punishment there."

Kelly's fingers trembled across the stubble. With her Mary necklace and the fringe of bangs, she looked like a Mexican cab, but without the character. She blubbered. We were put on probation. I realized I'd been secretly hoping for expulsion.

I was scared of turning to boys for survival. I'd already made that mistake in Asbury Park (which I missed too much . . . because it can rip the bones from your back. Yep, I listened to too much Bruce. I know Janey—I'll take your sorrow if you want me to and all the others. It would take years of therapy to untangle the influence of rock and roll in my self definition. Jane, Sweet, Sweet Jane. Or maybe music has just saved me an awful lot of time in my self definition. It's hard to say.) Michael Hanrahan still haunted me—the image of him stepping out of the twisted car, walking home, blood-soaked, his hand pinned to his chest. His thumb, had they ever found it? Was his hand sewn shut? Could he still shake someone's hand? Had he forgiven me? If I had nearly killed Michael Hanrahan—the tough boy of Asbury Park—what damage would I do to this pristine college lot? I felt like a cannibal who'd happened upon a picnic of churchgoers. I was trying not to devour anyone.

But I did sample a few college boys, delicately, like picking up a chocolate and trying to see if it's one of those pink cream-filled horrors without actually biting into it. Most were pink cream-filled horrors. I was undercome (why do we always have to be overcome?). Damn, they were emotional box turtles, skulking around in baseball caps, freshly beer-bloated, all pent up, shrugging the primary colors of their J. Crew jackets, lift tickets flipping from zippers. Sometimes they got drunk and unfettered and peed wildly in public. There was, in fact, a counselor whose sole job was to manage the fragile psyches of public pissers. Now, don't get me wrong, I like a nice box turtle. I had one as a child and scrubbed its shell with a toothbrush. And I might have actually learned to control my barbaric tendencies and endured college, coaxing these boys out of their shells with turtle food and scrubbing their tough backs . . . But then there was Elton Birch.

I'd seen him striding across campus. Head down, his cowboy hat strung round his neck—it bobbed on his back. People slapped his skinny shoulders. "L-tone! My man!" Sometimes he'd bark at people across the lawn, and they'd laugh and wave. "That's the El-man for you." I'd seen him once from a classroom window, galloping, quite alone, down a ramp in the pouring rain.

He stared at me when I was working behind the counter at the school-owned pizzeria where I had a part-time job to help with tuition, but I'd noticed that he often stared at people. I'd noticed because I stared at people too, which often made them stare back especially fellow-starers. So it was hard to tell where he stood, romantically.

I was walking home from the school pizzeria one night, cutting through a parking lot. Elton was zagging around in his dented red Saab, and pulled up sharply beside me. It was starting to get cold, but he had the top down. He said, "Excuse me. I'm in need of directions."

"I don't really know where anything is." I have a lousy sense of direction, and I still had a campus map in my backpack, but I wasn't willing to admit to something like that.

Elton said, "This is fine actually, because, well, fuck, I think I am where I'm supposed to be." He sat up a bit in the seat and looked out over the windshield.

"That's bad news."

"Exactly. See, Gloria's put me in her backyard this time so's to keep an eye on me, but I'm not so sure it's going to work." He always spoke as if everyone knew pretty much everything about him, and I didn't know it then, but a lot of people did. The Birches were old money, made more famous for their history of eccentrics—suicidal poets, weasel-raising million-aires, military psychotics. Elton was part of a long-standing tradition.

"Who's Gloria?"

"Glo and Ned. My parents. Good people. Good stuff. Let's go get a drink." He slid down into the driver's seat and revved the engine.

"I don't have an ID."

"Are you feeling sincere?"

"I guess."

"Sincerity. That's all you need. It's the most important thing to know how to fake, but I don't say that from experience. I'm unfailingly honest. It's a disease."

And so I got in the car. He put in "California Dreaming," and we slammed onto the beltway. It was cold, blustery. My eyes teared.

"What's your story? You look like you have one."

"I got kicked off the field hockey team, but I wasn't ever on it." I was trying to keep up. I was already pretty sure that Elton was dangerous, not in a way that the Asbury Park boys were. A topless backbend wouldn't do the trick here.

"I was once captain of something, some sport, but that was colleges ago."

He pulled into the parking lot of a dim little bar, Dick's Bar, the kind with a front window strung with Christmas lights year-round. He killed the engine, pulled his cowboy hat out of the backseat. "What's your name?"

"Jane. You?" I already knew his name.

"It's your choice, really. I have no real investment either way. My mother named me Elton. Do you like that?"

"Sure."

"Okay then."

We started walking to the front door, but he stopped me. One streetlight poured down on us, kind of held us there for a moment. He said, "I like you. I could follow you around all day. I've seen you at that job, and I think I would mope for a very long time if you didn't like me back. What do you think?"

Nobody had ever really asked me what I thought, or if they did, they didn't really expect an answer. And certainly nobody had ever asked me what I thought of them.

"Take a minute." He waited, gazing around the lot, down

WHICH BRINGS ME TO YOU   93

the street. He seemed suddenly anxious as if there were a lot riding on my answer. I was nervous, too. He stuffed his hands into the pockets of his shorts—baggy, faded khakis that, because of the wear and tear, made him seem all the more wealthy. He breathed up at the sky. He had a beautiful neck, a restless energy. He seemed already thoroughly corrupted, somehow. And me? What did I look like? Levi's, bought at a second-hand shop. My top probably looked new and cheap because it was. I wore too much eyeliner, and there was nothing subtle about my padded bra.

I was nervous. I said, "If you were a ride in an amusement park, I'd buy a ticket to see what would happen." I was used to Asbury Park, those metaphors made sense to me, but still the way it came out I immediately flashed on Michael Hanrahan, alive and healthy, lanky, naked, twisting around in the backseat of his car. And I wondered if I would ride Elton. Was that what I was saying? That I'd ride him?

"That works for now."

The packed bar was long and narrow, humid and yeasty. There were regulars, men with large bellies, and a few rowdy college kids, players of some sort, lacrosse or rugby. A few girls, not many. The Christmas lights were the blinking kind. They pulsed dimly.

Everyone seemed to know Elton. In fact, it seemed like they'd been in some sort of holding pattern waiting for him to arrive. They swarmed, and I realized he was famous in that way local people can be famous. People wanted to know who I was. "Jane!" he'd yell over the juke box. "Her name is Jane!" He pulled me under his arm, and he forced a way to the bar.

The bartended said, "She legal?"

"Doesn't she look legal, old boy," he said. "Put her on the tab."

We got drunk, the whole bar. Elton and I pulsed and flailed
on the cramped dance floor. He crooned along with "Brown
Eyed Girl," "Feel Like Makin' Love." We were an instant couple, celebrities. I felt like I was dating John John at Brown.
Elton was sometimes droopy-eyed and tender then he'd beam
at his entourage. "Isn't Jane perfect? Isn't she perfect? Look,
look, she's blushing. Don't you love it when Jane blushes?"

I was blushing, though it wasn't in character. But I'd never
been so adored before.

Every once in a while somebody would ask him about Ellen. Some drunk. "Where's Ellen?"

But he'd shrug them off. "No, no. No speak Ellen. Me no
speak Ellen."

Elton drove drunk as badly as he did sober, there was no
marked distinction; if anything I'd have to say there was im-
provement, which should have been an indication. He asked
me if I wanted to go home or home with him. I said I'd rather
go home with him. I felt absolutely blessed. I'd been a one-man
band, a horse-and-pony show in Asbury Park. But Elton was
the real thing—he was loved by an entire bar of people. This
was completely beyond my grasp. And, moreover, he seemed
to want to pull me into the spotlight with him, to help soak it
up. Why would I ever want to return to Kelly, dusty Kelly with
her horrifying half-inch bangs.

I hadn't realized that when Elton said *Gloria's put me in her
backyard this time so's to keep an eye on me* that he was being lit-
eral. He lived in a guest house behind the his parents' giant stone
house. Still in the city limits, the house must have cost a million
dollars, now two? I don't have any real concept of money.

The guest house didn't have any food in it although its
kitchen was bigger than my mother's at home. And so Elton
and I went through the back door to the main house's kitchen.

It was immense, gleaming, industrial, but also plush. I imagined my mother and father clipping around in there. Could my parents continue to wear their punctured hearts pinned to their overcoats if they had this kind of wealth—my father with his slack expression of defeat; my mother whistling her little livid tune. What kind of disgust wouldn't just lift to the twenty-foot ceilings and linger up there overhead, letting everybody breathe a little easier?

Elton looked smaller. His cowboy hat was left behind in the backseat of his car and the high ceilings seemed to shrink him. He was uneasy. It was easily two o'clock in the morning, but I could hear distant chattering.

"Are your parents up?" I asked.

"It's nothing." He hurried.

"Who's that talking?"

"What?"

"Talking, somebody's talking."

"Oh, Ned doesn't sleep."

Elton grabbed chips and cheese and pears, and we went back to the guest house. We ate and Elton asked me questions. "Will you be able to stick school out? Did you ever play field hockey? Do you want to be someone of consequence one day?"

I was answering. I'm sure that I was saying something, but mostly I was waiting for him to kiss me. Michael Hanrahan, the healthy, heroic version I could still glimpse, wouldn't have asked any questions. He'd have already been done by now, breathless, zipping up with a smile. But Elton was insecure. It was four o'clock in the morning before he fiddled with the buttons on my shirt. He kissed quietly, apologetically. In fact, he apologized throughout the whole thing—for pinning down my hair with an elbow, for bumping, squashing, for things I couldn't determine. "That's okay," I kept saying. "You don't have to apologize." And he apologized for over-apologizing.

Not that night, but some other night soon after, we fished our way through sex. It felt like fishing, like there was casting and reeling and a bobber bobbing. There was a condom, fiddled with the intensity of putting a worm on a hook. Eventually we caught something that flipped around. It was awkward. Elton was tall and thin. His skin held onto a tan and his nipples, I remember they didn't poke up. They were shiny and flat and smooth as ironed silk.

Eventually, we would make a little nest out of the guest house, and the sex, like Elton, was unpredictable. I never knew who'd show up. Elton, doing some horrible Woody Allen impersonation, or some borderline kinky duke who liked to take the wooden mirror off the wall and set it up against the headboard, and was fond of the expression: Objects may be larger than they appear. I would glance at the mirror and away again. I was always surprised to find myself there. The mirror seemed to be trying to tell me that I was not a girl in Asbury Park. I was here now. But I wasn't fully convinced. I guess it was also true that the mirror took me out of my body, and put me into the mirror as an observer, detached and restless. And so part of myself was just keeping an eye on my life instead of living it.

Elton, by contrast, was always living his life. He seemed reassured, as if asking himself, Are we in love? Are we beautiful? Yes, we are. It reminded me of the Elton who loved to be the center of attention, how sometimes we'd stop in at Dick's Bar just long enough for him to get a hit of adoration.

Sometimes I liked the duke. Sometimes I liked the shy, unlit, tentative sex of Elton's other self. And sometimes I had sex at Elton, like something thrown. Sometimes he barely existed, duke or not. I felt a little crazy myself, and sometimes I wanted

to be allowed to crash through sex—sometimes I still do—
beating the world out of existence, awareness coming down
to one simple, physical, all-consuming truth, beating my way
through to some utter exhaustion. Once after one these times,
I remember he said, "If you had a dick, you'd be dangerous."
It's the kind of comment that sticks with a woman. I let it stall
in the air. I didn't say anything, because I already knew that I
was dangerous.

Physical intimacy would never be Elton's thing. He was intimate in other ways. He was dying to hear about my parents.
And, for the first time in my life, I heard myself telling the
truth about them, or inventing the story of my life—a version
that couldn't be scrutinized by someone with their own set of
observations. We'd lie in bed in the guest house. It smelled like
mothballs and its damp little fireplace. I told him about my
mother spending her days staring out the window at a Chinese
restaurant.

Elton dotted the freckles on my chest. "I think she sounds
lonely. Is she lonely?"

I'd never thought of it quite that way. She was married. She
had a family. Of course she was lonely, but that word seemed
reserved for the single, the truly alone. "I guess so," I said.

He loved to hear about Michael Hanrahan, too, even
though he didn't really like him. I didn't tell Elton about the
accident. I couldn't. Regardless, Michael was a complete mys-
tery. Michael made Elton huffy, exasperated.

"Why, do you think, he didn't tell you his father was dying? I'd tell you. I tell you everything."

He wasn't telling me everything. Elton had secrets. He hid
them so well that I wasn't sure, looking back, that he knew he
had them at all. Sometimes he would refuse to talk about Ned,
but other times it was his sole concentration. His father was

manic-depressive. He'd tried to kill himself twice: once with a firearm, an antique from a dead general. It never went off. Gloria was there. She talked him out of it. And another time with pills. His stomach was pumped.

"A man who's gone through the humiliation of having his stomach pumped is sad and pale and sedated. He folds up and looks dead. He stares at you but like a dead man."

Elton got teary once or twice, and he didn't apologize for that.

Sometimes we went out driving. He'd pull raggedly onto golf courses at night and have sex on the greens. He piggy-backed me across campus. As it got colder, we drank yards of beer at this upscale place, eating oysters. We sat on the roof of the guest house, under blankets and talked. We were inseparable. Sometimes I got up to pee, and when I came back, he'd tell me that he'd pined for me.

Mostly we'd spend the night out at Dick's Bar, sleep at the guest house, and he'd drive me to my 9:00 a.m. class. (Elton was certainly annoyed by classes.) I'd smell like beer and sex. My eyes were smeary blurs, but I was there, nudging the dispenser for my bite-sized portion of knowledge.

I was basically hazy. I longed for Elton. It was like he was a country with his own anthem. And I adored the border of his soul, what became a familiar crossing, an outpost with weeds. I'd never met anybody who let me linger the way he did, on the edge of such usually highly guarded terrain. It was as if his border guard stamped my passport with a lazy formality, while whispering, *Take what's yours. It's all yours.*

For a while, Kelly didn't exist. Her bangs grew back, and she became invisible. My parents, I didn't dwell on them. During phone calls, I felt the weight. My mother would say: *There's a squirrel in the attic. I found droppings.* My father would tell me the neighbor broke a hip. They were passing information to each other so they didn't have to speak to each other. I would read despair, envisioning my mother writing a condolence card, my father rooting through the attic boxes for a nest. (He preferred the attic, the basement, any place where our lives were sentimentally boxed for eternity.) Did days go by without a word spoken in the house? I would conjure Elton and slip away.

I met Gloria. She liked me. I think she saw something in me, a toughness but also a steady ordinariness that reminded her, maybe, of herself. She had a swinging dry blond bob and broad shoulders. She was erect, poised, her words a little labored. "Ned is a lifetime project. A daily, hourly endeavor," she told me.

At one point Ned was feeling good enough, by Gloria's estimations, to go to the office. Ned didn't drive. He wasn't allowed to drive. "Take him to the office, Elton."

"I can't," Elton said, under his breath. "I'm with Jane."

"Please, Elton. She doesn't mind."

He looked at his mother in a way that said, *She doesn't, but I do.*

"Take him on your way to class. You're still going to classes, aren't you?"

This was a sore spot. That was evident. "Yes," Elton said, a little defensively, a little heated up. "I'm still going to classes." He was boyish here, borderline petulant, borderline unattractive, except that he was always so damn pretty, his blustery hair, his cockeyed grins at me, toothy and wry.

Ned Birch was a thin man with well-combed tan hair. He was chipper. He drank coffee, swung a briefcase. He said, "What beautiful eyes! Did you see this girl's eyes, Gloria? She can look right through you!" Then he turned to his wife in a hush. "The towels are out of order in the linen closet. Can you go over that again with Marguerite?" He turned to me. "If we can just keep ahead of the game. You know how that is."

"I always try to keep ahead of the game," I told him.

"So, I'm off to the office, I see. Here I am."

Gloria kissed his cheek, then wiped off her lipstick. It was almost perfunctory, but not quite. She loved Ned Birch, I think. He was *her* lifetime project, after all, and she hoped for the best. "Have a good day."

"I will!"

Ned insisted I sit in the front seat and he folded up in the back. Elton drove the two of us up one street down another.

"Where do you want to go?" Elton asked his father. I realized that Elton and his father had been in this position a number of times before and had not gone to the office.

"I don't know. I'm feeling Aboriginal. You can just drop me in the woods."

Elton was as nervous as I'd ever seen him, rubbing sweat from his upper lip, jiggle the gear shift when at a red light. He obviously didn't want me to be in Ned's company and so I tried to be invisible. "You could try the office," Elton told him.

"I could try a lot of things," his father said, a menace in his voice. He reared from his tie, suddenly weary. "I should eat pie. When will you pick me up?"

"I have class."

"When will you pick me up? Don't leave me at a diner all day with pie and a bowl of water. I'm not a beagle."

"I'll pick you up after class."

"I won't make it."

"Go to the office. They'll take care of you there." I had the feeling that Ned and Gloria owned the office, that Ned had no duties except to occasionally appear, to much backslapping.

"They'll stare at me. I'll only spend the day staring at that note from my brother."

(I never knew what this meant. What note?)

"You should throw it away."

"Oh, I should throw things away. Old things. The past. I should. How about you?" his father said. He dropped his voice, leaned forward between the bucket seats. "Ellen. Ellen. Ellen. Ellen."

The car was quiet except for Ned's breathing, which was rapid. I looked at Elton. He was struggling, I could see it, struggling not to wear an expression. They were torturing each other, but not exactly on purpose.

Elton stopped in front of a diner, and his father got out of the car. He slammed the door and then knocked on the window, pointing to his briefcase still sitting in the backseat. Elton ignored him and drove off. Obviously there was nothing of importance in it. It was a prop. Did it even hold stationery, a pen?

Elton and I hadn't ever talked about Ellen, but I knew from hanging out with him at that bar that she had been more famous than I was. I'd heard she'd taken a job somewhere. I'd heard she was engaged. I could tell that I was no Ellen. I didn't want to know about Ellen really.

On the way to campus, Elton turned up the tape player, The Cure singing loud and melancholy. He tore around, slamming through gears without really getting the clutch all the way to the floor. I felt a deep sense of dread. My hands were hot. I wiped them on my pants.

"Are you okay?" I asked him when he'd pulled up to my dorm.

"You mean Ned? You're not allowed to hate someone for being crazy. It's Gloria's rule. Her rules are unbreakable." He looked up at me. "You know the rule, right?"

I said, "Yeah." I hadn't known the rule. The rule made me anxious. I didn't know what was at stake. Elton looked unbearably fragile, his face stiff and pinched. His nose, his jaw, they'd never lined up, but now he looked distorted, pained. "But are you okay?" I asked. "You didn't answer the question."

"Do I look okay to you? Don't you see it? I mean, I'm that guy who could just disappear one day. Don't you know that about me? I've told you everything!"

I got out of the car, the door still propped open. "Not everything," I said, meaning Ellen.

He sat there, gave a gusty sigh. He said, "Damn," and tugged the idle wheel back and forth. "It isn't a complicated story. Ellen doesn't love me." I didn't like the present tense. I thought it should be that Ellen didn't love him, that it wasn't a complicated story. I felt jealous, but then he squinted up at me. It was a cold day, but bright. "But you do. Right?"

I wanted to tell him that I loved him. I wanted to say, Let's become Mr. and Mrs. Misterandmissuses and drive around and around for the rest of our lives, living on yards of beer and oysters. But my heart seized up. I realized at that moment I was afraid of him. It had always been there—a rush of fear, not knowing what he might do next—but this was a more desperate fear. I didn't know him. I didn't understand him, Ned, Gloria. I was afraid to tell him any of this. I barely understood it myself. I was afraid mainly because I wanted to say the right thing. Elton would be driving off. Telephone polls hemmed roads, cornered intersections. I was afraid to tell him I loved him. I was afraid to tell him anything more complicated. I nodded. But it wasn't a great big nod. It wasn't a yes, yes! Of course I do! And he could sense it. Elton needed excessive love. He needed an overabundance more than I had even though I had as much love for him as I'd had for anyone.

He smiled. "Don't sweat it. I'll call you."

This was about two months into the relationship. Exams were coming up. Elton said he was studying hard and he couldn't see me. We'd talked every day and then there was a three day stretch, no word. This made me a little frantic. I finally got a phone call. "I'm getting in shape. I've been running all day through this fucking forest." He was breathless, exuberant. "It's great. Mind, body, spirit. The forest is beautiful."

"There's a phone in the forest? You're there now?"

"No, I'm lying. There's no forest. I'm just running in the guest house. I'm running around the yard."

"Are you being sarcastic?" I couldn't read his tone.

"I haven't been home in a while. But there's no forest. I'm at a phone booth. Listen." He pulled the phone out of the booth, through the folding doors, and let me hear the whizzing cars, a horn. "I think hello is all wrong. I think we should use some other greeting. Something like, 'What the fuck?'"

"Okay," I said. "What the fuck?"

"Exactly. Right on. I love you. I really love you. Where are you going to be?"

"When?"

"In an hour?"

"I have to go to the library."

"I'll be there, too. I'm hungry. I haven't eaten. Ned's crazy. The old bastard. But you know that. Gloria wants me to go into plastics."

"What's wrong with you?"

"I'm pure! I'm running on unleaded Elton. Go to the fucking library. I'll be there. I'll be wearing bells and shit." He hung up.

Ned was crazy, and so was Elton. He wasn't just a wild character. Gloria knew that something was wrong, of course.

She was wired to. About fifteen minutes after Elton hung up, the phone rang again. It was his mother.

"Do you know where he is? Has he made contact?" she asked.

I wanted to prove that my bond with Elton was stronger than hers. "I'm meeting him the library in about an hour," I said, as if everything were normal.

"What are his behaviors?" She was a pro. She handled the Birches.

"I don't know," I said. "He's not a child. He's old enough . . ."

Gloria cut me off. "Look, you're very nice. You should go."

"What?"

"It isn't a healthy environment, and you need to go forward. I sometimes have to give this advice. A warning."

This "needing to go" was clearly a phrase that Gloria reserved for just such occasions. I wondered how many times she'd used it. "Did you give this advice to Ellen, too?"

"Ellen needed to go."

"Don't tell me what I should do. And Elton can take care of himself or is he a lifetime project of yours?"

"Look, you're quite lucky, to get away from your family as you have, scraping by, the little pot bust—how darling. You're lucky just getting to go to college at all. You still have possibilities."

Had Elton been confiding in her? "Who the hell are you to tell me that I'm lucky? Are you just afraid I'll replace you? That Elton won't need you anymore?"

"You don't know anything about us," she said, with great exhaustion. She hung up.

When I showed up at the library, Elton was already there. He was carrying a box of ice cream, Push-Ups and Rocketeers, things you'd buy from an ice cream truck or in bulk, cleaning out a Seven Eleven freezer case. I realize this might sound charming or simply quirky to you. But it wasn't. Everyone there knew that they were in the presence of someone who'd come unhinged. Elton, glossed in sweat, gleaming at the circulation desk.

"Hush! Hush!" The librarians were flapping.

Now Elton was asking them if they'd seen a girl he was supposed to meet. "The ice cream is melting, for shit's sake!"

But the librarians were giddy, lightheaded from all the hushing. They spun around each other, a little goosey and maybe a little in love. Elton was still gorgeous. He was valiantly handing out ice cream to people at tables. Finally he dumped the cardboard box on the floor where some of the softened canisters oozed.

"Call security!" one of the librarians called out.

"Elton," I whispered it at first. "Elton."

He turned around and raised his arms up. "She's here! She's here!"

But I was crying, and he caught himself. He turned around slowly, looking at the mess, the startled college kids, the librarians' shocked mouths. He looked past me and there was a flurry of motion, people storming in through the library's entrance.

"Elton!" Gloria called out, her bobbed hair swaying stiffly. "Elton!" The security guards filed in behind her. "He's fine," Gloria told them. "He's just fine."

Elton stared at me, his face fallen. He said, "I'll come back! I'll bust out!" And it was clear that he knew where he was going, that he'd been there before.

Gloria mouthed to me. "It's not your fault." I think that's what she mouthed. I want to believe that's what she mouthed. I needed desperately to believe it. I watched her, flanked by security guards, hold Elton's arm and guide him out through the double doors.

Then the doors swung shut and the hushed silence flooded the library in Elton's wake. The librarians scurried to the checkout desk where a line had formed. I saw Kelly look up from a book. Our eyes caught, but she returned to her page. I was jealous of her for a moment. She was in college. She was studying for exams. She'd made good decisions. Kelly knew, instinctively, that the world was dangerous in countless ways. One of the older librarians knelt to put the melting goodies back into the box. The copy machines strobed in the distance. Things fell back into order that quickly, that horribly fast.

Wasn't that the case with your sister? Didn't people demand normalcy? We should all be allowed our rage and grief. Shouldn't every half-lit street of Hoboken and Baltimore and Jerusalem be filled with people running past the pawnshops, the bodegas, the butchers because they're afraid or wanting or both?

Here are the confessions. My name remained in the computer as being on the field hockey team. I don't know why, but because I wasn't really on it, I never really got kicked off of it. And, so, at the sports banquet, I was later told, my name was called as one of the scholar athletes because I'd maintained a solid GPA while playing field hockey. It made no sense, but I was a scholar athlete for four years and I put it on my resume.

Like Ellen, I took Gloria's advice which was wrong, and I knew it. I was lucky—news to me. And my parents, with all of their cramped gloom, were lucky too. The neighbor with the broken hip died in the hospital. My father couldn't find the squirrel's nest. The animal weakened the walls. My father called an exterminator who, he assumed, would trap it and let it loose—not the case. You have to cross a body of water or squirrels will just return. The squirrel was offed. At Christmas, we opened our gifts like strangers at a bus stop. They were all wrong. We barely knew each other. But we were trudging on.

I began to realize that my life had been carted off along with Elton Birch, this wild other inside of myself. I was being taught that those who are truly alive don't make it. I was learning that Kelly, my pasty obdurate roommate would survive, along with my aching parents; but Elton would not, and my choices, from then on, would have to be made with that knowledge, that full unavoidable ugly truth. I'd been blaming myself for Michael Hanrahan's car accident and now I could blame myself for Elton's breakdown. But I was too scared to do that. This is something you need to know: I have a strong instinct to survive. It can be an ugly instinct, an ugliness inside of me.

Elton called me in late spring. He left a sedate message. "Hey, that wasn't a good scene. Sorry about that. Sorry. Don't hate me." He took a breath and then added lightly. "Give me a call sometime."

And I knew that I loved him with more than a nod. I loved him with a rush of tenderness, a lion's share. (Is that ever enough?)

I wanted to survive. I had to. I never called.

Blisslessly yours,
The Scholar Athlete

December 2

Dear Lioness—

So alright, it's kind of late here in the city and I'm writing to say how sad your letter was, true sad, good sad, and how bad I felt for Ned and for Elton and for you, too, everybody clinging so hard to their hopes. It got me kind of emotional. And I also want to say sorry (again) for not following through at the wedding. I've been thinking about that. The thing is, actually, the truth, is that I'm AMAZING in BED. I know this is weird to say, arrogant, borderline creepy, but it's the truth. And I'm mentioning it because, in addition to all the other stuff in your letter there were also clear indications that you seem to have some of the same rabid tendencies as me, the same needs, and this means—unless I'm just way off here— that we would have had VERY GOOD SEX like right from the start, a total homerun in the CUM DEPARTMENT and that would have clouded things between us, because it always does. But it's been a couple of months now since the COAT ROOM and I'm just thinking that maybe it would have been worth the risk. To get that started, you know. Because actually as you may have noticed, I can sometimes come off as too cautious. But the wonderful thing about me is that once the clothes come off all that melts away. I get lost in the motion, the wet tug of the thing, the body talk. (Did I just say: *Lost in the motion*? Will you promise to shoot me in the head if I do so again?) What I'm saying is I'd like for you to see that part of me, to feel that part of me—it's more of a feeling thing, or a rhythm thing, a rhythm-feeling thing—and I've been thinking about you, too, your body, those huffy little breaths you were letting out at a certain point, your fingernails digging in just a little . . . So we should consider this as an option. Not giving up on the letters. No. Love the letters. But also adding maybe like a SEXUAL ABANDON COMPONENT to the endeavor. It would be nothing like fishing, I promise you that.

I Am Nugent Hear My,

Roar

PS—I have been drinking a little bit

PPS—But I still mean everything I said

December 2 (again)

Jane,

Oh my. Okay, I'm not sure when you'll get this letter, but I'm going to assume you've read my previous note, which was not, despite considerable evidence to the contrary, written by my cock. (It was merely *ghostwritten* by my cock.) I don't suppose I need to tell you that I'd been drinking. Did I have the good sense to mention this? That the bottle seemed, toward the end, to be sucking on my tongue? It was a rough night. Anyway, I'm not going to labor the excuses. Things take a bad turn, we drink, we begin to fantasize, the old rope of love—bless the rope!—gets thrown sloppily yon.

Which is not to say I didn't make efforts to avert this embarrassment. No, I woke this morning in a proper state of panic and staggered downstairs and the sun was mean, intent on murdering my eyeballs if you want to know the truth and worse yet high, high overhead, meaning, actually, that it was close to noon and that the letter in question (the one I hope you have not read yet) had been carried away by my mail person.

A quick word about my mail person, which requires a quick word about my former mail person, Kenneth, whose loss and the significance thereof I have only just begun to realize. (Did I mention that I may still be drunk?) Kenneth was a large fellow, damp, lonely, not quite old enough to be a Vietnam Vet but with some of the same tendencies—jumpiness around dogs, chain smoking, frequent rhapsodies about Sir Charles and *the shit*. In short, a loon. And a very friendly loon at that. Kenneth, I feel safe in saying, would have happily helped me out of my crisis by retrieving my letter from his pouch. He might have handed me a few others for good measure. He was also chronically late on

Saturdays, all days actually, meaning that my letter would still have been in my mailbox. But no. Some weeks ago, Kenneth disappeared from the beat. It is unclear what happened to him. I initially thought vacation. I am now thinking Bellevue. (Have I made an inappropriate joke? Let us hope not.)

The point being: my new letter carrier, whom I have never seen and who is infuriatingly punctual. The letter was gone. I dashed back upstairs and called the central post office. I could not get a human being, so I tried the Chelsea local, where a man with an oddly sensual wheeze promised assistance then left me on hold for thirty-seven minutes. I eventually managed to ascertain that my letter had been, almost assuredly, dropped into one of those green storage mailboxes—called *dumpers* in the local postal argot—located at the corner of Broadway and Twenty-Third.

It was here that I waited, through most of the afternoon, in what probably qualifies as the most incompetent stakeout in the history of, uh, postal stakeouts. I tried to look inconspicuous and, in so doing, looked tremendously conspicuous. Several cops stopped to ask if I was lost. One mentioned that I might want to "move it along," which sent me scurrying to Starbuck's for refuge. I will not detail my loathing of Starbuck's, which is, upon reflection, tiresome. Finally, toward four o'clock, a large black woman in a postal outfit appeared.

This, though I did not know it at the time, was one Bethany Delacourt, Postal Courier. I had by this time partaken of two (perhaps three) coffee/sugar-related drinks, to keep myself at peak awareness, though I would describe my state as closer to electrocuted. So I dashed outside with perhaps a bit too much pep in my step and Ms. Delacourt gave a start when she heard my steps and—this should be noted—removed from her waistband a small canister of what would turn out to be pepper spray.

"I'm sorry," I said. "I didn't mean to startle you."

Ms. Delacourt rose to her full height and glared at me. "I'm not scared of you."

"Right," I said. "Listen. I know this sounds crazy, but . . ."

And I set about explaining the situation: that I lived at such-and-such an address, that I sent a letter to my aging mother (who was herself recuperating on a small Greek islet that did not have any phones) informing her that my brother had been taken off life support, but that—miracle of miracles—he had actually recovered, despite having been legally dead for several minutes, and so obviously the letter would cause mother incredible and unnecessary grief, enough maybe to kill her, given the heart murmur, and what I needed, therefore, was to retrieve the letter and make sure it didn't get sent.

I am, if you can believe this, making the story far more coherent than it emerged for Ms. Delacourt. Indeed, if memory serves, my depiction of the circumstances surrounding the letter were a bit more improvisatory, such that (for instance) I initially identified my brother as an interior decorator who had lead poisoning, which I later modified to a fireman who had suffered smoke inhalation.

Ms. Delacourt, impervious in her blue muslin uniform, her corinth of coppery hair extensions, shook her head and said, "That's no business of mine, sir," and "I've got a schedule to mind" and "You got to call the main post office."

We were not communicating.

"Oh listen," I said. "All I want to do is remove one silly letter, which I wrote myself. It will save poor mother so much grief."

Ms. Delacourt shrugged. "I can't help you, sir."

"But what if the letter just got lost. Don't letters get lost all the time? There's even a place where dead letters go, the dead letter office."

Now Ms. Delacourt rose from her crouch and faced me and

I could see at once that she was one of those minor officials for whom the protocols of her job have become a kind of spiritual exercise. The dark center of her eyes, which must have been, at some point, wry and girlish, hardened into an officious glint.

"It is a federal offense for me to tamper with the mail. You understand that, I assume."

"Nobody's talking about tampering," I said. "You misunderstood me. I'm just saying that the letter might get lost."

Ms. Delacourt bent down to unlock the dumper and began tucking the envelopes into her satchel.

I stood there, trying to spot my letter by its drunken scrawl.

"I'm going to need you to back away from the mail receptacle," Ms. Delacourt said. "Please sir."

"Oh come on," I said. "Have a heart. The letter's right there, in your satchel. I can see it."

(This was not true.)

Ms. Delacourt looked up at me, then past me, presumably scanning for a police officer. "Even if I wanted to help you," she said, "which I don't, particularly, I couldn't. Since 9/11 we can't have people messing with the mail. You should understand that." Ah yes, 9/11. I was living in New York City, after all, a mere twenty-seven months after the grievous events of that day. How could I forget? How could *anyone ever* forget? There was no possible way, because every single day of your existence you were reminded by some aggrandized delay, some tinhorn security measure, some tax expenditure in a rented uniform.

"So if you lose this one letter," I said, "the terrorists have won?"

Ms. Delacourt seemed to bristle.

"Who said anything about any terrorists?" she said.

"I was joking," I said. "Forget it."

"Joking," she said. "I don't think you should be joking about any terrorists, sir. Not on this city block."

"Oh come on," I said, forcing a little chuckle. "What are you suggesting, that I'm Taliban? That I pose some kind of threat? I don't even know what a box cutter is . . ." I should mention that my chronology is going to get a little fuzzy here. I will have to resort to certain postures of conjecture. For instance, I will have to, uh, conject, that Ms. Delacourt was (not entirely consciously) waiting for someone precisely like me to enter her life, a smartass, someone who lacked the proper respect for the authority vested in her, and who might make certain statements, or, actually, who might use certain words, such as *Taliban* and *box cutter*, words which, from her perspective, constituted a physical threat to her person and the city of New York and (what the hell!) the entire United States of America and which would necessitate the use of the afore-mentioned pepper spray, the canister of which was—as I later realized—still pinched between her ring finger and pinkie and which (again, more conjecture) she rather deftly shifted to her thumb and index finger as I was speaking.

It may be also true that I made some gesture, that my hand moved toward her shoulder, though I can assure you that I was merely hoping to establish a little human contact of a non-terrorist kind, that I was in my own inimitable-hungover-Taliban sort of way trying to *defuse the situation.*

What I can tell you, pretty definitively, is that she rotated her left shoulder away from me and brought her right hand up and suddenly my eyes were stinging and I was coughing and shouting, between coughs, "What the hell! What the goddamn hell!" It was at this point that the police officer showed up.

It was his voice I heard first, a voice straight out of central casting: firm, bellowing, gloriously accusatory.

"You're going to need to step back," he said, "right now."

I assumed he was talking to my assailant, and therefore

adding my own choked second to this notion, something along the lines of, "Yeah, for fuck's sakes! Back off!" Then I felt something clamp onto my arm, this being his hand (and not a titanium claw, as I initially thought). And I was quickly being conducted backward, bent at the waist and sputtering.

"Stay put," said the cop.

I still couldn't see a thing. Put I stayed.

I heard Ms. Delacourt loudly declaiming me. Someone handed me a cup of water and, oddly, a dinner roll. "Eat the roll," a voice said. "Use the water to flush your eyes." I did as I was told.

This helped considerably. My vision, though still kaleidoscopic with tears, began to clear and I could see now—based on the eager crush of citizens that gather in New York City at the least sign of potential public humiliation—that I was at the center of a large, unfolding drama. Ah yes, street theater, Chelsea style.

The cop was on his radio. He was bald and thick and alarmingly short, so short that I'd initially thought he might be on his knees. Delacourt was looming over him, her mail bag laid coyly across her chest. He, the cop, was asking her questions in a low tone and she was answering him, now softly. Her expression suggested a state of rapture. Everyone else was looking at me, the terrorist. If I'd taken a lunge at any of them—and I was tempted—they would have scattered.

At the same time, I felt a strange compulsion to perform somehow, to prove my normalcy. "Can I just ask who gave me the bun?" I said, holding up the half I hadn't eaten. No one said anything. "Well," I said, "that was very kind. Thank you."

The cop glared at me. Then he turned back to Delacourt and continued his interview. She was, by this time, weeping quietly. It had been quite traumatic for her, clearly, to spray me in the face with pepper spray. It's not every day that your hidden sadistic impulses are so flagrantly gratified. The cop set his arm on hers. She looked at him tenderly. They were, apparently, falling in love. This meant I was going to prison.

Given the circumstances, prison wasn't seeming so bad to me. I would have a lot of down time and perhaps, some solitude. But, in fact, before I could get to prison, the cop had to interview me, which meant he had to tear himself away from Ms. Delacourt. I regarded the crowd, failing to look not guilty.

A little red-haired boy, thrown atop his father's shoulders, kept saying, "What happened? What happened?" (Ah, let us pause here to bless the civic/paternal impulse.) "That man attacked that nice lady," the father stage-whispered.

"Why?"

"Nobody knows. That's what the police officer is trying to find out."

Can I just say that I was, like, three feet from this exchange?

I tried to ignore the crowd. I nibbled at my role. I realized that I had to pee. I spent some time marveling at the cop's stature. He was a bicycle cop. I felt certain someone had modified his bike, so he could reach the pedals. But even still, his legs were so short. I could see his stubby little thighs pumping away, in pursuit of an actual criminal. It didn't seem fair. Finally, the cop made his way over to me. He looked good and pissed off.

"ID," he snapped.

I handed him my license and he stabbed down my information.

"Okay," he said. "Let me ask you a few questions."

"Of course," I said.

"Don't get problematical with me, sir."

"What?"

"You heard me. I worked with guys who died at the WTC, okay?"

"Okay."

"Because I'd like nothing more, okay, sir? Are we square?"

I nodded. I was aware that I needed to remain very, very *calm*.

"Did you at any time place your hand on the victim?"

"No."

"Did you threaten her?"

"No."

He squinted at me. "You're telling me you didn't threaten her?"

"I made a joke, which was misunderstood."

"A joke," the cop said. He wrote this down. "What sort of joke?"

"A dumb joke," I said. "I forget the exact words. But I never touched her and I'm really very sorry about all of this."

"Did you attempt to tamper with the mail she was handling?"

"No."

"You made no attempt to tamper with the mail?"

To this point I'd been doing pretty well, because I had assessed the situation and realized that the less said the better. I had, in other words, *played within my game*. But this question was a tough one. I didn't want to lie outright. So what I did was I leaned toward the cop a bit and said, "Alright, let me be totally honest with you . . ." The idea I had in my head was that I'd be able to appeal to him, one guy to another.

Now, if I can offer you a piece of advice when it comes to dealing with law enforcement (though why you'd want my counsel in this area remains unclear) *do not ever confide in a cop.* Do not suppose that they want to hear your sad song of exculpation. Do not suppose that you can win them over. You cannot.

I will spare you an exhaustive accounting of the subsequent exchange. A typical sentence might have run like so: "No, I never told anyone my mother was on a Greek island, I said that she liked Greek salad, which is true, though she's in poor health and isn't supposed to eat feta cheese, we're not sure if it's a lactose thing or what, but my point is, I think Ms. Dela-court, not intentionally, might have misheard me, not because my speech was slurred, not at all, because I did drink last night, a very limited amount, two drinks, two watered-down drinks, but I've had nothing today, because, with the street noise and all, as well as I have a minor hearing problem." Not pretty.

In the end, I was issued a citation for disorderly conduct, for which I will have to appear in district court in six weeks, unless I want to pay a fine of $500. Nobody was especially happy with this result. Ms. Delacourt was livid. The crowd was crestfallen. ("Aren't they going to take the bad man away, daddy?") The mean, runty cop appeared disgusted with himself for failing to incarcerate me. And so my starring role ended, a mere forty-seven minutes into the second act.

I expect it will not come as too much of a shock that, on my way home, I seriously considered borrowing a car from my neighbor Briggs and driving to down Philadelphia, in the hopes of pleading my case at your local post office. (Yet an-other charming example of my problem-solving skills!)

But I am trusting, based on your own stated adventures, that your share my appreciation for the occasional criminally insane impulse. Let us hope.

Time now for a hot bath and a quick frontal lobe scrub.

> Pricing turbans for my day in court,
> Johnny Rotten

PS—Oh God. I CAPITALIZED, didn't I? It's all starting to CUM back to me.

PPS—My cock says "Hi!"

December 6

Hi Cock!

Y ou, sweetie, deserve a letter of your own—as does Ms.
Delacourt—a thank you for her courage and valor
under duress. She deserves a tribute really—to be read
with a national anthem soundtrack building steam in the back
ground—Whitney Houston's version, if I may be so bold to
suggest, Superbowl circa Roman-Numeral-Something. Because
without the likes of Ms. Delacourt and her belief in the sanc-
tity of the Federal Postal System—those employees who march
through our cities and towns in their woolly blue shorts like
Catholic boys playing hooky from the lower school—without
the likes of her, I'm afraid that attempts like the stunt pulled
by that bulky goody-two-shoes you're rooted to—attempts at
nothing short of cock censorship—would not fail, would go
unthwarted. And many (literate) drunken cocks everywhere
would be silenced.

Some would argue—not you, cock, no, not you—that this
wouldn't be such a bad thing. But I can't help but sympathize
with the plight of the silenced cock. You are conspired against
these days—what with feminism and psychology and Oprah
and vaginas having their own staged monologues. (You aren't
the best spokesperson, are you?) But still! Poor cock, so often
clipped at birth—while just minding your own business—
you're doing the best you can. (Did I mention I have a T shirt
that says Circumcision Is Circumspect? Did you know that I
was such a cock activist?)

By golly, even the English language is against you. Penis—who can say it without wincing at the weenie sissiness
of the word? Was it invented by a wordsmith whose mother

referred to his privates as his "tinky-dinky," someone whose confidence was so thoroughly wrecked that he could only combine the words puny and squeamish to describe his manhood? Penis is nothing compared to the word vagina—which is so gorgeous, nearly glam—or vulva, my God, it's like a Superhero or something!

What I'm getting at is that Ms. Delacourt deserves her praise! Ms. Delacourt, though she might not know it, is just the kind of pillar that cocks need! And because of her heads-up postal savvy, you, cock, you were set free into the world to speak your purposeful, single-minded mind, (by now Whitney Houston should be full-bore—*And the rockets red glare. The bombs bursting in air.*) And, you, cock, you deserve praise too—you who always keep your one eye trained on the essentials of this country's very foundation—life, liberty, and the pursuit of happiness—are a true patriot. For that, I, as an American, am very thankful.

> Sincerely,
> Jane, President of CRA
> (Cock Rights of America)

PS—For the big fella . . . You aren't stalling, are you? Don't you have something "filthy and lovely and true" to tell me? Haven't you warned me in the past: *Don't stop. I mean it, Jane.* And so, back at you, *Don't stop.* A confession, please.

MARIA EVANGELINA
FAJARDO CORTEZ

December 14

Dearest CRA Member,

As you are not doubt aware, recent federal cutbacks in penile funding programs have forced us to make some hard decisions. Regrettably, we have had to rescind the epistolary privileges of our member cocks. Proper supervision was proving too costly. The following letter, therefore, comes from Theodore Nugent (CRA #1025) with only an occasional aside by his cock . . .

You're going to miss some years. Two or three. I graduated, just barely, and went plummeting down to Santa Barbara. Why Santa Barbara? There was a girl there, at first, though I scared her off with my moods and erratic shaving patterns. I was going to learn to surf, too, like a real Californian. But I didn't have the patience for failure, so I took a job at a pizza parlor run by a Greek who dealt crystal meth on the side. How prestigious.

It was this gentleman who introduced me to another Greek, Patros, who threw pots. For a while I became his apprentice and followed him into the desert south of Pasadena, where we dug for red clay and camped under the stars. I sat and watched the fire and ate white beans slathered onto flat bread and grape leaves spiced with cumin, while Patros philosophized in his halting English. *Beauty was the truth*, he told me. *The sweetest fruit gives her pit.* I listened to this grave hokum and waited for some mystical tranquility to take me up.

Back at his tiny studio, Patros used his hands, long, hacked up things, to shape healing vessels. I was in charge of the kiln. They use tiny cones to measure the heat in a kiln and Patros favored a high heat for his pieces (cone nine). Sometimes, after Patros had gone home, I would fire up a joint and stared into the viewing slot—at the roaring flames and the glazes blooming with dead oxygen—until my eyes seared. I was not in the best of shape.

Then it was a job as a shipping and receiving clerk for a medical supply company run by an affable alcoholic named Sprat (everyone called him Sprat) who spent most of his time in my office, talking about the Korean War. He'd killed a few people and kept circling the graves. Years later, I would read an article in the paper about Medicare fraud and note Sprat among the indicted. His first name was, I believe, Thomas.

During this stint, I played in a punk band called Anthrax Ballet, one of several thousand in the Los Angeles basin at that historical moment, perhaps the worst. I played bass in the Vicious style, a concerted twinge only loosely concerned with notes. We made a grand total of one record, a self-funded seven-inch of our hit single, "Girl Fight." I'm going to assume that, despite your certain riot grrrrrl tendencies, you never encountered this seminal release. The lyrics ran as follows:

Scratch face
Pull hair
Girl Fight!
Girl Fight!

My father actually came down to visit around this time, and spent a few days pretending not to worry about me. He even schlepped out to one of our shows, at a club called the Black Nasty, and this memory seems more painful to recount than all the rest of it, my father in his dress shirt, gazing at the sad angry crowd, dodging gusts of beer, his ears battered by the endless feedback, and the way he looked at me afterward, this lover of Mozart and Verdi, his gentle eyes searching for a way in. I sent him away, beaten down in confusion.

Then I met Lina. Maria Evangelina Fajardo Cortez. She was a friend of a fan of the band and she was—choose your adjective: beautiful, ravishing, disruptive. She wore a blue, pin-striped suit, a man's suit, which was a strange thing to wear to a punk show, and sharp-toed leather boots. She stood at the edge of the mosh pit and kicked anyone who came too close. Afterward, she took one look at me and yawned. But she must have seen something there, under the hacked shingles of gel and safety pins. I was the band's pretty boy, after all (my mates were exceptionally ugly) and the only one to earn a college degree, a fact I tried desperately to conceal. Lina was someone I could love just looking at her. She had the face of a Mayan princess, retouched for Vogue. It was all there: the plump lips, the round cheeks, the dark eyes wet with embedded pleasures. She exuded, in how she looked and spoke and moved, an over-ripe quality I associated with glamour. Her figure was what us surfer wannabes called tragic. (Tragic, dude. No hope for you.)

I tracked her down, called her at the office, left what I considered a witty message. She did not call back.

My friend Curt asked his friend Ann to intervene on my behalf.

"She doesn't like scruffy guys," Ann told me.

"Am I scruffy?" I said.

"You might be," she said, "if you cleaned up a little."

A meeting was brokered. She stuck around long enough to let me buy her two beers, neither of which she drank. I asked her a few questions. I praised her outfit. I talked of the band's success, our grand ambitions. She gazed out across the bar. "Punk is kind of over," she said. "I mean, isn't it?"

I asked if I could see her again.

"I'm heading out of town for a while," she said.

I couldn't stop myself, though. She had turned me all goony and drooling.

It will sound odd, given all the humiliation I absorbed, but I felt I was taking fate into my own hands. This is the secret allure of the crush. People underestimate how empowering the arrangement is, particularly for characters like me, lost, feckless, in need of a magnetic pole. (Elton himself was, I suspect, doing some of this when he swept you off your feet and into his life.) The guys in the band despised Lina. Whenever her name came up, they played "Maneater" by Hall and Oates. But it was clear Anthrax Ballet was going nowhere. Punk was just an excuse not to practice much. Then our drummer moved to Oregon and the rest of us really began to bicker. Citing uncreative differences, we split. (Tell me if you've seen all this already on *Behind the Music*.)

I moved into a phase affectionately memorialized by Fish, our leader singer, as full-time grovel. Imagine a barn fly. Imagine a pane of glass. This was our dynamic. I wrote her poetry. I sent flowers. She began dating a soap opera star, a fellow named Tomas Panza. She was ecstatically happy (Ann reported) on the verge of getting engaged. Then Tomas landed a role on a sitcom as a beefcake doctor with a retarded sister, and took up with an underwear spokesmodel. They were pictured in one of the tabloids, tongue kissing at the Daytime Emmys.

Did this minor celebrity heartbreak set the stage for our hero? No. Lina continued to bludgeon me with her indifference. I couldn't get enough of the stuff. I was a whimpering dog. And Lina threw me just enough scraps to keep me around. She often mentioned a bar where she might wind up and never did. One night, at a jazz club, on the sloppy downside of a binge, Lina set her mouth to my ear and growled in Spanish. I felt the smear of her lipstick on my earlobe, the fierce edges of her push-up bra. I begged her to let me drive her home. She took a cab and didn't return my calls for two weeks.

I'm not going to go over all the other evenings. What's important is this: I got a job at her office, as a receptionist. This was an ad agency in Palos Verdes religiously devoted to Hip Lifestyle Buy Decisions. The people there worshipped at the altar of Clever. They threw parties where everyone sat around trying to top each other, where, if you stepped out onto the porch to clear your head, you could hear the bad jazz of ad-speak squalling away under a cloud of cigarette smoke.

I realize I'm sounding like a condescending asshole, which is not a nice thing to sound like. It's that snobbery creeping in again, as if *those people* were somehow divorced from me and my existence. This is easier than copping to how much of them was already inside me, which will become clear anyway.

So I did my numbed-out receptionist thing. One day the senior designer, a mean old bird named Alice Tewksbury, came tocking across the bright lobby of our office. She was haranguing some guy named Jed about the mockup for an ad, which she suddenly thrust in front of me. It was something involving penguins. "Johnny Thunder here could do better than this," she said.

(My nickname was the result of the perception that I had been in a rockabilly band—the excess of gel gets some of the blame here—a rumor that Lina might have dispelled but did not. It was also widely held, for a time, that I had played Bowser in a Sha-Na-Na tribute band. I will not attempt an explanation.)

The ad was for a golf resort in the Dominican Republic, the kind of place where colonialism comes with conch fritters and Coke. So what did I do? I went home and made a copy of Gauguin's good old nudes, sketched in a bunker or two, and a white fellow, naked and ecstatic, with a golf bag in front of his privates. The legend read: *Go Native.* Alice liked that alright. She made me her assistant. It was a heartwarming story, fit for a middle-brow romantic comedy. This meant more money, nicer clothing, something to do with my time. The big money was in television, where Lina worked, but I really was happy working on print ads. I got deeply into fonts, learned how to photo shop, indulged in the joys of clever. I began to take myself a little more seriously and stopped trying so hard to impress Lina.

I don't suppose I have to tell you what effect that had.

The night it finally happened was an office party with a good deal of sangria followed, unwisely, by tequila shooters. Lina got herself in a stumbling mess. She waited until most of the office staff had cleared out, of course. Then she began singing *canciones* and punched the jukebox for not singing along. The bartender suggested she slow down. She cussed at him, called him a wetback, dropped her shot glass on the floor.

Something inside me, a tiny voice of good reason, said: *flee*, while another voice hissed: *now, you fool! Now!*

Lina caught me at the door. "Where do you think you're going, Thunder?"

She pulled me to her and tried to get me to dance some kind of Latin thing.

"Happy birthday," she said to me.

"It's not my birthday," I said.

"Sure it is," she said. "You get to drive me home."

I'm going to skip all the swollen teasing (my cock can fill you in on that later) and proceed to the part where Lina stripped down to this kind of sharkskin body suit and straddled me.

"Are you a safe little boy?" she said. "Do you have any kind of nasty disease?"

"No," I said.

"From your skanky punk girl groupies?"

I shook my head.

"If you do," she said, "my *papi* will cut that thing off, Thunder. I swear to God. No more *pinga*." She plucked at her bodysuit. "Why don't you figure out how to get this off, so you can fuck Lina. Would you like that, Thunder? To fuck Lina?"

I had no idea how to get the garment off. There was no zipper, no buttons. I fumbled about, while Lina stared at me insolently. Finally, with a huff, she reached down and unsnapped the tiny, hidden buttons at the crotch. Then she looked at me, to make sure I was appreciating what was happening, and peeled the material away.

She arched her back and grabbed her breasts and twirled around so I could watch her bottom do its good work. She was limber, womanly, alarmingly thin through the ribs, and her smells were good, running to the scented balms. Her skin, which was quite cool under normal circumstances, got very hot. She yanked at my hair and, finally realizing what she wanted, I yanked at hers. This was how she operated—it was hard for her to separate affection from the infliction of pain.

In the morning, before the light could cut into her bedroom, Lina sent me away. I remember sitting on the steps in the pool outside my apartment. It was one of those primo Southern California days, with enough breeze to keep the sun from clobbering you. The palms swayed. Electric blue wavelets rippled the pool. I felt overwhelmed by joy. I'd really wanted this woman and I'd bedded her and she'd been just as hot as I'd imagined. That's the thing that really killed me.

There is such a thing as animal magnetism. I don't have to tell you. How ever nebbishy Elton may have been behind closed doors, he had that raw physical presence. Lina was the same way. Every time she walked in a room she commanded its full attention. Her face and her body never let her down. I don't mean to make easy comparisons. I only mean that we may have been driven by some of the same urges: toward reckless, absorbing forms of love.

I can remember heading down to Tijuana to go shopping with Lina. She insisted we get there in the early morning, to avoid the crowds. She didn't want to take her car into Mexico either, so we took a cab. A pale fog had rolled in from the ocean and it clung to the desert floor as we clambered over the bridge. I had envisioned a day trip, a lingering walk through tree-shaded plazas, tacos al carbon from a street vendor, the whole Go Native! shebang.

But Lina had a different itinerary in mind. She told the cab driver to stop outside a jewelry shop a block into Mexico and disappeared inside. A few yards away, outside the customs station, dozens of men and women were sleeping, curled on sheets of cardboard.

"Chili pickers," the cab driver told me. "They bus them up there to the fields. My cousin did that for a few years. Wrecked his smelling."

"What did?" I said.

"The chili oil. It gets up there and burns through the smellers."

I thought about the letter I'd received from Lisa, describing the first time she'd eaten a meal spiced with habanero. She'd guzzled water, which served to spread the oil across her tongue and throat. The women in the village where she was staying had come to her rescue. "The whole thing was hilarious," she wrote. "They were stuffing tortillas into my mouth, stroking my arms. I was laughing and crying at the same time. You should have seen me, Johnny. What a mess."

It was astonishing how quickly and vividly Lisa had returned, still alive, laughing, her throat on fire. I stepped out of the cab to clear my head and wandered over to the chili pickers. I knew I should feel something for them, pity or hope. But all I could feel was rage. Tijuana was so fucking ugly. The main drag was a grotesque cartoon, broken neon and gutters that stunk of vomit; a crust of diesel smog where the sky should have been. I ran back to the cab, and the driver started talking to me again, something about his sister, he had a sister who lived on this side, whatever it was.

Lina hurried out of the jewelry shop and jumped in the cab. "What's wrong with you?" she said.

My breathing had gone sort of jerky.

"I don't know," I said. "It must be an allergic reaction."

"You're allergic to Mexico, *papi*?"

I hadn't told Lina anything about my sister. She knew only the basics, a couple of parents in distant orbit. I figured I'd get around to the whole story at some point, but I didn't want to get too deep or intense, and Lina, with her endless self regard, made this impulse seem perfectly natural. She looked at me for a long moment, then out the window at the chili pickers, and I could see her own revulsion.

"Fine," she said softly. "Let's get the hell out of here."

The cabdriver grunted softly; he'd been expecting an all-day fare. I was ready to weep at how lovely Lina looked in her blue summer dress, the graceful curve of her neck, the red of her painted lips. It hadn't occurred to me yet that my new lover had anything to do with my dead sister, that I had chosen a woman who reviled everything Lisa stood for. All I knew was that I had to get away from the stinking poverty of Mexico, which was choking me. Lina leaned toward me to display the jewelry she'd bought, smooth stones of malachite and onyx set in sterling silver, and I dutifully examined each piece, though really I was gazing at her. The tops of her breasts made me think of the smooth healing vessels Patros had shaped out of clay.

Another delightful detail: Lina didn't want our thing public until she'd had a chance to clean up my act. I happily signed myself over to her. We went shopping for new clothes. I joined her gym. My hair was cut short. I became, basically, a yuppie asshole. This didn't happen all at once. I didn't really see it as happening at all. At the time, I felt I was getting my life back on track.

And, despite my own double-reverse snob jujitsu, I was happy. Lina stoked the old fires of ambition in me. I worked long hours and took late dinners at sophisticated restaurants with my hot Latin girlfriend and later we retired to her refrigerated bedroom and had rough sex with mirrors all around. In the morning, I got up and chugged a protein smoothie and went off to harden my muscles at the gym—tone and definition, these were the buzzwords—and zipped my new car (a Honda Del Sol) into the clever factory, where I now had my own parking space and office, and chugged one cup of coffee after another and, on those days when the blood surged unreasonably, dragged Lina down to an abandoned office on the third floor.

On weekend nights, we went to bars with names like Bang

and The Spot and did amphetamines in the bathrooms and danced to the DJ of the moment. We spent Sundays grooming our pubic hair and watching videos and swapping office gossip. Lina was smart about people and this seemed all the more impressive because of her beauty (though it was her beauty, of course, which required her to keep these circuits firing).

Her apartment was appointed in blacks and whites. The lone exception was a wooden diablo from Michoacán, brightly painted, with a wild red tongue, which sat on a high shelf in her foyer and stared me down as I waited for Lina to cinch herself into a new outfit. Her fridge contained: old broccoli, champagne, soy milk. Her diet consisted of various puffed grains: rice cakes, popcorn, cereal without milk. She was also subject to cravings: fried pork tostadas, fish tacos, chili rellenos slathered with asadero cheese. To watch her eat these delicacies! The sheen of grease left upon her lips and the smoky scent of pork on her breath. It made me want to tip God 20 percent.

After these binges, she was ill, soft and moaning, her little belly bloated. You should understand: she had these tender moments, during which her face expressed a tremendous concentration of feeling. Often alcohol was the impetus, or a good sweaty rutting. (Most of us need something stiff to dislodge the volatile memories.) I can still see Lina draped across her sleek leather couch, whimpering for her *abuelita*, describing for me, between hiccuping sobs, the way she used to prepare tortillas on her stovetop, the soft slap of her palms, the white of the dough, the pinch of cinnamon, and how her *abuelita* tore these hot tortillas into strips and dipped them in honey and fed them into her waiting mouth.

This was her mother's side of the family, the ones without money, who clung to the rituals of the campo, who regarded with quaint suspicion the dream of El Norte, with its electrified walls and atheistic plenitude. There was a germ of this nostalgia in Lina herself. It held a power that terrified her, and her terror thrilled her, though most of the time she spoke of her father's family, the noble Spanish blood flowing through her veins (they had papers to prove forebears from Castille) and the story of her father's shrewd ascent from indentured clerk to salaried executive.

So Lina was in retreat from that ancient poverty, embarked on journey into the upper class, and this was a point of connection, because I too was in retreat from my legacy, the arid world of ideas, loveless self-consideration, and the earnest liberalism that had killed my sister. I wanted none of it.

These are supposed to be confessions, so let's cut to the chase: I stopped giving a shit about the have-nots. I fucked my hot girlfriend with impunity and voted republican. I learned to eat sushi and ordered the most expensive meat, from the belly of endangered fish. I turned my talents toward a precise exposure of consumer insecurities and offered various perfumes and malt beverages as a solution. I believed wholeheartedly in glamour, not as an affectation, but a durable necessity.

Lina made all this possible to believe. She simply refused to yield her glamour. I kept waiting to catch her in an ugly moment. But even in the mornings, after a long night of booze, with her hair crimped and her eyes all puffed, she looked like delicious—a sugar-plum fairy in crotchless underwear.

We went to visit her family in Nogales, for the quinceañera of her cousin, an elaborate celebration held in the ballroom of the Westin. I assumed this meant that I had moved into a more solid romantic category. But I wasn't inspected very closely. I tried out my mangled-up Spanish on various relatives. They smiled thinly. Or maybe condescendingly; it was hard to tell. The family was occupied by its own dramas, the party most immediately, but also the misdeeds of various drunk uncles, freeloaders, fallen cousins. I was placed in a basement guest room, while Lina, chaste and sullen, stayed in the room next to her parents.

These were the glory days of free trade, maquiladoras were all the rage ("twin plants" they were called in the business press) which meant an American office with a few *jefes* and vast Mexican factories packed with young women assembling circuit boards. Hector Cortez was a neat, corpulent *jefe* in a dark suit. He received a steady stream of visitors at his table.

Earlier in the day, he'd taken Lina and me out to a gun range. I'd expected a wide open space with targets mounted on bales of hay. This was how archery had worked back at Camp Tawonga. But the range was indoors, a concrete bunker with stalls. Lina and her father stood side by side, squeezing off rounds. They were the exact same height and they assumed the exact same stance, legs wide and hands clasped devoutly around the weapon. Afterward, emerging from their stalls, they exchanged a tender glance. Lina's face was flushed and vindictive, as in the moments after our love. I myself took a few shots. The sensation was tense and thrilling. It shocked me how much the gun wanted to move. It leaped about in my hands, like a heavy fish. Hector had a fondness for weapons The Cortez mansion housed swords from Toledo, antique pistols, a suit of armor allegedly worn by the mad conquistador Aguirre. He urged me not to view these artifacts as evidence of his imperial nature.

"Investments," he explained, in his strangely Midwestern drawl. "Don't get the wrong idea."

Lina's mother was less forthcoming. She spoke to daughter in a sharp, conspiratorial whisper. Lina had told me (in a moment of besotted candor) that her mother grew up in a pueblo without running water. She might well have been one of the women working across the river. But her face had rescued her. It was a splendid mask, exquisitely plucked, glossed by emollients, with eyes that smoldered. Senora Cortez dressed in flowing white robes. She billowed about her tremendous kitchen, chopping the air with knives.

We visited my parents, too, during a weekend trip to San Francisco. It was supposed to be both of them, actually, but my mom bailed at the last minute. She'd been invited to deliver a paper in Prague. She called and left a halting message at home, after I'd left, and my father called me at the hotel, to apologize on her behalf.

So it was just the three of us. We went to the most expensive restaurant I could find and put it on my Gold Card. Lina was dressed to kill. She ate nothing and said little. I spoke about my success at work, a sports car I hoped to buy, the need to cut back the welfare rolls. My dad was stunned. What had happened to his son? He hovered over his plate of carefully arranged food.

Outside, in the parking lot, my father said, "You love this girl?"

"What's that supposed to mean?" I said.

My father laid a hand on the sleeve of my garish suit. He closed his eyes. The moon lit his eyelids, which were quivering. I thought he must have been frightened of me, and this gave me a perverse pleasure. Then, very quietly, not even looking at me, he said, "I miss your sister."

I felt my throat constrict, as it had in Tijuana, and on the night of her funeral, when, only half awake, I had wandered into Lisa's room and climbed into her bed and breathed in the musty scent of the sheets.

"Sure," I said. "Sure."

My father's grip tightened on my arm. He didn't want me drifting off just yet.

"Do you still think about her?" he said.

I was a good half foot taller than my dad. I could have stared down at his scalp, its wisps of peppered hair. But I knew he was looking at me. I could feel him. "I've been seeing somebody," he said. "A therapist."

"That's good," I said. "Good to talk."

We heard Lina emerge from the restaurant behind us, the sharp click of her heels, and we both stiffened, as if we'd been caught at something illicit. Off in the distance, the lights of the Bay bridge were screaming out against the black hills of Oakland. My father leaned into me and gave me a quick hug. I feared he might start crying and I hated him for just the thought of it.

Back at the rental car, Lina reapplied her lipstick. She had nothing much to say about my father (I was relieved) so she talked instead about some club in the Mission, owned by one of her clients. Later, we did some drugs, a combination of amyl nitrate and speed which goosed our aggression. Lina tore my back up with her nails. I thought of my father, the soft purple of his eyelids, and yanked her hair so hard she pinched a nerve in her neck.

I knew something terrible was happening inside me. I was burning through my life at cone ten, but I couldn't stop myself. Lina suggested I cut back on my work hours, ease the coffee intake, go to see her acupuncturist. For my twenty-fifth birthday, she gave me a portfolio of boudoir shots: Lina all greased up in a bustier, Lina in a pose suggestive of self-love, Lina with lollipop and naughty tongue. (I would later masturbate, angrily, repeatedly, to each of these photos.)

You're probably wondering at this point whether I ever

told Lina about Lisa, and whether this unburdening soothed me, or drew us any closer? The answer is, well, yes, and no. I did talk to Lina, just before our trip to San Francisco, and she said most of the right things, too. (Her shyness at that dinner, I can now see, was the result mostly of fear; she hadn't known what to say to my father.)

But I wasn't really ready for sympathy, if that makes any sense. I wanted her to know this terrible thing had happened, to have that excuse on tap, but I didn't want to face my own feelings on the matter, which I didn't understand anyway. The whole purpose of pursuing Lina, after all, had been to remove myself from the chaos of these feelings. However I might play it, she wasn't just holding herself apart—I was keeping her at bay.

The incident that comes to mind took place on a Sunday in March, just after our one-year anniversary. Lina had decided she wanted to wax my chest. We were bored and restless, eager to stoke the glands without disturbing the heart. Lina scattered newspapers on the floor of my apartment. She heated the wax on my stove and slathered it across my chest and waited for it to harden into a sort of shell, which she cut into strips. I looked like I'd been dipped in earwax. Lina tugged at the first strip, and I yelped.

"*Pobrecito*," Lina said. She licked her teeth and yanked again.

"That hurts!"

"Embrace the pain."

"I'm serious," I said. "It hurts."

Lina reared back on her ankles. "I get this done every three weeks on my fucking twat. Okay? Now quit being such a baby."

I realize that complaining about the discomforts of waxing, as a man, isn't necessarily the smartest play for sympathy. But I should point out that the hair on my chest was (and is) pretty thick in spots. And that Lina—for all her extensive experience being waxed—had no clue how to remove wax herself, that a brutal haste was called for, as with Band-Aids. And (finally) that Lina was enjoying my pain. She'd been enjoying my pain, feeding off it actually, as long as I'd known her.

So when she reached for that same first strip, still dangling pitifully under my chin, and began to tug, something in me snapped. I took hold of her wrist.

"Chill out," she said.

But I didn't chill out. I twisted her wrist. "You chill out."

I knew immediately that I'd gone too far. Not that there was some grisly snap, but just the feel of her wrist, the unnatural angle of hand to arm, the viciousness of the gesture, and Lina's shriek, which was not theater, but pain.

"I told you it hurt!" I said, as though this might be a defense.

Lina stood and cradled her wrist against her stomach. She was wearing a halter top and running shorts and her legs were glowing, because she'd waxed earlier.

"Fuck you," she said.

"I'm sorry," I said.

"Fuck sorry."

"Okay," I said. "Calm down."

I reached for her leg, and she kicked my hand away. "Don't fucking touch me." I could see that she was holding back tears. "I've had enough of your little psycho routine, John. I swear. Just because you've had some misfortune, that doesn't mean I have to be miserable."

I was stunned that she'd had the nerve to say this, actually. I looked down at my chest, where the spots of blood were already blooming at the torn-out roots. It was the sort of the moment in which we might have pushed beyond our raw narcissistic urges and found each other. But Lina wasn't one to back down. And neither was I, at that point.

"How dare you," I said. "You don't know a thing about it."

I kept waiting for Lina to say something, to apologize to me, to relent. But she only stood there and shook her head.

"What?" I said. "You don't! Because you don't give a shit about anyone but yourself! You and your fucking mother! What a couple of psychos." I could feel my throat tightening again and, as if to ward this off, I began to roar while Lina, still pressing her wrist, backed away from me.

"What? What do you have to say about that, huh? You could die, someone else could die, and you still wouldn't care, because you're dead already, aren't you? Your fucking heart is dead. Say something!" I shouted. "Say one fucking thing."

Lina was gathering up her things and placing them in her leather backpack. "I feel sorry for you." she said softly.

This might even have been an invitation, the best Lina could offer anyway, but I was deep inside my little self-pity bunker and I only screamed more, certain she would turn back, even after I heard her Beemer peel out of my guest spot and join the tide of Sunday morning traffic. "Where are you going?" I bellowed. "To the mall? To get some fucking new underwear for your waxed fucking pussy?" I was lying on my back, in my boxer shorts, alone, my heart encased in earwax.

I wound up cutting the wax off with a pair of scissor, then shaved my chest. It took an hour. And when I looked at myself in the mirror, I was overcome by an intense longing: I wanted to be this young and smooth again, to start over, construct a life that would lead me somewhere other than where I'd arrived, bloated up on protein shakes, in an apartment full of catalog decor, doused in some goddamn cologne that smelled like drunk lemons. What had happened to all my sweet lovers, to Jodi, to Eve, the ones who might have rescued me?

You asked, in your last letter, about this drive toward dangerous love. Why do we choose the ones who will leave us wrecked, or wreck themselves? The beautiful meanies. The screaming yayas. (Anyone, really, but the nice ones.) Is it a desire to feel alive at the extremes? That pathological fear of boredom? Or is it, in the end, something more like a fear of sorrow? That's my guess.

Lina began to travel more for work, to the New York office, which was charged with sexing up the new technology sector. We made up, officially, but she kept finding excuses to avoid dates. This made me desperate. There were various warnings. I needed to give her some *space*.

On a Friday afternoon, I caught her just before she could zip out of the parking lot and jumped into her car.

"What's up for tonight?" I said.

Lina sighed, fiddled with her new stereo. "I need some rest, John."

"We can order in."

"That's not what I mean."

"We can rent a movie and build a fort."

"I'm tired," Lina said. "Don't push me, John."

"Push you? I just want to see you."

I touched her cheek. Lina remained still, staring straight ahead. It was a terrible moment.

"I need to go, John."

"I don't get it," I said.

"There's nothing to get."

I slapped her dashboard. When that didn't draw a reaction, I punched the glove compartment.

"You're not helping things," she said. "That's not helping."

"It's not, huh?" I punched the dashboard harder. "How about that?"

"You need to calm down," Lina said. "If you want to talk to me—I won't talk to you if you're freaking out."

We went on like that. I was so sick of Lina. I was so sick of the part of myself that had thrown in my lot with her. And I was helpless for her acceptance. I began to beg. There's no need to repeat the words. Trust me: this was begging.

Lina had found herself a new man, of course, a German athlete-slash-model she met on the set of a TV spot for wrap-around sunglasses. (They had so much in common. Sunglasses, for instance.) It took a couple of weeks for me to figure this out—the unreturned messages, the sour looks of pity from my colleagues—and by then I was already four bars into that old country song, The Cuckold Is the Last to Know. I wanted to slap Lina so badly. Every time I saw her in the office. I wanted to slap the pretty right off her face. I hated myself for not actually doing it.

I realize, in writing this, how scary I must seem: the dead sister, the breakdown, the uber bitch girlfriend and violent fantasies. I'd meant all this to be funnier, lighter, more clever. (My wacky journey into the world of the weightless!) I hadn't realized how darkly the era would return. I wish I had someone like Elton on reserve, a colorful character with his own tragedy to bear. But then, Elton was nothing to laugh about either. He, too, was in a headlong dash from his madness. He seems to have been alive, though, Elton. He felt things. And, for better or worse, he honored his family.

I'm a little worried (more than a little) that this confession is going to scare you off. This is no doubt why I was stalling in the first place. You don't need another nutbag to survive. I guess I want to say, in my own defense, that I wasn't exactly myself in those days. Or, that I was an earlier incarnation of myself, living apart from the chaos of my feelings, and therefore unable to manage their expression. I do still believe in danger, Jane: the danger of connection, of weakness revealed and forgiven and repaired.

The strange thing is that occasionally, when I think back on this era, I miss it all: the cool pad, the long, useless weekends, Lina swaying on the dance floor of The Spot, holding the place in her thrall, her tragic bod, the sounds she made when we were alone and naked, the sweet corruption of it all.

Beauty is the cure of the weak. Yes. Understood.

But it was also, in those days, the safest truth I could find.

Awaiting the restraining order,
Nuge

PS—Unless otherwise advised, my cock continues to say "Hi!"

PASCAL LEMIR

December 22

Dear once-upon-a-time *Republican?*

Yes, yes, Lina Cortez and her guns. I can understand. On the one hand, I have to admit to a certain nostalgia: Where did my sweet boy go? And on the other, maybe I'm relieved by it all—you, stripped down, the wreckage, and that rarity of the truth, the whole truth. To be honest, though, I *am* looking for absolution. The Catholic high school, with all of its contorted efforts to save me, actually did instill some otherworldly desires that I can't dismiss. But that's not your job. Absolution will have to be granted elsewhere. The truth. Right . . .

(But first, please note: I manned the phones for the telethon pledge drive to help boost penile funds. I was in the trenches on that one, and, well, it was a battle lost—what with the issues of phone sex manners being inappropriate for telethon fundraising—but, by God, it wasn't for lack of spunk.)

At twenty-four, I was living in Baltimore—a grunty, industrial city that was desperate to swell into something new and shiny, but still most charming in its old giant neon Domino Sugar sign reflected in the harbor where you can still rent rusty dragon-shaped pedal boats. I waited tables at Charles Village Pub and was under the mistaken impression that my life was a work of art. I lived in a house burdened with the similarly deluded. There were tattoos and piercings as well as some avant-garde work with toasters, body paint, a perversion of a garage door opener that would just take too much explaining. The world was senseless and so it was our duty, our high calling, to reflect that senselessness. We were artistes. (Did I mention that you'd have to suffer my artiste phase?) But we shrugged off the term "art." The notion had been so sourly confused with life that it no longer existed on its own. I was painting dicks and Wellington china, most often combined. Oh, how your swishy high school art teacher would have loved it! A steamy objet d'art. It was all quite heady and very now.

I don't think I have to state this but we weren't really artistes. We were Pez dispensers with pink candy pop ideology. Our mouths opened, not because we had ideas, but because our necks had hinges. I was sad because Elton was gone. And I hated myself for letting him go, though I didn't really know why I was sad and why I hated myself. (Wouldn't you and I have hated each other? There's only so much self-loathing a couple can cart around.)

By any set of standards, my friends and I were failing miserably and we were miserable. Things accumulated: My car got towed; it wasn't worth the money to get it back. I couldn't one-up my kettle and cock piece. I quit my job because the boss didn't understand me, and finally got kicked out of the house. The last thing I remember is two of my fellow Pez dispensers, high on meth, licking the screen door.

I retreated to my parents' basement in Jersey. They'd turned my bedroom into storage space, the choked attic's overflow. And so my old bedroom was filled with things that they refused to throw away. My father is the hoarder. He has a deep sentimentality. The hoarding can appear to be just a lesson in frugality reinforced by those inevitable moments when someone suddenly does need ribbon or extra dice, and my father disappears, then emerges, often hours later, vindicated.

The basement was two rooms divided by a wood-paneled partition. My father's workspace—he still repaired clocks and things—was moved to the room with the washer dryer which left the other room open for a makeshift bedroom. It was damp. The washer ground through its cycles. I memorized the various whines from agitate to spin. The dryer, overstuffed since I'd come home, sounded choked, raspy. There were spiders, the overriding stench of mildew. It echoed lonesomely.

Now that she'd had a few years of not being restlessly stuck in motherhood, my mother was working on a new persona. I didn't know it, but she was planning her divorce, and she was trying to set up the new life she might waltz into.

She'd taken a part-time job at my Uncle Jack's store, Super Jack's Record Shack. She was hired as a family favor. She should have worked in a shoe department somewhere handing out nylon peds, talking up StrideRites, whispering, "These'll be half off come Tuesday." But she really didn't have the confidence to charge into an interview holding a blank resume.

Uncle Jack is a white man with an Afro, so devoted he uses picks instead of combs. He wears leather vests and still says, "Dig it," with grave sincerity. My mother was completely out of place. She tried to study the different bands, but I had to tell her more than once that it was Run DMC not Run DMV. She confused the bands Boston and Chicago, Bad English and English Beat. We had conversations like:

"Just ring things up. Just give people their change. That's all they want."

"What if they ask me questions? What if they want to know what I think?"

"They won't."

"But what if they do?"

"Tell them that you like Johnny Cash. Offer to fill them in on Johnny Cash."

Once I saw her at her post behind the glass counter, the bowl of hacky-sacks, the register. "Oh, Poison! Nice choice. They're quite popular!" The patron scowled at her, but she didn't seem to mind. "Here's your change. Come again!" There in her denim vest and her helpful smile, she was in the world. She broke a penny case with a hard whack on the register drawer and rearranged the change and bills. At home she played heavy metal, funk, rap. My father didn't say anything about it. The change befuddled him. It was possible that this might work in his favor. He was a religious man who prayed every night—like a child prays, kneeling, that humble—he'd been asking for a change for a long time. How couldn't he believe that this might be it?

I was the silent charge now. I wanted to see Michael Hanrahan, his stitched, thumbless hand. I wanted to know that he'd gone on, forgiven me long ago. I drove by his mother's apartment. An Asian family lived there now. I wanted find some truth of who I'd been then and who I'd become. I wanted to linger over the old bruises, but I was also dying to get out.

I'd heard about the nanny posts from a friend who'd done a stint in Switzerland. And this is a notion that had come to me: European men are big slobbering farm dogs of love, great, happy, howling, shameless, tongue-hanging, leg-humping, too-big-to-be-in-your-lap-but-there-they-are-anyway   farm dogs. I knew certain European exclusions: the British, for example. But in general I was sure that European men knew how to lift a woman up by an outpouring of love and adoration (and perhaps forgiveness). I guess, too, years after Elton Birch, I was looking for someone to replace him. I was looking for a country of Elton Birches, minus the insanity (though I loved the insanity of Elton Birch, too) and it seemed to me I'd find that country somewhere in Europe. I was hoping someone else would define me for a while. Like Lina. I understand why you wanted Lina. Aside from all of the obvious, stunning reasons, there are some sadder reasons, but you know these. I think you're clear on all of that. I hope you're clear on all of that. (What I'm saying is, yeah, you were a little scary, but by saying you were scary that makes you less so.)

Also, I wanted to go to a place where I could fail anonymously.

My mother was the one who drove me to the airport. It was still summer. She was wearing a pant suit, something too formal, really, for just dropping someone off at the airport. But I imagine she bought the outfit especially for the event to match some image she had in her mind. She kept her eyes on the boards, the signs.

When we got to the gate, she covered her mouth with her hand. There was a muffled pause. She started crying. She said, "I'm not good at this."

"What?"

"Mothering," she said. "Here." She handed me an envelope of cash. "It's from your grandmother." This was a shock. My mother and grandmother hadn't spoken for years, as far as I'd known. This is all I remember of my grandmother: cranberry juice and a poodle that was allowed to poop in the house. I don't know the details of the war between the two women—or any war, for that matter, the kind of ignorance that really hits you when in Europe—but we'd heard through my aunt that my grandmother was sickly, and my mother had garnered a little confidence now that she was a woman out in the world of Super Jack's Record Shack. I don't know if my grandmother said, weepy and weak and deathbed-inspired, "All is forgiven between us, now." I doubt it. Probably she just gave a good old-fashioned wad of cash and let that do the talking for her.

My mother said put on her sunglasses. She held out her shaking hands and stared at them. "What's wrong with me?" she said. It was the first time she'd ever asked herself the question out loud, though now looking back I'm pretty sure that she said it to herself often enough. "Here's the only advice I can think of, and it's probably the opposite of what I should say." She sighed, always resigned to everything. "Don't work too hard while you're there. Do you know what I mean?"

I nodded. "Sure. I should have fun."

"More than that. Just, what I'm saying is, don't waste." She took my hand and squeezed it. "Sometimes I feel too tight in my own skin. I just feel like my own skin is too . . . well, too tight." For the first time, I understood her. I understood her completely.

She opened her purse and clicked open a box of Tic Tacs. She kissed me awkwardly one of those left, no you go left, no your left, right, right, okay done, and then she turned and swiftly clipped up the airport's wide corridor.

The nanny agency had assigned me to an elderly couple whose baby was a twenty-three-year-old playboy still living at home. They'd tricked the agency or the agency had tricked me. There was no need for a nanny. I was a maid. This was fine, actually. The whole spoon-full-of-sugar mystique was beyond me. I preferred the straightforward work of ammonia and Brillo while I dutifully spent my off hours the way my mother wanted me to: in Parisian bars wearing liquid eyeliner and a leather bolero jacket with twenty-some zippers. I had this Janet Jackson layered look and a don't-slap-me-cause-I'm-not-in-the-mood stare.

The best thing about all of this, I think, is that I was really free for the first time in my life. And being freed, for the first time is much more interesting than being free, in general, to do what you want when you want to. I had the overwhelming feeling of having been let loose. Sure, the boys of Asbury Park had let me loose once upon a time, but this was worldly. There's something especially liberating about the fact that you're just not going to run into anybody you know.

At first I was in love with Paris itself. I loved the idea of putting chocolate in flaky bread. I loved that everything was so damn ancient. I loved how men rode bikes and not because they'd gotten busted for DUI.

For a week or two, I ran almost everywhere I went. I showed up breathless so often that I was asked more than once if I was asthmatic. And, just like the billing, the French were tirelessly romantic—my housemother finally gave me a vase for the random roses given to me in restaurants, on the metro, in long white boxes sent to the house. But slowly I learned enough to tell the difference between a gaze, and eventually, I realized that it wasn't exactly my glorious presence that inspired hearts to soar. These hearts soared pretty easily, regularly, like homemade rocket-launcher kits. I'd been mistaken, taking it all so personally.

Plus, there was the added irritation that Frenchmen didn't like the fact that I was American. They often couldn't place my accent, but when I placed it for them, they'd say things like, "I find most American women are fat and stupid as cows." So I spent a lot of energy giving them the finger, throwing drinks and what not.

After this new understanding, Paris wore me down. It toughened into a real city all around me. The elderly couple and the playboy son detested me. The playboy occasionally dressed as some mascot—a squirrel?—to do promotions in grocery stores. Had he wanted to be an actor? Nothing was clear, because the host family didn't speak to me. My room was at the end of a very long bent hallway lit by push-button wall switches, and I was encouraged to go straight there upon entering the house (and not to bathe too often, a waste of water). I remember that the shower and the sink were miniature, like so many things in France, as if all midgets there are encouraged to become architects, elevator and appliance designers.

And so I felt alone, single, (underwashed and yet steeped in wood polish and cleanser) in a way that I hadn't ever been before. The feeling of being let loose felt more like untethered.

This is the mood I was in one night when I was hanging out with another exchange student, Mira, who was living on the eastside in Chinatown. She was odd and sophisticated—a giant-eyed blond wearing a leather jacket she'd plucked off of the metro tracks. This one night she'd walked up to the bar, ordered something ridiculously beyond her years, like a Dewars straight-up. She'd asked the guy next to her for a cigarette, lit up, and addressed the men in general. She stood on a table. "Who has a yacht? Who would like to take me to Morocco?"

It so happened that there was a Brit that night, a rich guy, a little older than her father, who said he'd be happy to take her to Morocco, and so we ran up his tab and smoked his cigarettes.

And this is all I know: Pascal was in a corner booth with a crowd of guys and then, I'm not sure how it came to be, I was sitting next to him, his arm wrapped around me, our faces an inch apart. He had a French nose and full French lips and those French eyes that tilt up. His English was shoddy and my French improving, jumbled but fast. Pascal and I kissed in the bar, on the street.

Pascal was the perfect Frenchman to fall in love with because—and I'm not making this up—he was about to be shipped off to Antarctica for fourteen months to do mandatory military service. It's not everyday that someone meets an amorous Frenchman who's about to be shipped off to Antarctica. And it's my belief that when someone does meet a Frenchman about to be shipped off (he actually took a flight out, but shipped off sounds so much more romantic) they should take full advantage of it.

It seemed like I'd walked into the premise of a good movie, and all that was expected of me was to play my role. It promised weepingly orgasmic sex, a grief-stricken airport scene. There would be months, perhaps, where we could languish painfully, wandering around like wounded romantics, and always the hope of a torrid reunion. And I was looking forward to saying: I once fell in love with a Frenchman who was shipped off to Antarctica. It has a certain Molotov cocktail quality, a certain—as the French say—I don't know what.

Also, the relationship had an expiration date. No, this time there would only be a doomed hopelessness that made everything sweeter in an overly-ripe-fruit kind of way.

And so I started out thinking of Pascal as unreal.

Pascal lived in the north of Paris near a fish market. We did a few date-like things, but mostly we lazed in a cot in the blue kitchen of his tiny apartment. We lingered over each other's bodies. I remember high small windows that poured blue light and the light would change, diffuse, fold back in on itself. It was getting cold and the heat purred weakly only every once in a while, and we would breathe each other in, consume, swim each other's bodies like we were taking turns being summer lakes. He was skinny and his hipbones made beautiful bruises on my inner thighs.

Sex aside—and sex wasn't usually put very far aside; it was our clearest form of communication—I became an ambassador of sorts, explaining American culture. He was most interested in song lyrics. I did the best I could, but may have taught him that "Stop dragging my heart around" was the more pragmatic concern: "stop driving my car around," and that "a rose in fisted glove" was "a road and a distant love," but, well, I prefer mine there.

He worked with "transmissions" and so I assumed that he was an auto mechanic, and, hey, I was okay with that. I wasn't going to be like my mother, pouting over a man's lack of professional ambition. I accepted him. But there was never any grease under his fingernails and he seemed to talk about an office where he went to work, but neatly dressed. Eventually I realized that he did something more along the lines of radio transmissions, airwaves.

At first, this lack of information had great appeal—a good old-fashioned language barrier. I didn't want any pointed questions about my childhood, my parents, about Michael Hanrahan, Elton Birch, about the boys I'd now been with since Elton Birch—two years of crusty, lackluster gimme-gimme boys. And I wasn't really looking for long drawn out explanations from him, either. I'd had my fill of being brought home to meet the folks. I was looking for the smile, the shrug, the blissful reliance on chemistry to do the talking.

I knew French pretty well. I could rattle on, but I was so used to nodding along, hoping to catch on eventually, that I missed a good bit of what Pascal was saying. And there were those aren't-we-a-silly-darling-bilingual-couple miscommunications, sure. Like when I thought I was telling him that I had a pain—cramps, really—pointing to my lower stomach and I was actually telling him that I had a penis. I insisted that I did. He insisted that I didn't, that he should know. I insisted that I should know. It was my body after all.

But the thing about writing about this kind of floaty, hazy period in my life is that I don't remember things in French very well. It's as if the words melt away from their meanings too quickly, and I'm left with the gist. Basically, I had only that, the gist. Everything Pascal and I had together was based on the general idea. If the relationship had been a three paragraph essay, it would only have consisted solely of a thesis statement about vague amour.

It was a devouring, nearly wordless love, a constant wind-swept rush, and I couldn't help but be pulled in. I know I'm not being very specific this time around. I know I'm not be-ing as grounded and clear and declarative. But nothing was grounded, clear or declarative around me. I didn't exist, in a way. I was foreign to myself even. I was scrubbing tile, pick-ing at grout, polishing silver, and then making love in a blue kitchen.

One night we took a train to a small fishing town on the West Coast to meet his parents. Their house was small and antiquated with a large garden that took up the back yard. There was a big family dinner at a long table set up in the middle of the living room. His sisters looked medieval—black hair, red faces, bulbous noses, even the pudgy little sister. His mother was a flushed busty woman in a flower-print dress. And there were a bunch of ruddy uncles, all fishermen. Even though I spoke French well enough, they didn't speak to me directly. They treated me like abstract art, like something their boy had made himself—out of leather and zippers and liquid eyeliner—in an art class in the big city, something you'd put on the mantel and try to ignore as best you can.

They did offer me cigarettes, because, they told me, all Americans smoke. I tried to explain that there was a fitness craze in the States, but I was met with blank stares. His mother, confused by it all, petted me, which I took as a signal to stop talking.

After I accidentally locked myself in the bathroom during the dinner party and had to knock and knock to get their attention to let me out, Pascal's mother made one of the uncles fix the doorknob, although there was nothing wrong with it aside from it being backward from mine at home.

His family was hard to deny. They were real in a way that Pascal's blue kitchen wasn't. I couldn't overlook the fact that they were involved now, that we weren't just this love-swept couple in Paris.

We slept together in Pascal's childhood twin bed. It was still a childish room and the closet was packed in such a tender, frugal way that I thought of my father. I tried to tell Pascal this story: One summer when I was around eleven, my father would wake me up in the middle of the night, on Tuesdays. He'd whisper, "Fishman's here." And because some buddy, a trucker, owed him a long-lost favor, my father and I were allowed to load up the back of the station wagon with boxes of cod and tuna and processed fish parts. We met the trucker behind the Howard Johnson's. My father's face would shine in the streetlight, ecstatic, electrified by the luck of it all. Once he pounded the roof of the car as we sped over a bridge. It was the happiest I'd ever seen him. At the end of the story, I started to cry.

Pascal told me he understood. He said, "Your father is a good man who provided for his family. If he was a thief, then it is okay. He was the good kind."

This was a very nice answer, but the story had nothing to do with my father stealing fish. I was trying to explain how so little made my father really joyous, but the thing that did was small, unimportant. We didn't need free canned fish. It was impossible to explain. Pascal and I made love quietly under a homemade solar mobile—the planets bobbing and turning around a yellow ball, and it dawned on me that I had no bearings.

Despite the lack of communication, I loved him, and he loved me. Self-help books on love will tell you it isn't, but it is. What was clear most of all was that the relationship wasn't going to end when Pascal got on the plane. I was in deep, even more so now that his family had embraced me. I was scared, for the obvious reasons of my past.

We went to bon voyage South Pole parties. And the day came. The sex was weepy and orgasmic, yes, but it was also real, true. The airport scene was awful. Do I have to go through it? I was breathlessly sad. What had happened to the storyline? The role I was playing with poignant grace?

There was a dismal Christmas with Mira in the pimp district of Rome. She'd fallen in love with a French musician despite the fact that the rocker didn't think much of women in general. This and the vicious pigeons made her edgy. We pooled our money to buy a chocolate display cake that must have been two months old. It looked beautiful but tasted bitter, brittle and dusty. Finally, we went back to Paris. I said goodbye to Mira and the French family and their playboy son and went home.

For a few days, I found myself mentally pointing out Americans—something that had become a habit; backpacks, baseball caps, Nikes—but soon caught on. It took a month or two before I lost the liquid eyeliner and didn't replace it. And eventually it got too hot for the bolero jacket which went to the back of the closet. I only spoke French with a Haitian woman who worked in the drug store. I confused penis for pine tree this time, telling her that I found it depressing to see all of the old Noel penises lining the gutter waiting for trash day.

This was all pre-email. Once the ice stopped the mail ships, Pascal and I faxed. Phone calls were ten dollars a minute. When the ice thawed, there were boxes of letters that arrived day after day. There were photographs of penguins and the stories of somebody losing a frozen toe, part of a hand.

I was now working at a small private school, teaching social studies. The schoolroom smelled like the kids' dirty heads and chalk and glue. I read the letters during my rare breaks, sitting alone behind my desk while the kids were upstairs at art or music. I read the letters in my parents' basement while the washing machine jawed and the furnace ticked. (I was saving my money.) They were beautiful letters, but as time wore on, I wondered if they were someone else's love letters? A foreign housemaid's, someone who smiled a lot even when she didn't understand and smelled of silver polish and bleach?

Finally, a taxi pulled up to the house, and Pascal climbed out, looking thin and pale. My heart gave a little, collapsing in my chest. I'd been afraid that I wouldn't love him, but I still did. We hugged and kissed in the street. I didn't want him to see my bed in the basement, though I'd talked about it in letters. We only stayed for dinner.

But it was long enough to see that my mother wasn't my mother, giddy in her denim vest, trotting out her clunky French, "Bonjour!" and "*Passez du beurre, s'il vous plaît!*" She didn't say so but I knew that she loved the idea of a Frenchman in the family. She wanted him to stay, to give her French lessons, to come to her bridge parties as a kind of show-and-tell. She wanted me to marry him, too. She wanted to have French grandchildren who called her *grandmere* and wore miniature

berets. It would air-lift her out of this reality. It turns out that
Pascal was exactly what she'd meant by "Don't waste," maybe
even more than she'd let herself hope for.

My father looked at me, too forlorn for words. I heard him
grumble something like, *If it weren't for us, you people would
all be speaking German,* though he'd been to young to serve in
the war. He meant, I think, *We gave you your freedom and now
you want our daughters, too?* He was betrayed, wounded. He
worked on the lawn and got an American flag to flap above
the front door.

Fortunately, the timing was good. Pascal's arrival coin-
cided with the school's spring break. I borrowed a family car,
and Pascal and I went to stay with friends at my old digs in
Baltimore. There were only two of the original Pez dispensers
there—a video clerk and a part-time youth counselor. Pascal
looked alternately blindsided and bored. He drank coffee and
smoked cigarettes and acted French, which had worked so well
in France, but fell flat here.

But it was more than cultural. This was a shift in power. I
realized that I'd needed him in Paris, and here he needed me.
I translated conversations, jokes. (Jokes don't translate, neither
does garage-door-opener art.) He was living in lapse time, being carted around. I wasn't talking down to him, but I hadn't
realized how empowering it had been for him to take care of
me in Paris, to tend to me—the lost American housemaid.

And who was I here? Some ex-artiste? Some woman who
taught watered-down history to sweaty kids, and lived in her
parents' basement? The daughter of an odd, unhappy couple?
I zigzagged out of traffic, sang along to loud radio, pointed out
unusual cultural conundrums. "Look, Americans often hang
up flags of hummingbirds and watermelons on their porches.
I don't know why."

Sometimes he'd tell me not to translate. "I understand. I'm not stupid." But he didn't really understand, and even if he'd understood English, how could he have possibly made sense of the American phenomena of my friends. I wanted him to understand my life here, but when I tried to explain, he got impatient. "Just put me in the car and drive me around," he'd say. "Like my luggage."

He wasn't being a jerk, not really. He'd fallen in love with someone else. And he wanted to know where that woman was—the sweet one in the bolero jacket who smiled all the time and shrugged a lot.

We flew to Florida and fell apart. Pascal and I argued on the Florida beaches—Naples and what not—creating mini-French dramas in front of families with umbrellas and coolers and toddlers.

The undercurrent was simple: There was one thing that he didn't want to say: I loved you and now I don't. And so he said everything else that he could think of. He didn't know the word for claustrophobic. He drew a picture of himself in a small box. He said, "This doesn't translate, this relationship doesn't translate. It doesn't work." I wanted him to tell me that he didn't love me. I wanted to be punished—for old crimes, I guess. But I wasn't sure that I could take it. So I would goad and retreat.

After fourteen months in Antarctica, you can imagine he burned easily. I bought a gallon of milk at a Seven Eleven and, back in the motel room, poured the milk into hotel towels. I laid them on his bare red shoulders, his stinging back and legs. It was something I remembered my mother once doing for me when I was little. The air conditioner chugged. The room smelled old, worn, the coming and going of bodies, layer after layer of what we leave behind. The milk towels were cold but quickly they drew heat from his skin, turning warm and then hot. I put on another cold milk compress and another, like someone trying to extinguish a patient fire. The room soured.

On the last night, he finally told me the truth. "I'm not in love with you anymore."

I screamed at him. I felt like I'd been through a lot—the waiting, the painful letters, the lonesomeness—and he owed me something. I told him that he was a bastard. Maybe I seemed crazy all of the sudden.

He slapped me across the face.

My eyes teared immediately from the sting. I touched my cheek and stared at him. And then some ancient, dormant ferocity rear up in me. In that second, I was sure that I could kill him.

But Pascal was already contrite. "You'd gone crazy," he said. "You needed to be brought back. I'm sorry."

This is something you should know about me. I took the slap, but I held onto it. I wasn't going to do anything in a motel room—too private, too unprotected. I am obsessed with stories of women's bodies found in basements, public parks, in marsh reeds, stories of girls who don't ever come home.

We flew back to New Jersey in the morning. That evening, I was standing next to him in a station waiting for a bus that would take him to JFK. There was a Mexican family, a few backpackers, the woman behind the desk. Occasionally, someone would squawk over the speaker, but mostly the place was quiet.

"Pascal." I said it softly, my hand curled into a fist. And when he turned to look at me, I punched him in the mouth. He was stunned. His hand flew up to his mouth. His lips were bleeding. My hand was ringing. He looked at me, bewildered. The people's heads swung around to watch.

"I didn't like the slap," I said.

"No," he said, his face tight with pain. "I don't think you did." He pulled out a handkerchief and held it to his mouth, but refused to give any bigger response.

We both looked around at our small audience. They seemed to know that it was over. That there wouldn't be a brawl. They went back to peeling oranges, reading paperbacks, buying sodas.

I was thinking: Who does a thing like this? What kind of person softly says someone's name and punches them in a bus terminal? I thought it had something to do with Pascal. I thought it was because I was so crazy with love.

And, of course, I didn't like that Pascal was dumping me. What I hated most was the fact that I still wanted Pascal to love me. I wanted him to tell me that he'd been wrong, that we could work it out. And there was a panic, a deep irrational panic, in knowing that I'd probably never see him again. (I told you how I hate goodbyes.)

I watched him get on the bus with his swollen lips. I waited for him to change his mind, to jostle off of the bus, and run back to me. I waited for him to turn his head toward me, to look at me one last time. But he didn't get off the bus. He didn't turn to look at me. He stared straight ahead. The bus lurched and rolled away. And I stood there, feeling like a struck gong, my chest still ringing, my knuckles tight.

I waited a week before telling my mother about the break-up. We were standing in the kitchen. I was dressed in a skirt and a button-down shirt. I had an interview for a job in Philly at a bookstore. I was already thinking about grad school. I needed a new plan. My father was in the car waiting to take me to the train.

My mother didn't take the news well. "I hope you love this crappy house. I hope you love mowing grass!" As if there isn't grass in France. "I hope you like this . . ." She picked up a well-meaning saltshaker. "And this . . ." She threw a Tupperware container onto the floor.

At any other time I would have gladly entered in, but I wasn't allowing myself drama. I'd cut myself off. I was sure now that it was better to pinch off emotion. But I wanted to throw things too, and cry, and tell her that I knew that if she'd had the chance to trade me and my father in for something else, she would have. It was what I'd wanted to say all my life.

But, no, I said, "I'm heading out. Dad's waiting." I turned and walked away, but she followed me.

"I hope you like that stupid K-car!" she said. "I hope you like it all!"

My father looked up from his spot behind the wheel. I jogged to the car, sat down, but he was frozen, looking up at his wife who was standing on the front step in the freezing cold, hands on her broad hips, breath steaming from her mouth. She was flushed and fuming.

"I don't know her," my father said, quietly. "Sometimes I swear I've never seen her before in my life."

So now the difficult part. I'm supposed to be mantling things here (why only dismantle? Why not mantle every once in a while?).

I'm afraid that there are endless versions of myself—one broke Michael Hanrahan's heart and let him go racing off on wet night into a telephone pole, one deserted Elton Birch because she wanted to survive, one was a sweet, innocent housemaid in Paris and one punched Pascal in the mouth in a bus station. I am afraid that I'm like my mother, and I feel sorry for my father who fell in love with a debate team champ, a debutante, and that's not who she turned out to be at all. I'm afraid that someone will fall in love with one version of me, but that version will shift and change until a new me emerges, maybe wholly from an old wound. It's a confession. It's a warning.

I broke a finger when I punched Pascal in the face. It hurt like hell. It turned fat and blue. I didn't go to the doctor. I didn't get it x-rayed. I just let it pain me until eventually one day it didn't pain me anymore. It healed crookedly, and so now when I try to point out a direction straight ahead, my finger is veering off-center to some unintended locale.

One more thing.

Maybe there is a problem here, in all of these letters, you know. You can feel it, too, can't you? This addiction. This tallying of loss. We're harboring the half-life of what we've let go. See, it can become a kind of hoarding, not unlike my father's habit. My mother left my father not long after the Frenchman left on that bus—this will come up later—and my father went rummaging through our boxed-up lives. He laid it all out and waded through. It was an awful thing—all of that gazing. It becomes unhealthy. Is this too much?

Mantling my past in search
of sorrowlessness,
The French Maid

REBECCA "SUNNY" DARLING

January 5, 2004

Dear Sonny Liston,

I am going to restrain myself, just barely, from making any cracks about your French maid outfit. You're raising a serious concern and all I can say, really, is that the past is always too much. That's what makes the past such a tough customer. One minute you're waltzing down memory lane, the next you're besieged by what could have been. Pascal doesn't sound like a guy who would have survived your twenties. But who knows? Maybe he would have. And, at any rate, the possibility of Pascal persists. He remains dreamy and tender, bathed in milk and bleeding from the mouth. (Note to self: Jane punches. *Hard.*) And frankly, who wouldn't rather live in France at this point, given how dumb and murderous America has turned.

Which leads me to my next order of business, a quick word about the republican thing—in short, I was hotdogging, mugging for effect, making myself romantically despicable. I did vote republican, but only in one local election, and mostly because the Democratic candidate wanted to turn this one toxic beach area into a Superfund site, which meant all of us surfer wannabes wouldn't be able to pretend that we boarded there and we were all like, *No way, those waves are* our *waves, dude. Don't go harshing on our gnarly. This is, like, America. Civil rights and shit.*

I was probably also trying to test your mettle. But I realize that the word *republican* has, of late, acquired a more sinister valence. I can't begin to describe how sad this great country has become. Never mind the conniving nutbag who stole the election, or his minders (nakedly devoted to greed) or the lazy chickenshits of the press. What upsets me most is the royal we, We the People, our lonely and deranged populace, cheering for death on TV, renouncing the sick and poor at every turn, choosing to fear and hate at the precise historical moment when love seems most essential. How very Christian of us.

So you see? All better.

A final possibly relevant note: I need you to not get a big head about the whole Arctic lover thing, because most of my former lovers wind up in the Arctic sooner or later. They've got a kind of support group going up there, last I checked. (Out of sheer charity, I'm not going to mention the hottie Laplander I was balling during Clinton I.)

No, the one I should tell you about now is Rebecca Darling. Yes, Darling. Rebecca of Sunnysnatch Farm, I used to call her, soon shortened to just plain Sunny. (And she did have a sunny snatch—a natural blond down below. Not even Jodi Dunne could match that.) This was a few years removed from Los Angeles. I'd moved on to Miami, to a design firm, and stumbled into a therapy that helped me understand just how furious I was at my mom and how much she frightened me. I'm not going to burden you with all that. You don't strike me as the sort who needs any further immersion in the Province of Damaged Mothers.

That's not the story, anyway. We're talking lovers here, though I should mention that it was Sunny who kept me marching into the Good Doctor's office, Tuesday and Thursday afternoons, long after I'd declared the whole thing bogus, because she knew I needed to simmer off some of the rage, let the better angels of my nature emerge, and she knew, more important, that this wasn't her damn job. She was a fabulous woman, nurturing but no-nonsense, a genuine foxy grown up. She was also a mother.

It was her child, an indomitable six-year-old named Zoe, that I met first, at a potluck dinner. There was a faint knock on the door and I, being closest to the door, opened it up and there stood a pretty little girl with her hair in a very sophisticated French braid. "My mom's parking the car," she announced.

She walked into the apartment and looked around her, at the rest of the guests, seated politely on various couches. "Is this going to be one of those things?" she said. "One of those adult things?"

The hostess Patty came running over. "Isn't that a lovely gown?" she said. "Did your mommy get that for you? Look at those sleeves. Aren't those sleeves pretty?"

Zoe inspected her outfit for a second. "It's a dress," she said calmly. "It's not really a gown."

Patty clapped her hands. "Isn't that funny! I'm Patty! What's your name?"

"Zoe."

"I'll bet I have some shoes that would look great with that, Zoe!"

"I don't think we're the same size."

The kid wasn't being cheeky, either. She was just trying to get Patty to ease off. (In my recollection, she set her hand on Patty's arm in a gentling manner, though I may well be making that up.) The other women in the room were itching to descend on Zoe. You could see it. She exuded thermo-nuclear cuteness, owing to the delicacy of her features. One felt the slight urge to pinch her nose, to make sure it was real. She was clearly used to entering rooms full of panting adults, because she immediately asked Patty if she could go some place and draw. "I'll be back when you guys eat," she said.

Then Sunny appeared, her hair sort of floating around her. We all looked up.

"That's a pretty poised daughter you've got," someone said.

Sunny smiled. I'd never met her before. We were part of the same clique, vaguely cultural people trying to transports ourselves from the comforts of office labor to the wild prairies of art. I liked her looks, blond, a bit washed out, and I liked her manner, which was friendly in a matter-of-fact way. There was no sign of a dad, and no mention of one. But Sunny had a daughter and that put her off my radar. Anyone with a child was already way too mature for me.

Besides, I'm not exactly a natural when it comes to children. You may have deduced this from my adventures in camp counseling. The truth is I find kids excruciatingly self-conscious. I don't blame them. They're constantly getting all this panicky energy thrown at them. So I tend to take the opposite approach. I'll acknowledge a kid, but that's about it. If they want more, they can ask. Zoe must have appreciated this, because she took the seat next to me when she came back into the room. Dishes were going around the table and I got passed a quiche with broccoli and some kind of redolent cheese. I have serious broccoli issues, so I didn't take a piece, but I offered Zoe one.

She sniffed at the thing. "It smells like farts," she said, sotto voce.

"You think Patty farted on it?" I said.

"Gross."

"You're the one," I said.

Zoe paused to consider this. There was some kind of dish involving chicken and prunes and capers and she took a little of that. She jabbed at the prune with her fork and held it under the light. Her expression suggested the basic question: *Wherefore prune?*

There was some other stuff, a pasta salad with too much vinaigrette, a grease-mushed effort at homemade tostones.

"My mom cooks better than this," Zoe said quietly.

"Which dish is hers?"

"She brought dessert."

"What kind of dessert?"

"A torte."

"You mean a tart?"

"No," she said. "A linzer torte. It has jelly and powdered sugar. I put the powdered sugar on. You have to sprinkle it carefully. If you put too much on, the whole thing gets wrecked."

The guy on Zoe's left, Randy, was one of those guys who makes a grand display of his rapport with children, as if auditioning for fatherhood, badly. He kept saying things like, "Zoe likes the chicken! Zoe likes the pasta!" By the end of the meal, Zoe looked ready to stick a fork in his eye.

Sunny didn't worry about her kid. She was at the other end of the table, listening to Patty discuss, in punishing detail, her plans for a vacation to Florence. She glanced at me a couple of times, flashed a patient smile. And the linzer torte—my God! It was ridiculous. Half butter, half raspberry preserves, with a pinch of flour thrown in to keep up appearances. I ate half. Zoe ate the other half. What a couple of pork balls. We sat on the couch together, woozy, the remains of the torte between us.

"You weren't kidding," I said.

"She's a pastry chef," Zoe said. "That's how she makes money."

"You're one lucky little son of a gun."

Zoe scanned the room for her mother, who was nowhere to be seen. She looked at me for a second. "What's your name again?"

"John," I said.

"Right. John. Excuse me, John."

She got up and marched out to the balcony.

There was some kind Trivial Pursuit thing starting. I always find those games depressing, as they force me to acknowledge that I know more about obscure television shows of the seventies than, say, literature. Zoe was still out on the balcony, so I wandered out there. Zoe and Sunny were standing side by side, both staring down at Biscayne Bay, which had gone rosy in the late-summer dusk.

"Howdy," I said.

They both turned at once. It was the first time I'd seen them side by side and the resemblance was a little eerie, the cant of their lips, the nervous balling of their fists.

"I caught her smoking," Zoe said.

"Half a cigarette."

There was an awkward pause, which I tried to fill by introducing myself to Sunny. "She knows who you are," Zoe said sharply. "That's still smoking, mom. Half a cigarette is still smoking. It means you get cancer and you die and I'm an orphan."

They had gone over this a few times before my arrival.

"Please don't say that," Sunny said. "I'm going to be around for a long time, my love. I promise." She reached down and stroked her daughter's cheek.

But Zoe squirmed away and began coughing ostentatiously.

"Maybe the wrong moment to interrupt," I said.

"No," Zoe said, "you talk with her. I don't have anything else to say."

We watched her slip back inside the apartment. From inside, we could hear Randy booming out, "There she is! Zoe, you're on our team! You can be our secret weapon!"

Sunny smiled dryly. She was showing exceptional poise for someone just dressed down by her six-year-old. "This was a mistake. Zoe hates potlucks."

"Why'd you come?"

"I thought there might be other kids here. Patty said there would be other kids. I'm trying to make sure Zoe gets to spend more time with kids her age."

"She does seem a little on the precocious side."

Sunny stared down at the bay. "Sensitive," Sunny said. "She's more sensitive than she lets on." She blew a strand of hair from her cheek. "Death is her latest thing, that people die, they no longer exist. Her father let her watch some fucking Discovery Channel special on her last visit and now she's convinced I'm a goner."

"That must be tough," I said.

"Anyway, she's right." Sunny stubbed out her cigarette. "It's a terrible habit."

We both stood there for a second, watching the sun make another one of its flamboyant South Florida exits. I snuck at peek at Sunny. She looked drowsy, adorably so, the tendons of her neck standing out a little.

"On a brighter note," I said, "the torte was amazing."

"Thanks," she said.

"John," I said.

"Right. John."

So this was hardly a case of instant fireworks. Sunny was a busy woman. She had this kid and a new business as a caterer of upscale desserts. I was busy with my own late-twenties shenanigans, rebuilding myself, basically, after the degradations of

Lina Cortez. What did this mean? I slept with younger women who were easy to impress. I rid my hair of gel products. I ditched my TV. My life drifted, not unpleasantly, in a bohemian direction. I kept a sandy studio apartment on South Beach, in an art deco building painted like a Mondrian. This was pre-Armani, pre-Versace, pre-DeNiro, the new gay money doing battle with the old Jewish poverty. The result was a beach town with slum cred. I strolled Washington Avenue on Sunday mornings and took in the entire human travesty: transvestites, altecockers, Peruvian playboys, lipstick lesbians and Lubavitchers. It was not unusual to see a man traipsing around half naked, with a twelve-foot python slung over his shoulders.

My Sunday routine was to rise relatively early, hit a grungy Cuban juice bar for a pint of fresh carrot/orange, pound that, then jog to the beach. It was criminal that no one swam in that ocean. But most mornings, I had the run of the place. I'd dive in and muck my way out to the buoy. The water was so clear you could see the sunbeams bouncing off the bottom. I used to lie on my back and take in the hotels of Ocean Drive, with their jaunty portholes and rails, the tourists fried pink, wandering hangovers.

A few weeks after the potluck, I emerged from the water on just such a day and heard my name being called. Zoe was wearing a yellow bikini that showed off her pot belly, and matching sunglasses. Sunny was behind her, lying on a towel. "Hey," she said. "I remember you. Come here, John!"

Sunny said something, but she waved her mother off.

"You were at that picnic," she said. "At that fat lady's house."

"Don't bother the man," Sunny said.

"I'm not bothering him," Zoe said. "Am I bothering you, John?"

"Not at all," I said.

"You really shouldn't swim in the ocean," Zoe said. "There's bacteria in there."

"Bacteria?"

"Don't say that sweetie," Sunny said. "It's rude."

"You're the one who said it."

I sat down beside them. "Is there something I should know?"

"One of my mom's friends found a needle in the water," Zoe said gravely. "A poison needle."

Sunny smiled, just enough to dimple her left cheek. "That's not something we're going to talk about, okay sweetie? We're going to talk about something nice."

Zoe looked at me. "You've got good muscles." She leaned over and felt my bicep, gave it an appreciative little pinch.

Sunny laughed. "Stop being a flirt. Honestly, Zoe."

Zoe wheeled on her mother. "You're the one who said it!" The kid could see she'd hit the mark and she pressed her advantage. "You said yourself, mom. 'Look at that fine spaceman! Don't we know him?' You said that.'"

"Spaceman?" I said.

"Specimen," Sunny murmured. She was blushing sweetly.

I did look pretty good at this point in my life. I'd gotten rid of all the dumb muscle from my El Lay days, and the swimming had helped lean me out, which was important, because I still had the chicken legs to contend with, a bequest from my father. I was, like every single Miami native, tan year-round.

It hadn't occurred to me, until just then, that Sunny might be interested in me. She was in this category of mother and suddenly she had slid into this seemingly-remote-but-actually-adjacent category of woman, sexual being, potential hoochie-coocher. She was wearing shorts and a halter top, a

terribly modest outfit given our location, the infamous Four-
teenth Street Beach, where the gay men sunbathed, and, as a
result, where the models came to lay down their tans, all of
them quite topless. Boobs everywhere, the natural ones swaying prettily, the fake ones standing straight up under the sun,
little womanly mounds of saline.

It was a weird spot to take a kid, actually, particularly a
girl like Zoe, who was so—what do I want to say here?—alive
to the adult aspects of her environment, though, in Sunny's
defense, it was still early. Most of the models were still asleep,
and the gay men were just slipping into their banana sacks.

"We're going to have breakfast at the Front Porch," Zoe
said. "Do you know that place? We're going to have hash
browns. Do you like hash browns, John?"

"I love hash browns," I said.

Sunny made a ceremonial effort to protest, but she could
see an axis had formed. It turned out that Zoe and Sunny lived
just off Espanola Way, a few blocks from me, and this meant
that I could come over, if I wanted, and see how Sunny made
crème brûlée. Zoe extended this invitation. The smell of that
kitchen alone was enough to sink me: vanilla, cinnamon, chocolate, and eggs. I was supposed to meet my latest dumpling
for an early dinner, but I arrived at her place half an hour late,
still in my swimming trunks and stinking of caramelized sugar.
This wasn't hard to explain. I'd met a woman, a much younger
woman, and she'd somewhat kidnapped me.

"It's, like, what, a Big Brother/Little Sister thing?" she
asked me.

"Right," I said. "Yeah."

So I played that angle for a while. It wasn't far from the
truth. We kept meeting up, each Sunday, on the beach. Zoe
needed a non-threatening male presence in her life. Sure. I

could handle that. We went and bought gourmet sandwiches from Stefano's and watched Sunny make these insane desserts: mocha pound cake drizzled with Valrhona chocolate, hazelnut cannoli, key lime napoleons. Oh, it was sexy as hell, this cute little mama bear whipping all those ingredients into obscene shapes, while Zoe showed me her seashell collection; like a play date with erotic charge.

And then one morning, no Zoe.

"She's with her dad for the weekend," Sunny said.

There was an awkward stretch there, in her absence, both of us stumbling around in our clumsy adult bodies, trying not to eye the adult equipment. Sunny filled me in on the details. She was from Buffalo. She and her sister Tess had been raised by her mom, an irony not lost on her. It was her mom who'd taught her to bake. Seven years ago she'd left Buffalo for good, gotten as far away from the snow as she could imagine.

Then she met and quickly married this Swiss guy, Marco, who she thought was a sexy European-variety box turtle. He was a snapper, though. "No papa genes," Sunny said. "The lack of sleep made him crazy. He hated changing diapers. He thought there'd be a nanny involved, someone to bring him this sweet-smelling bundle when he came home at night." He'd done a few dumb things to force Sunny out; the obvious ones.

I nodded at all this. What else was I going to do? Keep nodding.

Here was one good point: Marco's family was loaded. They were the heirs of that ancient European money you always hear so much about, and happy to provide some of the seed money, via Marco, for Sunny's business. (This was the least they could do.) Sunny didn't like the arrangement one bit and she was determined to pay this loan back, every penny, as soon as possible. Thus the brutal work schedule. I was incredibly impressed.

To engender such chaos! To withstand this chaos with such aplomb! I had to remind myself that she was the same age as me, twenty-eight.

On this particular Sunday it was her duty to prepare tiramisu for eighty. I'd never given much thought to tiramisu—though I'd wolfed down my fair share—and so I hadn't realized the precision required. Sunny had to prepare two pans of light sponge cake, a mixture of mascarpone and sweet cream, a syrup involving butter and Kahlua. These had to be chilled, warmed, tempered, all just so, then layered like a lasagna and sprinkled with powdered chocolate and cinnamon. Her kitchen technique was her life: frantic, hopeful, spilling over at the edges. It was the Kahlua that got us in trouble. Not that we needed much encouragement.

This is going to sound sort of lame, but I really hadn't had much good sex through my twenties. I mean, it hadn't been terrible. I certainly didn't see it as terrible at the time. But there wasn't that true sense of abandon, the ecstatic rhythm that begins with a desire to eat the other person and culminates with a bang for both parties. That was how it went with Sunny. I'd thought, in my idiotic twenty-something way, that a woman with a child would have been somehow depleted sexually. It hadn't occurred to me that the female body was a regenerative instrument. Sunny hadn't had sex since the marriage went south. There was a lot of desire stored up in her not-very-large body, and some darling creative capacities. So, yes: kitchen-related monkey business. How could there not have been? Sunny had access to all these ingredients: honey dust, coconut butter, almond paste. She didn't have the world's most shapely bottom, but it tasted awfully good lightly slathered in ginger flan. The whisk was put to good use, as was the basting brush, the pastry sleeve, and, improbably enough, the garlic press. The second or third time we were together, Sunny ran to her big fridge and retrieved a bowl of chilled cake batter. We stripped naked and dipped our paws into the bowl and rolled around until our hair was crusty. It all sounds kinky and flagrant. But these innovations were more childish than adult, the result of natural gastronomic curiosities. Come and get it. There was some biting, too. Sunny was a biter. Oral aggression, she said. I could rally with that. It's amazing, really, what people can rally with when they're in love.

(And here, I should confess to something in the present tense, which is that my moment of panic in the coat room did have something to do with your having bitten my shoulder, which should have been, and was, incredibly sexy, but also a powerful reminder of Sunny, though, as you'll see in due time, there was more to my idiotic abstention than this.)

Sunny didn't want her daughter to know anything. So for the first couple of months our coupling was covert, fit between assorted maternal and professional duties. We had sex—hurried, ardent sex—in one of the storage closets at a local elementary school gymnasium, while Zoe performed an array of cartwheels and headstands for her gymnastics teacher.

After a while, though, the allure of being a secret wore off. I began to suspect Sunny was using the kid to keep me at bay.

"You're being ridiculous," Sunny said. "You have to look at my situation. Zoe's at a very precarious stage. Give her some time to adjust to the idea."

We were lying on my futon, the remains of a banana flambé scattered across the floor like wet coins.

"She can't adjust if we keep running around behind her back," I said.

"You can't just expect to barge into her life."

"Nobody's barging. But at a certain point, you know. Does

she really expect you to remain celibate for the rest of your life?"

"Celibate? Jesus, John. What are you talking about? This isn't about sex. It's about what kind of role you're going to play in her life. You're not her father "

"Did I say I was?"

Sunny lifted her head from my chest and studied me. Her eyes were light blue, with flecks of gray. "This isn't an issue of you and me," she said slowly. "Just so you understand. There is no you and me, really. It's you and us. I can't just invite a man into my life, okay? It's a package deal. And I'm not going to get Zoe involved until I feel comfortable." Her eyes slipped to the bedside clock. "Shit," she said. "Shit, I hate this. I've got to run." She got up from the bed and began hunting for her clothing, while I lay there in a sulk.

Sunny glanced down at mess we'd made and smiled to herself, bemusedly, and came and kissed me on the forehead, then, more tenderly, on the lips. "I'm sorry about all this. Listen. I am. But I've made one mistake already. I can't afford to make anymore. There's no margin of error for me. Try to trust me. Can you do that, baby?"

Well, of course I could. The math here isn't very complicated. She was a mama, a true mama, fiercely in love with her daughter. I was in love with her, and, if this makes any sense, I was also in love with the love they felt for each other. Often, late on those lazy Sundays, I'd sit in the living room and listen to Sunny and Zoe enact their bed-time ritual—the coy, whispered negotiations, the stories read then reread, the soft, clicking kisses—and tears would well up, a sudden messy surge of sadness and joy. More than once, I crept down the hall so I could watch them from the doorway, Sunny leaning over her daughter, murmuring, the soft light from the hallway on Zoe's cheeks, Sunny circling these cheeks with her thumb, kissing her forehead, the scent of the room (bubble gum and baby shampoo) making me dizzy. The ritual took an hour some nights. I knew Sunny was over-indulging her child, giving a little more than a mother should; and I was helpless to resist the gentle spell of their love.

I did a good deal of lobbying to spend the night. I was enamored of the idea that Zoe would slip into the bedroom one morning and cuddle between us. It wasn't just a matter of wanting things out in the open, you see. I wanted, in a way that I can see now was emotionally perverse, to absorb the love that flowed between them. But there was something needy in the way I clung to their lives, overstepped what Sunny calmly referred to as boundaries. She was leery of my jones to play Big Daddy Savior. It was the Good Doctor's opinion that I wished to resurrect my mother and sister, this time as capable of loving each other and—heck, why not!—me. I'm not disputing the matter.

Fast forward six months. February 14 on South Beach, down to a frosty eighty degrees, the streets full of human peacocks, the clubs booming out house music. Nights like this, you could gaze through the windows of a restaurant like Divine or Oggi and see grown men and women, fashion editors and drag queens and sheiks, skulled out on overpriced champagne and dancing on the tables.

For caterers like Sunny, pliers of the upscale dessert, Valentine's was crunch time. She'd worked forty-eight hours straight, preparing 180 heart-shaped puff pastries (filled with courants and puréed pear) two dozen pecan-and-white-chocolate pies (also heart-shaped), and 4000 hand-rolled truffles. I didn't quite realize how busy she was, though.

I'd made reservations at Bella Napoli, our favorite Italian restaurant, and instructed her to meet me there at eight sharp, because I'd hired these guys to play violin for her. Sunny had a weakness for such gestures, exorbitant and softly lit. I'd arranged with the owner to reserve a corner table on the balcony, away from the clamor of Washington Avenue, with a view of the ocean.

So there I sat, at eight, all scrubbed and sweet-smelling in a light green guayabera and khakis. My hair was loose, a little wild. I'd swum a triple buoy earlier; I felt that pleasing ache of having exercised. I kept imagining Sunny in a sun dress, smiling, her eyes going misty at the violins.

She was late. At 8:20 p.m., the violin players showed up, three of them, mustached and grim in rented tuxedos. They were Hungarian (I think) dark little dudes with long noses and scuffed violins, which they held under their chins with great tenderness. The shortest of them spoke Marx Brothers English. "We play," he said. "Make-a good song for love."

"I'm still waiting for my love," I said.

"Sure," he said. "We wait till the lady come." He nodded and motioned for the others to join him behind a pillar.

I went to call Sunny at home. No answer. I sat at my table again, trying not to look stood up. Down below, on Lincoln, couples were strolling past. I was watching for Sunny, of course, but the figure I saw, just past the public fountain, was (cue the ominous music) Lina Cortez. She was dressed in a red skirt and a sheer white blouse and she was walking in that smooth, hippy way that always ruined me. I hadn't recognized her at first, had actually thought she might be a child, because the guy next to her was about eight feet tall, a ridiculously muscled black dude. He was—I realized in a rather unpleasant flash—the starting center for the Miami Heat. They were drawing rather a lot of attention.

What followed was a sitcom moment. Instinctually, as if to duck out of view, I rose from my chair. The violin trio, taking this as a cue, stepped out from behind the pillar and began playing a strenuous version of "That's Amore." This drew the attention of well, basically, everyone, including Lina and her companion, whose name was (and presumably remains) Marvelous Williams.

Lina glanced up and saw me standing alone over a candlelit table, in my idiotic guayabera. I saw her raise her hand, the beginnings of a smile, but by then I was backpedaling and the violin players, in a state of eagerness endemic to professional serenaders, gave chase, all the way through the restaurant, sawing frantically. I knew that Lina would seek me out. The potential for male shame was too delicious for her to resist. ("Marvelous, this is an old friend of mine, John.")

And so, very heroically, I hid in the bathroom. The violinists eventually got the basic message and stopped playing. They did not find any of this particularly funny. Their leader stomped into the bathroom and explained that they had another *geeg* at nine. I started thinking in a paranoid way. Were Sunny and Lina in cahoots? This was ridiculous, but it helped me convert my rotten luck into a convincing rage. So I sprinted to Sunny's place and banged on the door and finally snuck in the side entrance. Her kitchen told the whole story. She had used virtually every utensil she owned. The walls were spattered with dark chocolate. The floor was sticky with karo syrup. A giant keg of butter, left on the stovetop, had melted into a shiny yellow lake. I found Sunny in her study, asleep with her head on her mousepad. She'd been printing out invoices.

I didn't know what to do. I felt all queasy and amped, solidly forsaken. But Sunny was completely wrecked. She barely knew where she was. I carried her to bed and began taking her clothes off. She was mumbling apologies, thanking me, clinging to my neck.

"Don't go," she murmured. "Stay."

"You should sleep."

"I'm all naked now," she said. "Please stay."

"What about Zoe?"

"She's with her father."

Sunny woke up in the middle of the night, famished. We both were. She heated up some potage and made a salad and we had our candlelight dinner amid the wreckage. I told her about Lina. It got me a little teary, actually, thinking about how doomed I'd been, tumbling through my life like it was a beer ad.

Sunny touched my cheek and said, "That's over now."

Then she threw some kiwi and pear slices into her food processor, splashed egg yolks on top, grated orange peel, sugar, and spooned the result—it was a kind of fruit mousse—into my mouth. We were in bed by this time, stripped down to our skins. Love with Sunny, when time allowed, was long and concerted. There was an awful lot of appreciative staring. And then, at some point, Sunny's features began to pinch and her lips slid back to reveal her teeth and those teeth found my shoulder and bit, soft, hard, soft. (The bruises looked like plum skins; I touched at them incessantly.)

Sunny was still zonked at eight. Toward nine, a car pulled up and the door slammed and Zoe's voice rose up to bid her father farewell.

"Bye-bye, Daddy-o!"

I shook Sunny awake.

"That's Zoe," I said.

"It's okay," Sunny said.

"What should I do? Should I hide?"

Sunny looked at me and smiled. "No. No more hiding. Just put some clothes on, sweetie. We can have brunch, the three of us."

I dithered into my pants, dizzy with gratitude, and grabbed one of Sunny's oversized tee shirts and headed out to the kitchen, looking as nonchalant as possible.

Zoe was just letting herself in the front door. She marched into the kitchen and looked at the mess and then her eyes fixed on me. "Where's my mom?" she said.

"She's just waking up," I said. "We were going to make you breakfast."

"I had cereal already."

Usually, upon meeting, Zoe would give me one of her sly sidelong glances, a mix of affection and conspiracy. But her expression now was knotted with suspicion.

"Why are you wearing my mom's shirt?"

"I'm just borrowing it," I said. "Just for today."

"Don't you have your own shirt?"

"I do," I said. "But it got dirty."

"Were you helping my mom cook?"

"Yes," I said. "I was."

"And it got dirty while you were helping her?"

I nodded.

"I don't believe you."

Zoe stood there, in all her lisping, Type-A glory. She was wearing a tiny black lycra top with Girl Power spelled out in rhinestones. This was the kind of garment little girls wore in Miami.

"Did you sleep over?" she said.

I nodded.

I could hear Sunny emerging from the bathroom. I thought for a moment, I was worried actually, she might embrace me from behind.

"How about some waffles?" Sunny said.

"I told him," Zoe murmured. "I ate breakfast already."

There was a tense pause, during which I could feel the energy of the room shift. It was as if I had sunk right out of view. Sunny and Zoe stood facing one another on opposite sides of the counter and the look that passed between them was simply terrible. Sunny was trying to smile. Her hand twisted at the cord of the food processor. Zoe wasn't giving any quarter. She had her mom pinned to that one spot with an expression that wasn't rage exactly, but something more calculated and menacing.

"This place is a big mess," Zoe said.

"I was working," Sunny said.

"It's gross."

"I don't like your tone," Sunny said.

Zoe mimicked her then, *I don't like your tone*, and when Sunny stepped around the counter, Zoe turned and ran back outside.

"Shit," Sunny said.

"I should go," I said.

"It's alright," Sunny said. "She just needs to adjust herself to the idea."

Sunny gazed at the state of her kitchen—everything congealing, everything starting to turn—and collapsed a little.

I tried to help her clean up, but she wanted me out of there. Hell, I wanted out there. I hurried down the front path of her place. Zoe, hidden away in the gnarled branches of a banyan tree, shrieked down at me: "I don't care! I don't care! I don't care!"

I didn't give up, though. No way. I was determined to win Zoe over, to recapture the easy rhythm of our early days. I wanted to see Sunny and Zoe in love again. I still thought there was some chance for me to get mixed up in all that. I remember taking to the two of them to the Stoneman Pond, this fancy public swimming pool in Coral Gables. Sunny was happy. She'd made another big payment to her in-laws. I was feeling good, too. I'd been asked to show some of my photo collages in a group exhibit. It was one of those rare breezy autumn days you get in Miami, the wind raising whitecaps on Biscayne, the blue sky a little higher than usual, cruise ships slipping past the government cut like giant floating wedding cakes.

We'd gotten sandwiches from Stefano's and a bottle of wine and dessert was a butterscotch pudding with chocolate covered almonds. Zoe had just learned how to swim without water wings. She wanted her mom to go in the pool with her. "Soon," Sunny said. "Give me a few minutes to digest."

"That's a fable," Zoe said. "Mrs. Fallows told us."

Mrs. Fallows was Sunny's kindergarten teacher, the current ranking authority on all matters related to the universe and its contents.

"Ask John," Sunny said. "He's a better swimmer than I am."

Zoe considered this proposal. She scratched at a mosquito bite on her ankle. Then she walked up to me and said, almost solemnly, "Will you go swimming with me, John?"

We weaved across the hardtop, hand in hand, and she jumped in the pool and bobbed around, like little kids do. I held her under her belly for a while. She showed me her kicking exercises. It was a whole thing. Then Zoe asked me to throw her.

"I don't know," I said. "It's pretty crowded in here."

"Come on," she said. "Just a little throw."

She gave me one of her devastating air kisses and my heart leaped. This was my big chance, to prove my worth, to stop feeling like such a lousy interloper. So I chucked her around a little and she howled and cackled. The problem was, each time she came paddling back, she would cling to me a little longer and her hands—how do I want to say this?—she was kind of grabbing at areas that a little kid shouldn't be grabbing. The first time, I figured it was a mistake. But then it happened again and I got a bad feeling.

"Last throw," I said. "Okay?"

Zoe fixed me with the creepy grimace and she was clinging to me, rubbing her legs against me and saying, "Come on, John! Come on!" Her hands were messing around with my shorts. I don't think she knew what she was doing exactly, but she knew well enough to freak me the hell out. I tried to lift her away from my body, but she held on, and I could feel the struggle between us building. Her nails sunk into my ribs and my own hands began to pry at her more roughly. If you were watching from afar, it would have looked like the standard shallow-end play. Zoe was laughing, in a dry, hiccupy way. But under the surface there was all sorts of vicious churning. Every time I got a solid hold on Zoe she would wriggle free and re-attach herself, until finally I pinned her arms to her sides. It was the only way I could figure to solve the thing. Then she kicked her leg out and nailed me you-know-where and I just lost it. I sent her sailing high into the air. She landed on her back with one of those gruesome back-flop smacks, the kind that cause people to wince.

Zoe went into diva mode immediately. All the weeping that kid did—it was like something out of "Camille." I apologized. I apologized my head off. Later, I tried to explain to Sunny what had happened. But I couldn't bring myself to mention what Zoe had been up to, not the worst of it. I knew it would only screw things up. Sunny wasn't blind to Zoe's will. But she couldn't really see how wounded her child was.

Sunny and I carried on for another six months. But more and more, it was just the two of us, when Zoe was with her father, or with a sitter. The sex became kind of desperate. And we ourselves started to feel the steady seep of self-consciousness that is, in some final way, the death of love.

My shrink had this all figured out. Hadn't my own mother and sister been terribly close before I came along and broke up the clambake? Was I not, in a certain fashion, reawakening the trauma of my youth, that house haunted by a brutal variety of feminine gazes and counter gazes? I didn't know. Sometimes that seemed to make sense. There were other moments when I wanted to say: "Look, doc, I was just trying to find love!"

I do believe I was getting better, a little less angry each day, a little closer to forgiveness. But I'm not the strongest guy on earth. Those last months were agonizing, all that ringing hate. And I hate to say this, but I think Zoe was drawn to me— and pulled me into her mother's orbit—because she knew my heart was too fragile to bear divided loyalties. Certainly, she had a crush on me, a dumb physical thing half-transmitted from Sunny. But at a deeper level, she sensed my weakness. She knew I would abandon the two of them if things got too messy.

In those charming moments of self-loathing to which I am still prone, I tend to regard the end of the affair as my doing. I was greedy, I wanted only dessert. If only I'd showed the patience, I could have battled my way into Zoe's heart. But the truth is I don't believe love should be a battle. It should be a struggle (a sweet struggle) in which both parties are fully available to push and pull and relent. The pitfalls are there, waiting for us, after all, as we expose more and more of the soft flesh.

Dreaming in chocolate,
Ted Nougat

PS—My cock wishes you a prosperous and tumescent New Year!

MR. AND MRS. PAGLIA

Jan. 19

Dear man chased by obsessed Hungarian fiddlers,

I have to say that I'm a little fed up with my subconscious. I've been trying to will it to hand over a little piece of you, a dreamy bite-sized portion, or more—I'd be willing to accept more—and possibly a boathouse scenario. Is that too much to ask? Evidently, it is. In my dreams, I've had sex with, thus far, Bill Buckner (still comforting him after the World Series of '86), Jon Stewart of the Daily Show (with wry commentary and the studio audience), most of the big playwrights—Sam Shepard, a young Neil Simon (played by Matthew Broderick, per usual), David Mamet (cussing all the way through)—Beyoncé (who hasn't?), Emily Dickinson (awkward doesn't quite describe it), Bon Jovi (ashamedly), the Wilson brothers (from their Bottle Rocket days), Starsky (without Hutch) . . . but not you. Never you. Well, once, almost, kind of you, but there was this accordion and a constant interruption by Cary Grant.

I'm tapdancing here, though, and buttering you up. This is a buttery tap-dance routine. You can tell. Enough.

I have to admit that after reading your last confession, I went through a series of thoughts. I suppose that Sunny seems to me like the first one who you were ready and capable of settling down with. She's your first real what-could-have-been, as you put it. And so this started me off: My God, what if this works out? What if there's a closeness here, an intimacy that becomes undeniable and we fall in love and we get married and honeymoon in Greece and have those children, the ones we would tell our story to, that begins with a dead cat on a golf course that came back to life. And what kinds of children would we create? Perfect angels? Perfect church-basement-pageant angels in cardboard wings. This is highly doubtful. We'd produce complicated stock. I know I'm making superhero leaps, but stick with me for a minute because I want to know, to really know how much struggle, sweet or otherwise, you can take. Life promises harder challenges than Zoe Darling. Not that I claim to understand the world of life with children or to know that I would be up to the challenges of our (delicate? hysterical?) offspring. But what I'm saying is that I want to know: Did you love Sunny or didn't you? Did you really love her, by your most idealistic definitions? If it's at all possible, I want you to tell me.

Wasn't I the one who said we shouldn't discuss the other's failings? I was. It was a rule, and now I've inched in this judgment, this questioning. I hope I haven't broken something irreparably, but I'm trying to be honest. I'm trying to respond honestly. (How many times has that been an excuse for bad behavior?) And you've been so well behaved, letting Pascal soak in the milk of memory, allowing me my crimes, my somewhat gory fascinations, my familial ruminations. And, frankly, I only have one more confession after this one . . . if we're to stick to the biggies. And you? I think you're probably catching up with your present day, too. This doesn't leave me much time if I've got to make amends. Well, I should stop now, go on and confess. I will lay bare so on that score at least we're even. Here goes:

The irony isn't lost on me: during my parents' divorce, I dated a happily married couple.

Alex and Deirdre Paglia. The Paglias, as in Mr. and Mrs.

Were they happily married? Were they *sadly* married? They were in love. That's undeniable. They were unbearably in love. And it felt good to be with them (for a while), to be weighted in all of their lush, restless helplessness. The Paglias were helpless with love. They were weeded over, despairing, lost in the wilds. I remember their greenhouse most of all. It took up much of the small back yard. Hot, moist, swimming, the flowers were lewd, perspiring with the effort of their vivid destinies. The tomatoes were red, fat, rumpy things, weighted, pendulous—too heavy, too ripe, so full they split their skins. Everything seemed to be twisting, inching with purpose at every moment. But I'm getting ahead.

Alex and I met accidentally, oddly, uncomfortably, illegally; I was trespassing. In fact, maybe this is what I was, a trespasser, throughout it all.

I'd left my pocketbook in the back of a friend of a friend's car. "I'll put it on the kitchen table," she told me, tossing out directions over the phone. "It'll be unlocked. Just walk in and get it. Nobody will even notice."

She lived in a row house with a group of foreign students—Koreans, Turks, Brazilians. She'd said the night before that living with Koreans was like living with cats and Brazilians like living with dogs. It was supposed to be a revelatory cultural theory not a demeaning stereotype. She was thinking of writing an exposé.

I was living in Philly now, a friend had quit a job at a bookstore that she lived above in a tiny apartment. I could have the job and the apartment, complete with her futon. I was in grad school, going after my PhD in poverty. It was an offer I couldn't refuse. I was dating a lot, though not seriously. I loved, for this brief time, mostly musicians and athletes. (No one famous. No one you should know.) It was a phase. I loved them not because they were onstage, not because they were heroic, but because I loved watching men become ecstatic, unabashedly emotional. I loved how they were finally allowed to be affectionate to each other, in fact, more than affectionate, passionate, tender. A shirtless drummer, a teary first baseman, these were, for a time, irresistible. And I did once date, with much disappointment, a basketball player who was sixteen inches taller than I am. If it's any consolation, maybe Lina wasn't having as much fun as you might think on that kind of amusement park ride of a man. I can say that the discrepancy in our sizes made me feel like the sexual equivalent of a leg warmer, a scarf. He could have worn me like a boutonniere. Sometimes I felt like I could have used a map with a little arrow You are here. (Is any of this helping? Maybe not. Sorry. Let's just go on.)

I was prepared for the apartment's oily fried foreign meat smell, those hot curdy yogurt sauces. I was expecting a barren living room of unmatched furniture, the anonymous tidiness required of a lot of people living together, an accumulation of bicycles.

I got to the place, and the door—heavy, old, with a thick glass crescent—was in fact unlocked. I walked in and the living room did seem foreign, but not in the way I'd thought it would be. Dark, woodsy with Persian rugs, lush leather sofas, massive bookshelves. It had an incubated feeling of moss; the walls were painted a dusty green. It made me think of the word *parlor*. The living room was small and filled with antiques, a mahogany fireplace, candelabras, smoky oil paintings, bookcases—and dead animals, bearskin rugs and gazelle hooves sticking out of the wall in lieu of coat hooks. It seemed like the home of a hermit—a quiet life of avid contemplation, but, no, a man who'd also had to fend for himself in the wilds, killing beasts to survive—in Philly?—so that he could . . . read? I breathed it in, and felt a thickness in my lungs, like I was a little high, like I was downing ether. It was the kind of place where ether could exist, or absinthe.

Of course, it was the wrong house, and I knew that right away. But I had an excuse to be there and I was willing to hold onto the idea of the pocketbook to see more. I turned down a small hallway. It was lined with monkey faces—preserved, terrified, frozen. I stopped there. I could see the kitchen table—a bowl of enormous eggs (emu? ostrich?) arranged on it. No pocketbook. Was I still expecting the pocketbook to materialize? I didn't move. It dawned on me now—the monkey faces were arresting—that I was in the house of a killer, a madman, a freak hunter who wore pith helmets, someone who'd gone dotty, but was still fully armed.

I heard a shuffle in the kitchen. A clatter of pots. The clicking of a gas stove top. Humming. I stepped backward. The wood floor squeaked. The monkeys glared from the walls.

"Deirdre?" A man's voice. "You home?"

And then Alex Paglia stepped out from around the corner. He wasn't a mad hunter—well, not the one I'd imagined, but he was some kind of hunter, I think. He was naked except for a pair wire framed glasses and white boxer shorts, the pink of his penis nudging the flap. He was holding a grapefruit and a glass of wine. It was three o'clock in the afternoon. The sun was streaming in the window.

I said, "I'm not supposed to be here."

This was the perfect thing to say to Alex Paglia, I would

come to find out. He liked it when things weren't the way they were supposed to be. He was good looking—or maybe he wasn't good looking, just amorous. He wasn't just looking into my eyes; he was taking in my whole face, lingering on my mouth. I didn't know it then but Alex Paglia was falling in love with me the way he often fell in love. Most men will say they love women, but it's not the same thing. Alex deeply achingly fell in love with women all day long. I understood this, of course. I suffered a similar affliction with men. (Maybe we were both insane hunters in pith helmets, fully armed.) I love men, and not just the idea of men, perfected in polished recurring dream. No, I love the restlessness of their corrupted souls, the way they hide their heavy, murderous hearts, their sudden delicacies and small shocking acts of tenderness. There is nothing like the stories a man will tell you—beautiful, simple, transcendent—if he truly trusts you and trusts that you will soon leave. (Is that what we have here? Are we sharing a confessional booth, its black screen? Are we even aware of the fact that the rules state that we have to resurface, surface, face each other?) And Alex loved women—the way their bosoms swayed, the way they arched their backs. He loved the way they read books and shopped for fruit. And there he was, standing in just the right slant of sun, and there I was, in the hallway, a little sweaty—it was summer, my dress clinging. Well, that was enough for both of us.

He smiled, blushed, and his penis bloomed before him, a gracious offering.

Now we didn't take each other right there in the monkey-lined hallway or on the kitchen table with its bowl of giant eggs (dinosaur?). There's no need to cue the porno synthesizer— bownt, micka chownt, da-da-da-da, bownt, micka chownt.

Alex turned. There was a well-placed oven mitt. He said,

"Well, are you lost? Looking for some porridge and a sturdy chair . . ." He didn't finish the final Goldilocks plot point—a comfortable bed, not too hard, not too soft, but just right. It lingered in the air around us. And I felt like I was in a house of bears—there was one skinned and yawning, enormous yellow teeth stretched out on the living room floor. "Let me get dressed." He brushed past.

"I was looking for, well, this exact address. The address is wrong though." I was yelling to him up the stairs.

"I don't know my neighbors. I'd try to help, but I really don't know any of them. Is that a bad thing? To be so unneighborly?"

"No, that's fine."

"Neighbors make me nervous, the way they stick around. Do you want wine?"

"Sure. Are you expecting someone named Deirdre?"

"Deirdre. I'm always expecting Deirdre. She just doesn't usually show up and so I get lonesome."

He reemerged on the word *lonesome*. Sunny, elegant, blessed with a certain wistfulness and a chipped tooth I wanted to run my tongue over. He was wearing a white linen shirt open at the neck, shorts, and sandals. He had great hip bones and the shorts hung on them just so, his loose leather belt not really doing a damn thing.

"Let's eat Limburger cheese and brie on salty crackers," he said, "and get drunk."

I had nowhere to go. As a grad student, I had a good bit of thinking time. Think, think, think. I had big ideas, colossal, and they took time to just bake with minimal basting on my part. (In what field? Do you really want to know? Well, I've made a career out of the boys of Asbury Park and Self-Esteem Warfare. There are Feminist Studies scholars who at least pretend to appreciate my theories on the female psyche. Irony. Go ahead, I know. Folks usually go into fields where they have the least business being, evidenced by Barbara Walters and Mugsy Bogues.)

It was my day off from a part-time job at Festoova's Bookstore run by a woman who called herself Festoova—the name reminded me of an infestation of oompah bands, and Festoova had the unfortunate build best suited to the tuba. (When she showed up with her similar-looking sisters one afternoon, I called it an Infesttuba, in my head.) The name was her invention. Once someone called for a Nancy, and as I said, "Nope, no Nancy here," she grabbed the phone out of my hand and started yapping. I lived in the apartment over Festoova's, one grimy room. It smelled of books and my old paint set; I could no longer paint dicks and Wellington china or anything for that matter. I was uninspired. I was lonesome, as Alex Paglia had said, despite the boys or maybe more lonesome because of them. I hated the apartment and that my mother would call from her wall-to-wall carpeted condo where she'd taken up residence. The machine would beep, and she would ask, "Did it beep? Did I miss it? Is this thing recording? Can you hear me?" And then she would cry and hang up. She was still working at the record shop, but the divorce was proving more difficult than she'd expected.

Cheese and drunkenness sounded like as good a plan as any.

I found out that Deirdre was Alex's wife, that she had an apartment across town, and she traveled a good bit.

"On business?"

"Sort of."

Alex Paglia didn't work. He said, "I don't partake. The employed depress me. Nine-to-five, water-coolers, coffee breaks. I wasn't cut out for it." He was embarrassed to admit it, but he seemed compelled to go on. "Women in offices with shoulder pads in their dresses, well, they break my heart a little."

The dead animals were inherited from his father. He'd hated the old man—a great hunter, but loveless. His father had called him weak, and his mother had raised him to be weak, meaning sensitive, tenderhearted. He showed me a picture of her when she was young, and it was obvious that Alex was the product of extremes: the manliest of men, the womanliest of women. He was also one of those boys who shoot an animal, by mistake maybe with a bee-bee gun, or on purpose because they're told to, and start to cry. I happen to like this kind. (I suspect you might have been this kind of boy once. I'd guess you nailed a squirrel—do they have those in California? Maybe not—with a homemade slingshot because your liberal parents wouldn't have let you have a BB gun, and maybe you didn't cry right then, but you did later. (Hey, there ain't no shame in it.)

Alex's father's work had been international and so Alex had lived all over the world as a kid. "The animals are my homestead, my hometown, my childhood. They were the only things that remained the same and I grew attached." I understood, although back then I hadn't really put it together that my youth existed in the bodies of men.

This led to a short discussion about my past, and the current situation with my parents. My mother had broken the news to me flatly: "Your father and I are splitting up. It just isn't working."

"Did I miss a point when it was working? I didn't know that working was part of your definition of marriage."

"Don't be fresh." She was diverting the focus.

"I'm not being fresh."

"Yes, you are."

"Are you scolding me?"

"No, we're in the same boat! We're two single girls!"

This horrified me for all of the obvious reasons. My mother and I were in the same boat? We were both single girls out in the world? She couldn't scold me because we were one and the same! (How many splintered versions of my mother can the world contain?) By this point, my mother had already moved into the one-bedroom condo. She announced that she'd stopped wearing shoes in the house—had my father insisted she wear shoes in the house? She also stopped cooking. She ate pre-packaged meals, diet food in frozen rectangular portions, and went on crying jags that I erased from my machine. She wanted to get personal, but it was too late for that. I'd needed her once, and she'd been only a flimsy version of herself, a flimsy version of someone's mother. She'd defined the relationship early on. I wasn't punishing her. I simply wasn't up for a change in the rules. Also her barefooted independence, her rebellion in the shape of frozen diet meals depressed the hell out of me, and her lonesomeness—decades of it spilling out in choked sobs—was terrifying. I didn't want to learn anything from her, even by accident.

As far as I could tell, my father's life didn't change much. I'd only talked to him on the phone. He'd learned how to cook pasta with white clam sauce from a can. He liked it, and gave me the impression that he was therefore pretty content.

My parents' divorce shouldn't have been a complete surprise. But it was. I felt homeless although I hadn't lived at home in years. I was old enough to know better than being all bent up about a divorce. I wasn't a twelve-year-old who was going to be exchanged from one parent to the other at a Texaco. Rationally, I thought it was the right thing. But it didn't erase the feeling of hopelessness. Love, the lost cause; I didn't make a banner and wave it, but the deep nagging suspicion I'd had all my life that love was a fake Santa seemed confirmed. I pretended to have ideas like: The question wasn't *How will they live without each other?* It was *How will they live without their discontent?* But really I didn't believe they could live without each other, and yet they were.

When I met Alex, I was wondering why anyone would ever get married at all. He wouldn't help clarify the sacrament any. Out of the back sliding door, through the patio with its small stone garden, across a narrow slip of grass, the greenhouse stood—a shining glass house, it seemed, oddly enough, more solid than anything I'd ever come across. Clamped to the ground, biting into the soil, it was a part of the earth itself, swollen on its own breathy fertility. When the sun hit it right, the whole structure reflected in such a way that it seemed it was made of light. And within it, Alex and I were too. Our drunken breath rising up into the thick air, humid, tight, we undressed each other and fell into each other, plush, brimming. Flowers, their mad excesses, their misty, floating pollens, dazed, they bobbed, swayed, and we lurched, breathlessly among them.

I stayed the night, went to work the next day, found my way back, spent the next night and the next.

The Paglias had an *open marriage.* I'd heard the term before, but I'd never made the associations—an open door, an open space, open mouths, open legs, Alex lying arms spread open, on their wide bed, open, open. And Alex was the perfect lover. He had practiced skills, but those don't impress me. He was sincerely appreciative, astute. He admired all of the right things—not the obvious, but the subtle—I shouldn't say what exactly, should I? (There's still the possibility of unfolding if we ever meet. Will we ever meet?) He'd stand at the bottom of the stairs just to watch me go up. He was just taking it all in. He was an admirer and not just some punk amateur. He was a connoisseur. He should have given lessons, as a public service, alongside wine tasting and defensive driving lessons at the Y.

Deirdre. I found her in pictures, in her toiletries, in her closet, filled with gorgeous scarves, long narrow skirts, swooping necklines. She was gorgeous. Her skin was always an even tan, her hair golden. She was leggy, effortlessly striking, like his mother. She gazed lazily at the camera or, caught off-guard, she was laughing wildly, one arm locked onto Alex.

I told Alex that I was fairly sure that Deirdre wouldn't like to find me here, despite the open marriage. But he assured me that Deirdre would love to meet me. "I told her about you when she called. She said that you sounded charming."

"I think she was being sarcastic."

"Deirdre isn't the sarcastic type."

One night, a woman showed up at the door. It wasn't Deirdre. It was someone else. She talked to Alex on the front step. I watched from the kitchen window. She was a little older than Alex, perfectly groomed with a square handbag. She was teary. Alex talked calmly, nodded, but she became more and more alarmed. She waved her arms and then started sobbing. Alex held her, and she melted into the embrace. He stroked her hair and then they let go. The woman turned and walked quickly to her car. Alex stood on the stoop, watching her.

"Who was that?"

"I don't always have good judgment," he said. "She didn't understand."

"What's her name?"

"Marsha. It's too bad, but she'll get it together."

And so I felt sorry for Marsha. Poor Marsha. She didn't understand. It's too bad. She'll get it together. Let's hope. Poor, poor Marsha. I wondered what she could have done to get kicked out. She'd gotten too attached, maybe. She'd wanted Alex for herself. She'd had little jealous fits and tried to split up the happy couple. I would never do any of these things, surely.

It was the kind of mistake that only a desperate woman would make. I was convinced that I wasn't desperate. And I was comforted by the fact that I wasn't the only woman. Less chance of scrutiny. Less chance of having to make the necessary improvements in myself—I knew I was pretty sorry, but couldn't figure out why. Poor Marsha. Poor well-groomed Marsha. She didn't even know that I was there, that she'd been replaced.

Now Lillian, she came by for money. She wasn't invited past the front stoop either, but I saw him hand her some bills. She had wreath tattoos around her biceps. When I asked about her, Alex said, "Lillian just got herself into a bind." Lillian was unemotional. She took the money, smiled, gave Alex a big kiss.

June was invited inside. She had a glass of wine with us and told us that she was dating a mime. "Tedious!" she said. "Absolutely tedious!"

Ellen, Mary, Karen. Karen was a poor Karen. Mary didn't get beyond the stoop either. Ellen had lost something. She had funky glasses and short black bangs. She wanted to see if Alex knew where the lost thing was. While he was upstairs looking, she said, "He's a handyman."

"Is he?"

"I mean like the song. He fixes broken hearts. What's wrong with yours?"

"Nothing," I said. I really believed it at the time. I was wrong. My heart was in bad shape. I was sad. I was as lonesome as my mother, but toughened to it. Was I after a handyman? Alix was no rank amateur. I must have appreciated that I was in the care of a professional.

"Sure. Right." She laughed. I felt self-conscious. "Have you met Deirdre? I never did."

"No," I said.

"Maybe she doesn't exist."

Alex appeared with a diamond porpoise necklace on a long chain.

"Thanks!" Ellen said. "He'd kill me if I lost this!" And she left.

I hoped that Ellen was right, that Deirdre didn't exist, but her presence was everywhere. I tried to insinuate myself into her life. I used her deodorant and her shampoo and a pantyliner from her box under the sink. Meanwhile Alex and I had these little domestic moments. He was reading the paper and I interrupted to ask him where he put the vodka. We were a little old married couple, sometimes drunk, sometimes horny as mad, sometimes ordinary, plain old ordinary. That's what I loved most of all—the plain old ordinary. I seemed to be saying to my parents, "Look, this isn't so hard! This is easy, in fact. It's a snap!" My parents were failures—from the starting block. Their mismanagement was only just starting to catch up with them. No one was surprised by their separation—least of all me. I had no hope of a real reconciliation between them, but I wanted to be able to believe in marriage. And so I was proving marriage was absolutely workable, but proving it with somebody else's husband. An obvious kink.

After I'd been living at Alex's for about two weeks, more or less ignoring my one-bedroom flat over Festoova's Bookstore, Deirdre came home. It was the middle of the night. Alex and I had been asleep in their bed for an hour or so when I heard the door open, keys hit the coffee table, high heels in the kitchen.

"Alex," I whispered. "Someone's here."

He rolled toward me. His skin warm, his dick hard. "Really?"

"Really. Downstairs. Is it Deirdre? It could be an intruder."

"An intruder." He pulled my hair back, kissed my neck.

He seemed to like the idea of an intruder. "I'll have to get out a golf club and chase this *intruder* down the street."

But there was no need. The light flipped on. And there was Deirdre, sunny, leggy Deirdre. "It's just me," she said. "You're Jane. Alex has said great things about you. And look, here you are!" She was sincere, a little tired. Her lips were full, glossy. Deirdre. The real thing. She turned to Alex, "I'm exhausted, sweetie. Don't get up." She was breathy, her voice was small. She listed to Alex. He propped himself up on an elbow, his hard-on still visible under the sheet. She leaned over. They kissed, and I loved them. I'd already kind of fallen in love with Alex, but it was this moment that finally tipped the scales. They were graceful together. And how can I explain the way they looked at each other? Heartbroken and nearly weepy. They were dying, in some way. They were glorious and strong, but I had the impression that they were deteriorating, too. They were in a state of collapse. Something about them gave the impression of ruins.

"Sorry," I said. "I should go." I started digging around under the covers for my clothes. I yanked on underwear, grabbed my tank top off the nightstand. I didn't want to be there, and yet I didn't want to be anywhere else. I loved the frothy green house breathing in the yard below the window. I loved the petrified animals, the horror of them, and that Alex took them in although he hated the old hunter, his father. I loved the bed with its light comforter and the beamed ceiling. It's strange, I know, but I didn't want to leave. I didn't want to be one of those other women—Ellen, June, poor Marsha—those other women with their square handbags, their wreath tattoos and funky glasses, those other women of the front stoop, of the lost items. And I knew that I was. I had no real bearings, no true place in the world. My existence was easily abandoned, a PhD that seemed out of reach, a job in a bookstore, an apartment with a month-to-month lease. Yes, I was one of those women set apart from the world, like my mother in her condo, eating rectangular food, barefoot—living my messy, solitary life. But I wasn't one of them while I was in Alix's house, in his bed. I wasn't one of them at this very moment, or so it seemed to me.

But Deirdre surprised me. "Don't go," she said. She stood at the end of the bed, crossed her arms, let out a gusty sigh and then started crying. "Tell her not to go, Alex."

He turned to me. "You don't have to go."

I should have gone, of course. I should have insisted on it. This was private. A bedroom. A husband and wife. A homecoming. She was crying. He needed to comfort her. And I assumed that she was crying about me or about the open marriage, the awful concept that gave way to scenes like this. The only polite thing would have been to excuse myself, but now it seemed more awkward to leave than to stay . . . and I wanted to stay even though it was so uncomfortable. I didn't want to be cast out. "It would make the most sense if I left," I offered.

"I didn't know I was going to cry," Deirdre said. She was still crying, and she cried beautifully. The tears slipped down her cheeks, pooled at her chin, pearling, actually, pearling, they hung shimmering. Her nose ran a little too, like Jane Fonda in *Klute*, and she wiped it with the back of her delicate hand. She unzipped the back of her skirt, took off her blouse. She was braless. Her breasts were full, loose, tan which struck me as Mediterranean. She shrugged on an big T-shirt. "Arthur's dying. That's all. It isn't news. He's going to die and I'll miss him."

"Arthur's sick," Alex told me.

"He's dying," Deirdre said again.

"Arthur is Deirdre's lover. He's the one who keeps her . . ."

"Ten years!" Deirdre said. "And he's dying on me. People

think lust is our undoing, but I think it's love, which is worse much, much worse."

And so I was wrong. The crying had nothing to do with me. It was about Arthur. Someone named Arthur, her sugar daddy? Deirdre flopped on the bed and crawled up it, still crying. Her perfume swirled around her. She got under the light comforter and lied down between me and Alex. She was hiccuping and sighing, trying to calm herself, like a girl who was lost but got found and can't shake the feeling of almost having disappeared. "Does Jane know the whole thing? I mean, I could go on about Arthur, but I shouldn't unless she knows. Do you know, Jane?"

"No," I said. "I don't know anything about Arthur."

And so Deirdre turned to me and told me a love story. It went something like this: When she was twenty, Deirdre's mother died and she was flying to the funeral. She'd spent every bit of money she had on the ticket and a friend in the airline had bumped her to first class where she met Arthur. They fell in love. He was married, but he took care of her, set her up in an apartment, paid for her to take classes—she chose languages, Italian, French, Japanese—and they traveled together. His wife understood the arrangement, vaguely, but didn't seem to care. And when Deirdre met Alex, Arthur was all for the wedding, because Alex understood. Alex would need his own amendments to the normal wedding vows. Arthur had paid for their honeymoon. Now Arthur was aging. He'd had bypass surgeries. His heart was weak. "One day, I'll be waiting for him and he won't show up. And I'll find out that he's dead."

"Or he'll live for ten more years," Alex said, weary. "I have a feeling that Arthur may just outlive us all." He punched his pillow and rolled over. "It's the middle of the night. We should get some sleep."

"It's late," Deirdre said, ignoring the huff in Alex's tone. "It's late."

When I thought they'd both fallen asleep, I snuck out of bed, got dressed in the half-light from the hall. I crept down the stairs and left through the heavy wooden front door.

I thought it would be difficult to explain to you my Asbury Park days, crazy Elton, that punching Pascal in the mouth, but this is the hardest thing to explain. Why I loved the Paglias. Why I listened to the messages left on the machine again and again, "Deirdre is making something with glazed ham and shiitake mushrooms. Come over. It's all these foods that taste good just to say." And why I called back and came over. And what did it all mean: the dead hunted animals, the well-tended glass greenhouse teeming with fecund potting soil, swollen tubers, tongue-wagging orchids. Something, I guess about holding onto what's handed down, something about the abundance of love, the delicacy of it, too. We're hunters. We nurture.

We ate salty ham, shiitake, and drank sweet, limey g and t's. Deirdre and I clapped while Alex juggled the giant eggs. It was like that. He entertained us. We were delighted. The eggs had been blown out by natives—natives of I-don't-know-where—and the shells were tough as hell, unbreakable. Alex dropped one. Deirdre squealed, but the egg bounced. He caught it and we clapped again.

Deirdre wanted to sit in the sun before it dipped behind the house, but it was dark by the time we made it outside. We laid down in the small grassy strip between the rock garden and the greenhouse. We looked up at the stars. Alex knew the constellations, and we let him rattle on. At first, it was boyish and maternal. We said, "Oh, you're so smart." "Isn't he a smart boy!" And, "Look at you! Knowing all of those stars!" It was like tussling, like chucking him on the chin, and ruffling his hair and calling him a good boy, a good smart boy. It was that stirring feeling of being with your sister's friends, I imagine. What did you call it? Vicious and sweet? And then we were lavishing him and then the excessive doting slipped over into something else, not maternal at all. It was dark. Skin and skin and skin. There was the lost feeling—drunken, hazy—of not being one person with two other people, but of being one larger animal, ample and sprawling, an animal that pours over itself and back again, that stretches and claws, that tightens into itself, then loosens, then spills open, a fat naked bloom in the yard.

I don't have to tell you what it's like to have sex with a woman. But I can say that, for me, everything came as a surprise. Like that first time with Michael Hanrahan, I hadn't thought of how warm his body would feel. That alone, the warmth, was something to love. And why should Deirdre's smooth skin come as a surprise? Or the sweet smell that collected at her neck? Or her soft lips, her gentle moans, the dip of her stomach? I have all of these things, an anatomy complete with nipples and clitoris. But it was so different in those moments when the two of us pressed against each other, pelvis to pelvis, breasts to breasts. Sometimes Alex seemed unnecessary. He seemed like some other breed, like a muscled ox trying to barge in. (*Go away, ox.*) Alex was wonderful, don't get me wrong. I loved Alex, and he was gentle and good, but there were moments, that's all I can say, when we didn't need him, when, maybe, we didn't even want him.

One time when Alex wasn't around, I asked Deirdre if she ever thought of herself as a lesbian.

"I tried to be a lesbian when I was younger, but I lacked the necessary discipline. I longed for dick."

So, don't worry about Alex, just in case you were about to. We both longed and he was well attended to. In fact, he was spoiled, very spoiled. Sometimes it was too much—like feeding brownies to a fat boy wearing an I-love-bon-bons T-shirt.

They would have seemed like the kind of couple to have a lot of sex toys. They joked about toys, but there weren't any. "Toys are for the bored," Alex said.

"And the bored are just the boring in disguise," Deirdre added.

I knew not to come up for air. I made excuses to Festoova. I'd been a good employee and so she believed a flu, a summer flu, the worst kind, I told her. And the three of us lived on this way. There were more ordinary moments that I still loved them. Coffee. Books. Alex spouting politics. Deirdre, who'd been raised without any money to speak of, combining soap slivers. I padded around the house, swayed in front of the rotating fan. We ate cereal. Once I saw Deirdre pet the bear like it was a golden retriever. She rubbed its ears and whispered some kind of endearment, patting its head. She could be very girlish. And I loved that about her. I wanted to take care of her.

And sometimes I felt like an orphan who'd been taken in and loved, given hand-squeezed grapefruit juice with a dollop of honey. I felt lucky. I felt at home. Alex and Deirdre never fought. They touched each other when they passed. They patted me too. They loved me. They eyed me with sweet sugary love. They eyed each other with the same thing. We were happy.

But I knew this wouldn't last. My answering machine, sometimes I thought of it. Friends calling to go out, a date or two that I'd left hanging, and my mother, of course, filling up the tape with her muffled sobs. "Did you get my last message? Does this machine work? We should get together . . ." I could hear her, "us, the two single girls, we should really get together." I would have to re-attack my research. I would have to go back to work at some point. I would have to pay rent.

And soon there was a new air of restlessness. Deirdre wondered why Arthur hadn't called—had he had another heart attack? She became anxious. She threatened to call his friends. Alex spent time plugging along in the greenhouse, pruning, snipping, tying tomatoes to thin stakes. Little silences pooled and then dissipated. The phone would ring and he'd jump to answer it. It was usually one of his women. "Alex has a girlfriend!" Deirdre once sang out. I thought I was his girlfriend, but I wasn't. I was above girlfriend. I was something more than that. Isn't that what she was saying? I didn't ask for clarification. I was a grad student in feminist studies. I didn't need to ask for clarification.

The boundaries manifested themselves in the sex too. Instead of each of us bending and following, there was more leading, more nudging, more directives and barriers. I don't really want to go on here. I think that any girl-on-girl action gets caught up in this eroticism that men seem to think they deserve. I realize I could be riveting here, if I wanted to be. I could go off in gorgeous detail, but I'm not going to play that card. I want it to be clear that Deirdre and I weren't using each other to make Alex a happy man. We were happy that he was happy, yes. But Deirdre and I loved each other too.

That being said, the sex got harder to orchestrate, or, more plainly, it started to seem like something orchestrated instead of something natural. We all knew that things weren't going well.

I can think of one conversation that pointed to a fundamental difference between Alex and Deirdre. They were talking about the older woman who came to clean their house. Alex hated to see her work and would tidy before she arrived. "No one should ever have to clean up after another human being," he said. And although this sounded thoughtful, it was actually just self-reliant. Deirdre said, "No. Everyone should have to clean up after another human being." Deirdre cleaned up after herself and her lover, Arthur, and Alex didn't.

Eventually the phone rang, and it was for Deirdre. Alex handed it to her, walked to the living room and sat down in an overstuffed chair. I took his lead, assuming that Deirdre needed privacy. I walked to the French doors that led to the back yard and looked out through the glass.

There, I saw a woman. It was poor Marsha of the front stoop. She had that stiffened hair and a boxy backside, but this time she was haggard. She was wearing a sun dress more suited to a picnic. She looked like she was a little sunburned as if she'd spent the day at a outdoor family reunion. She was walking around the greenhouse, jaggedly. She had a stone in her hand, a heavy stone from the small rock garden. She pressed herself up to the greenhouse, holding the stone to her chest, and peered inside. Then she shuffled backward.

"There's a woman in the back yard," I said. "She seems imbalanced."

Alex didn't answer. Deirdre was finished talking on the phone. She ran upstairs.

The woman picked up another rock from the garden. Her fists now looked engorged. She turned circles. She was crying, muttering to herself.

"There's a woman in the back yard," I said again. "I think she's gone crazy."

Alex still didn't say anything.

Now Deirdre was downstairs. She must have kept a bag packed and ready to go. Her makeup was freshly polished. She said, "Okay, then. I'm off for a while." She walked over to me and gave me a kiss, a small, soft kiss. She smelled of perfume again, like that first night. I looked at her. How could she go? How could she love Arthur? How could she leave Alex and

me? How could she do it all so breezily? Of course, I knew
that this was practiced. She'd left Alex for Arthur time and
again. And I'd known it was coming. I'd been warned. But still
I wasn't prepared. You know I never really sought out women
as friends. I wasn't good at those ties. And Deirdre's leaving
seemed to hurt more than anything else. It seemed like an
old pain. She was dipping into a deep, unresolved well. My
mother? Was that it? I wasn't sure. I'm still not sure. I looked
back out the glass doors.

"There's a crazy woman in the yard," I said.

Deirdre stared out and saw the woman with her heavy
fists. "Yes," Deirdre said. She called Alex.

He was up, walking slowly. He stood in front of the two of
us, and Deirdre looked at him and back at me.

She said, "It's one of yours, loose in the yard."

Just then the woman let out a cry and she hurled one stone
and then the other at the greenhouse. There was the shatter
of panes. Alex took his place next to us at the glass door. The
woman turned to the house. First her eyes were searching the
upstairs windows, but then they fell and found the three of
us staring out at her. The woman's knees gave. She wilted on
the grass. And it seemed right and sane, the most reasonable,
graceful thing to do.

But I couldn't watch. Alex walked out into the yard. Deirdre stayed at the window. I walked deeper into the house. My
eyes ran over the walls—the gazelle hooves, the bear's gaping
mouth, the monkey heads screaming from the walls. The
house was full of death. How couldn't I have seen it before. I'm
fairly good with metaphors. Death, but not just any death . . .
death suspended, frozen, unchanging. The Paglias were dead.
The sex was just an ongoing argument in which they tried to
convince themselves otherwise. I was dead, too.

After Deirdre left, after the incident with the crazy woman, I saw Alex now and then, but it was never the same. I slowly lost track. Arthur died. Last I heard, Alex was going to take a job. He and Deirdre were set to move. I decide to try to be more alive again. I started simply. I talked to my mother on the phone. We had occasional lunches together. We ate salads and iced teas. Sometimes my mother teared up. She said, "Well, I'm just unsuited to this kind of life, but I'm out there, making a go of it! I'm committed." More than once she said, "Your father isn't taking this well."

But I didn't believe her. I was pretty sure that this was something she'd made up to make herself feel better.

My father, my father . . . I finally visited. I went to his house one evening, unannounced. I wanted to see him for myself. I found him in his favorite chair. He was fishing artichoke hearts out of a small jar with his fingers. He'd dropped a water glass in the kitchen and cut his foot. He pointed to the trail across the rug from the kitchen to his spot. "I hadn't realized," he said. "I didn't know I'd done it. It didn't hurt at first."

His foot was still bleeding. There was no glass in it. I pressed the wound with a towel. He fished for more artichoke hearts, rubbing his oily fingers together. He started to cry. "She's gone, you know. She's gone."

I was wrong to date the Paglias. It was a bad decision. I'd like to say that the Paglias had it all wrong. That their marriage was a sham. That they were lust-driven swingers without regard for others, wrecking balls gliding and colliding through life. Arthur, I never knew him, but I could say he was a bastard to cheat on his wife. And while I'm at it, Alex's women should have known better. I should have known better, and my mother should have gone home.

As it turns out, the Paglias reveal my greatest act of faith-lessness. It was a time in my life when I couldn't rely on myself as a source of love. I was only willing to give myself over to a relationship that had abundant proof, the way an unbeliever who wants to believe is drawn to the church with the most obvious altar healings *(Get up and walk!)* and the loudest choir, but doesn't comprehend that the real work of faith—or love—has to start inside of the dimly lit soul without any discernible proof or general sensibility to go on.

Oh, but there was so much proof, so much love and sex. Deirdre loved Alex and Arthur. And I loved Alex and Deir-dre. And Alex loved Deirdre and me and Marsha, too, and all of the other women. My father loved my mother and my mother loved my father, though neither could express it. And I couldn't understand how so much love could come to so much ruin. Marsha. In the end, she was the only one who made sense. Her staggering grief was so blessedly simple. Now I'm convinced more than ever that Marsha was the lucky one, actually, because she knew how she felt and why, which is more than I could say for myself.

And, having said all of this, I'd like to say that I know, I know; it was more complicated with Zoe and Sunny. I know that you were reopening old wounds there. I understand. I get it. Everything is more complicated the more love infused into it. Sure, you loved Sunny, Zoe, your sister, your mother. You don't have to explain yourself. I've reread the confession, looked at it again and again. It's all there. We're weak, all of us. We can only withstand so much. We can't know what we'll come to rely on or how we'll give out or how we will, miraculously, forge on.

My confession is that I wanted to see my father like this. Broken. I wanted to believe that he'd lost something, because I wanted to believe there was something to lose. I told him my mother was sure to come back to him, even though I knew it wasn't true. And we sat in the blue haze of the television; we soaked in that gracious light; and we enjoyed the lie.

I never did find the right house filled with foreign students and bicycles or my pocketbook. A month later, my driver's license arrived in the mail in a plain white envelope with this note: *Is this you, yourself? Did you lose? I think you need it. Congratulations!*

And congratulations to you!

Sincerely,

The Crazy hunter in a pith helmet

MAGGIE LESKY

February 12

Dear Benign Home Wrecker,

I'm sorry this is arriving so late. I could tender a bunch of excuses, all more or less reasonable, but the truth is I've been stalling. Based on your last letter, it sounds like you're coming into the homestretch, in terms of major romantic disasters, and the truth is—actually, I'm a little embarrassed to admit this, but—I'm not even a third of the way through my catalog. Having come this far it seems wrong, really, for me to ignore the freckled lesbians I bedded in Glasgow, the former soft-core starlet who pulled a gun on me, the Fulbright scholar with penetration issues. This is not to mention the Hankey triplets, the Indonesian dominatrix, or the park ranger with sexy callouses.

Am I just supposed to pretend these women don't exist?

Or, okay, I guess maybe they don't.

The point is we need to be fair about this, and if you're only writing one more, than this letter is my last and after I'm done . . . yikes, what? What next? I get your last. And then . . . You see what I mean?

And another thing. A pre-confession confession (I'll offer a post-confession confession as well): I've been marking up your letters. I know this isn't a very romantic thing to do, but I can't help myself. I'm an active reader, a marginalia junkie, a restless heart, a Bryan Adams song.

So, for instance, last time around, when you wrote, *He had practiced skills, but those don't impress me,* I scribbled in the margins: *Oh, thank God!* And when you wrote about your deep nagging suspicion that love was a fake Santa, I wrote back, *Now hold just a goddamn Kwanzaa-loving minute . . .* And when you asked whether we were actually sharing some kind of epistolary confessional booth, I slipped into a pair of lacey black underthings and—wait a second, scratch that. What I did was jot down a joke my dad once told me, which goes like this:

Old Jewish man slips into a confessional booth and says to the young priest "Father! Father! I'm ninety-six years old and I just made love to a woman who's only twenty-two!"

"But sir," the priest says, "this is a Catholic church. Why are you telling me this?"

"What do you mean?" the old Jew says. "I'm telling everyone!"

I could go on. But counter-punching only gets you so far. I've got business to take care of, more splendid ruin to unspool.

Let me say, though, before we duck back into the confessional—say, what are you wearing over there? Am I the only one in this booth wearing sexy underwear?—that I don't blame you for getting into it with the Paglias. Not one little dirty-girl bit. If I put myself in your shoes (what size are you again?) it feels like a no-brainer. Those Paglias, they were full of love, sexy and sure of themselves, destructive, sure, but in a way that offered an expansion of your world. That's what you seem to be after.

Nor do I take any umbrage (whatever umbrage might be) for your questions about Sunny. On the contrary, I'm honored to have you call me out and somewhat less honored to plead guilty of Vagary in the Second Degree. I can see now that I ducked too quickly away from those last months with Sunny, and not just because the sad and peculiar facts of my upbringing made them painful to relive, but because I did love her, might even have made a life with her and Zoe, and because my decision not to fight for that possibility still shames me. I don't want to be thought of—by you especially—as someone not willing to fight for love. I'm going to try to deal with all of this down below. And if I fail, I trust you'll hold me accountable.

Lastly but not leastly, I should mention my childhood attitude toward small, furry animals, which was one of fetishistic benevolence. Meaning *not* that I entertained prurient thoughts about the squirrels that leaped precariously from limb to limb in the willow trees behind our house, but that I worried about them, their mortality, incessantly. This had to do with a widely-trafficked rumor concerning the detonation of a squirrel by one Eric Pankey, a cruelty memorialized by Pankey's myriad human victims as "the old M-80 suppository." I had no idea what a suppository was. My sister had to explain. Nightmares ensued. So yes, in the rodent category, I was a stanch pacifist, though I did develop an unfortunate pre-adolescent tendency to drown the small, reddish spiders that presented themselves in abundant numbers in and around the tub in the downstairs bathroom. I do not recall mounting any of their heads, or legs.

Let me now move on to the confession, which, I'm happy to report, includes a brief cameo by you. That's only toward the end. The beginning runs like so:

I left Miami for the wilds of New York City. I did this because I'd been offered a hideously lucrative job (this was the heyday of dot.com idiocy) and because I suffered the belief that my art would flourish in a place where consciousness ran so thick, and because I couldn't quite imagine returning to my own homeland, the loveable west, just yet.

It wasn't a great decision. New York, once you get there, proves to be a lot more letdown than billed. Everyone arriving all starry-eyed, their hearts murmuring: *I'm here, I'm here*, staring down Madison at dusk, picnicking in Central Park, and then, after that wears off, they find themselves living in some sooty box with brown water, getting dumped on by some lousy boss, paying too much for drinks, complaining on the phone, under-appreciated and taking it out on the rest of the nation. It's the immigrants who make New York bearable, the ones who drive cabs and sell kabobs and clean toilets. They, at least, wear the mantle of the city with some dignity, unconflicted about the crud and the freedom, out for wealth, pure and simple, rather than notions of sophistication.

That's enough about New York. The whole place is such a cliché, at this point, so full of its own glamorous bloated misery.

I will say this: the women of New York. Good Christ, there are so many of them, out on the streets, lured out of the great yawning mouth of the Midwest, the dead cities of the Rust Belt, the tank towns that become amateur comedy routines in the bars late at night. And the ones raised right here, life-time members of the Avenues, their hearts tucked away like concealed weapons, always a little bored, a little polished, all dressed up but sick of the available options. (I dated a few of them, mostly to see if they could be roused from their stupor.)

These were my own Sexscapades, the early thirties, having learned to fuck more or less, earning good money for very little actual labor, and, on the weekends, stuffing my head with modern art and ice cream. I managed to undo fifteen years of relatively good male behavior in, oh, seven months. I wasn't as bad as I'd like to believe. I couldn't stand the guilt. But I did go a little wild there. It was like being a teenager again, having Lisa's friends pawing me, but this time, remarkably, they were willing to go down on me.

My living arrangement didn't help matters. I kept a loft in the East Village, with a cubby-hole studio up a small set of stairs, where most of the sex took place. I took portraits of most of these women, at their behest. They wanted to be shot. (New York is the kind of place where everyone gets to be a narcissist.) The smell of peanut oil wafted in from the Wok N Roll four stories down and made their mouths water, their teeth shiny.

I was gradually learning the lesson of art, which is sustained attention. I spent a long time looking at these women, waiting for them to reveal themselves. They could dress however they liked. Or not at all. It was up to them, in the end, how much they revealed. The precise mix of desire and fear, weakness and strength. This was them, along with the angles of their body, the particular bumps and hollows, the smooth patches and secret outcroppings of hair.

What people want, in the end, is to be perceived. That's what Eve had taught me, ten years earlier, and I still thought about her. Sometimes, I would gaze across the river at Hoboken and wonder. Once, in a bit of a mood, I drunk dialed her old number, and later, a friend of hers told me she'd met a carpenter and moved upstate. I took these yearnings as a good sign. I didn't want to become one of those artist/cad types, rehashing my adolescence, gorging on the low-hanging fruits of urban loneliness.

Which brings us to Maggie. Not that she was lonely or low-hanging. She worked in a small gallery in Chelsea, the Delano, named after the owner's Chow, fearsome, purple-tongued, a prolific crapper on the nearby sidewalks. The Delano was the first gallery to show my work, a series of nude studies I'd diced up and placed in porcelain bowls, Chop Suey-style. (My aesthetic was half shenanigans, half bogus gravitas, unduly influenced by Braque, but I was learning.) A few days after the opening, my phone rang.

This soft voice said, "It's Maggie."

"Hey," I said.

"Maggie Lesky."

"Sure," I said. "Right."

"I hope you don't mind that I'm calling."

"Not at all," I said.

She asked how I was doing. I said fine. We chatted a little. There was a pause.

"You don't have any idea who this is, do you?" Maggie said finally.

"Not really," I said. "But you sound nice."

"We met at the Delano," Maggie said.

"Right," I said.

"I must not make much of an initial impression," she said.

In fact, she'd made no initial impression. This wasn't her fault entirely. It was an opening for several young artists and one of them had mentioned that his friend, little Ms. Such-and-Such from Art Forum, had talked about dropping by, so all of us were in a state of abject, unspoken panic. Maggie had been pouring the wine. She was one of those art history grads who dreams of curating a small wing of the MOMA, but must begin that long and hopeless mission as well-spoken window dressing. Gallery Assistant was the preferred term though I and my pathetic posse of fellow aspiring artist called them Gallery Girls, GGs for short, with their discreet lipstick and baby-sized purses, their dingy Brooklyn flats and drag queen roommates.

"I shouldn't have called," Maggie murmured. "I knew this was a dumb idea. Stupid Maggie."

"Don't say that," I said. "I'm glad you called. I'm just lousy with names."

Maggie took a deep breath. "I'd like to sit for you," she said.

"Sit for me?"

"For a portrait. I think your work is astonishing."

Astonishing?

I found the idea that anyone would find my work astonishing *astonishing*.

"One other thing," Maggie said.

"Yeah?"

She took another breath. "I'd like to be naked."

"Sure," I said. "Absolutely up to you. How ever you feel most comfortable."

"I want to be naked," she said. "Nude."

Well.

A couple of nights later, Maggie turned up at my apartment. She was wearing red jeans, a black silk top that showed a tiny triangle of belly, chunky shoes. She'd brought a bottle of wine and as she handed it to me her hands were trembling. I gave her some wine. We talked some more. Maggie was from Portsmouth, New Hampshire. Her brothers still lived there. Her parents were divorced. She'd left home at sixteen, gone to live with a friend, dropped out of high school, gotten a GED, enrolled in a community college, earned a scholarship to a small liberal arts college. None of her family understood what she was up to. When she told her father about the scholarship, he urged her to study computers.

But Maggie was hooked on art. When I told her about the class I'd taken back in high school, how Mr. Park had darkened the room and shown us painting after painting, she sighed. "That sounds like heaven," she said.

Her interests were scattered and obsessive. She read Clement Greenberg religiously (I had not heard of him). She felt it was the role of art to rescue people from the spiritual indolence of the era. She praised the stark beauty of Walker Evans, the juicy red hearts of Jim Dine, the languid sensualism of Modigliani. She told me, that first night, the entire life story of Modigliani, how he had come to Paris, beguiled Picasso, shifted from painting to stone carving, how he had dumped almost every sculpture he ever made into the Seine during a fit of depression—she fantasized about some day leading an expedition to retrieve these pieces—how he had been cut down by tuberculosis at thirty-five, how his mistress, the long-suffering redhead Jean Hebuterne, had flung herself off a balcony upon hearing of his death. The account brought a high color to her cheeks.

Then we were done with the bottle of wine. It had stained her teeth a pleasing violet. She asked to see my work and we tottered upstairs to the studio. She examined the pieces while I stood by, embarrassed at the quiet intensity of her attention.

It was pretty late by then. I asked if she still wanted to pose for some photos. She smiled and nodded. She disappeared behind my changing scrim and I could see her silhouette frozen for quite some time. I worried that she might have overplayed her hand. I wanted to say something, to tell her she could head home, no harm done. But then she appeared with her hair pinned up, and her neck was blazing. "Here I am."

Her body was a solid piece of human sculpture, narrow through the torso, pleasantly bottom-weighted, plump at the hips, with shapely, muscular legs. I set up the lights and she sat under them, pale, glowing a bit, with her small breasts trembling as her hands had earlier. She was a pretty woman composed of not especially pretty parts, a bumpy nose, small brown eyes, a thin jaw. Her most notable feature was the scar on her upper lip—her older brother had struck her there on the back swing with a baseball bat which shaped her mouth into a sweet, embarrassed sneer. The effect was that of an extraordinarily sexy hockey player.

I watched through the viewfinder as she twitched.

"What should I do?" she said, softly. "Do you want me to do anything?"

"Just what you're doing."

The struggle between her excitement and her shame was irresistible. I thought of the figure I'd seen on one of the Greek vases Patros showed me, a mortal woman gazed upon by Apollo while bathing, her eyes cast down, the corners of her mouth hitched in secret pleasure, one shoulder bared, the other demurely tucked.

"Do you have anything else to drink?" Maggie said.

I fetched her some vodka and began to take photos.

Maggie began to shift from one position to another. I watched her muscles flex and loosen. The sudden poise of her movements was startling. Later, I would realize that she was—consciously or not—imitating the postures struck by the women who posed for Modigliani. There was one in particular, a full frontal shot in which she tilted her head and stared directly at the camera, her chest pushed forward. I'd been playing some music, Mingus probably (the onset of spring had me on a Mingus jag) but the music stopped and then it was just us and the city, a stray siren, someone screaming for someone named Mickey, the click of the shutter. Maggie stared at me. Her mascara was crumbling a little. Small tears began rolling down her cheeks.

I asked her what was wrong.

"Keep shooting," she whispered.

I realize that this whole scenario, in the retelling, suggests a certain dismal Slick-Rickitude. The details—the wine, the studio, the nude sitting—are one errant sketch from collapsing into cliché. It might help to remind you that I wasn't much of artist and that she wasn't much of an art historian. (Or maybe that just makes it worse.) But I want to convey how brave and lovely she was to watch, all that vulnerability rising from her skin, shimmering between us. What was she saying to me? What are any of us saying in such moments? Here I am. Rescue me. Please.

There was plenty of sex after that, but I've blabbed enough about sex. What's important is how I treated Maggie.

I did not treat her well.

It was nothing close to despicable, given what men often do to women. (How's that for the bigotry of low expectations?) I never fooled around on her. I took a genuine interest in her life and fed her many fine meals. But I never made her feel entirely safe within our love. I took advantage of her adoration. I treated her, to a greater extent than I liked to admit, like something on the side. My favorite trick was to break up with her—to spare her a greater hurt down the line—but in such a way that we remained friends who could still sleep together. Every few months she would wise up and declare herself done with me, though never in a cruel or angry way (she was cruel and angry mostly toward herself) and I would praise her good judgment and we would speak winsomely and hug somewhere semi-public: a fire escape, an alley doorway. Then a few weeks would drift by and one of us would call to check in on the other and jump-start the disaster.

I thought I'd gotten rid of all my bullshit in Miami, in the Good Doctor's office. But it turns out I still had plenty of bullshit to inflict.

Lisa had told me once, after my freshman year of college, right before she flew off to Nicaragua, "Don't be one of those men."

"What men?" I said.

We were in the backyard, letting the sun wash down on us. Lisa was wearing a peasant blouse and Vaurnets. She was so beautiful it hurt me to look at her. And I must have looked good, too, more like a young man than the boy she had left behind. I'd caught her gazing at me earlier, when I'd taken off my shirt.

"You'll know what I mean," Lisa said.

And I did.

But there were things I needed from Maggie. Belief was the main thing. She believed in me. She thought my work was important. She had a whole theory about it, my need to simultaneously save and destroy women. She talked me up to the few people she knew in the gallery world. She gave me space to do my work and encouraged me to get back into pottery. I had an aptitude, she said. After a while, I realized that I was making my work, in large part, because she expected me to. (This provoked, if memory serves, break-up number seven.)

Maggie also allowed me to play the role of the kindly big brother, which, as an aggrieved little brother, I liked a lot. I gave her advice and encouragement and bought her books and vanilla candles and I came to her aid when her family did a number on her. I let her stay in my apartment while she was looking for a new place, because her roommate had moved to Queens. I was kind to her, in small, day-to-day ways, and spent many happy hours exploring the ecstasies of her body.

Maggie did manage to get a few of my pieces into a private gallery in Soho, one of those places on the tenth floor of a business building, a couple of rooms subsidized by a stock portfolio. It was a group show featuring several more established artists of the conceptual bent. One older lady talked about buying one of my pieces, but mostly she wanted to touch my shoulders and breathe Roquefort on me.

I don't need to deliver my bitter little sermon on the sadistic insecurity of the New York art scene. It will be enough to note that I didn't belong in such company. My work was representational to begin with (how dull) and the media I worked in (photography and pottery) were considered prosaic and minor. Couldn't I do something with feces? Or internal organs and Vaseline?

Afterward, I trudged down Prince through a sharp wind, tawdry and humiliated in my mock turtleneck. Maggie clutched my arm. I could tell she wanted to say something—to tell me, perhaps, about Modigliani's first show, which had been shut down for indecency (she loved this story). But she knew not to try anything sweet, that I would only punish her later.

There was another show, a few months later, at a bar called the No One. I'd managed to funnel some of my rage into a new series called Love at What Cone? Photographic studies, raw clay figures, and, after the intervention of a small kiln, the fired skin of each woman. Depending on the heat of the kiln, the glazes turned them different colors: kiwi green, beige, a bloody scarlet. The women reclined on a bed of melted cones. It was gimmicky as hell, but people loved it. There were a few write-ups in the free rags.

And the crowd! Swarms of ebullient GGs, testing the seams of their thrift store dresses, weaving through clouds of smoke and vodka. Maggie had broken up with me a week earlier, but she couldn't resist coming out and she circled the whole night, watching me flirt and swill free drinks. She was the one who got me at the end of the night and I let Evil Maggie, her sexual alter-ego, wring all the baby juice right out of me. Later, I listened through the bathroom door as she wept. She thought I was sleeping.

The next day, I called the Good Doctor down in Miami.

He listened to me deliver all the wonderful news about my job and my art career and my not cheating on my not-girlfriend. He knew about my mother and my dead sister and all the other bodies. So he just listened and listened.

"It must be nice to have so much control," he said finally.

"What's that supposed to mean?"

"You know exactly what it means."

It wasn't an official session, so he couldn't ask me what I was thinking about, and I wouldn't have told him anyway.

But I was thinking about Maggie, of course, slipping out of my apartment at dawn, hitting the corner market for a bagel, writing me a cheerful email an hour later (multiple smiley faces), trooping off to work, withstanding the bad parents of New York for another day, confessing the whole mess to her hairdresser while he burned red highlights into her hair. I saw her returning home to her apartment and gently touching the spines of her art books. I saw her at seventeen, chubby, her hair hot-kinked and puffed like Cyndi Lauper, driving her Chevy Cavalier through the dodgy neighborhoods of Portsmouth, delivering pizzas to damp men in bathrobes. I saw her taking a bus into the city and floating through the bright exhibition halls of the MOMA, dreaming of a way out. I saw her buying me gifts she couldn't quite afford and wrapping them in paper she had stenciled with elongated nudes.

The Good Doctor cleared his throat. "Have I upset you, John?"

But there was no way I was going to give him the pleasure of my anguish. So I told him I had to go, and we tidied up the conversation, said our polite goodbyes.

And still, I spent the rest of the day fuming. What was I supposed to do: marry the girl? I should just settle? Was that his point? But she didn't make my heart zing and thump. (Didn't

I deserve zing? Didn't I deserve thump?) On the other hand, Maggie made me feel calm and loved. That was true. I had no real desire to bed other women. This must have been a sign of something. I knew she was a strong woman, that she'd fought her way out of a terrible hole. She was only twenty-seven. Who knew what poise she might acquire, what she might become, if I stopped treating her like a lease model.

And sometimes, as I stumbled around the city, I imagined what it would be like. It felt like a surrender. Was that a good thing, or a bad thing? I was tired of being a dumb, lonely predator, tired of crashing into women's lives and leaving a mess behind. But then I would think of Sunny, whom I had loved without restraint, a little stupidly, even. We drifted on for six more months. And then, just a few days after my thirty-third birthday, my old friend Curt from Santa Barbara called to tell me he was getting married. (This was happening more and more.) He asked if I might want to swing down to Philly for the ceremony. There was a pleading undertone to this request.

"How bad is it?" I asked him.

"Pretty bad," he said quietly. "We're pricing tents tomorrow."

I didn't want to go, but I felt a special loyalty to Curt, because he'd allowed me to stay on his couch for a couple of months, during the lean years, and another time he'd almost gone to jail on my behalf, after the cops pulled him over in my car, which was uninsured, unregistered, and in violation of twenty or so equipment/emission laws. He'd never gotten mad at me because I was a rock star (of sorts) and therefore entitled to self-destructive extravagances.

I tortured myself a little over whether I should bring Maggie along. She'd been waiting for just such a gesture, patiently, waiting for me to relent. "I don't get it," she told me. "We could be so great if you'd just let me in."

So the truth is I wasn't in the best of shape at that wedding. The whole thing left me a little unbalanced. There was Curt in his tuxedo, shaking hands with the desperation of a losing candidate, and his chubby honeypot cinched into that awful gown and all the mothers (there were four, remember?) gushing sweat. I started thinking about Maggie, where she might be, what I was doing to her. I'd told her I had a conference for work, in Pittsburgh.

You'll recall I was wearing that absurd boutonniere. The bride had asked all the men to wear one. But I had no idea how to affix the thing to my jacket, so her stepmother helped. She'd been drinking already; I could smell the vermouth. "It'll be you walking down that aisle soon enough," she said, letting her hand rest on my lapel. "A handsome fellow like you."

I stood there watching the festivities and my breathing wasn't really so good. I imagined that I'd contracted TB and would soon die and that Maggie would be afforded the chance to fling herself off a balcony, though she lived on the first floor of a low-income residence for women. My hand had drifted to my lapel; I was crushing that cheery boutonniere in my fist.

A couple of drinks, I assumed, would help, but the tent was too much, so I wandered out onto the golf course and found that dead cat. Perfect.

And then you showed up and we did our little tap dance—clickety tap, clickity tap—and I felt that jolt I'd been waiting for. When you reach a certain age, you know what you're seeking. It doesn't take long to figure out if someone has the juice. The rest of it, whether you can hammer out terms, that might take months or years. But the basic wiring of the thing, the heat of it, is pretty much instant.

So we were driven into the coat check and happily unwrapped and you bit my shoulder and I thought of Sunny and escaped into your pleasure and then, a bit later, our bodies were ready for love and I wanted you so badly. But all I could think of was Maggie, whom I didn't love as I should, and my promise to Lisa, that I wouldn't be one of those men, and I thought of you, as well, lying beneath me with your mouth slightly open and your red neck, and I needed to know more.

A few more confessions.

This letter wasn't late because I was stalling. That's not the main reason, anyway. I had to fly west to see my mother. She's had some trouble with her health. No need to go into the gory details, but she had to have surgery, not a pleasant surgery, and I couldn't stand the thought that my father would have to bear up alone. As you'll have observed by now, I tend to avoid thinking about my mother. But it's all connected deeper down, the love we sought from our parents, the love we seek from our lovers. We return to those feelings sooner or later, to re-learn who we are.

My father picked me up at the airport. He was in one of his moods of buoyancy. The surgery had gone incredibly well. They'd gotten everything, every last polyp. Mom was doing great. He was doing great. He'd been walking a lot. (His scalp looked freshly pink, tender.) And the doctors. They were just sensational. They deserved the Nobel Prize, several of them. I was not to worry. And how was my life?

Good.

Good.

Good was good.

At home, he showed me the cards he'd received from mom's colleagues. He flung open the refrigerator. There were about twenty banana breads in there, wrapped in Saran. (An email had gone out at school.) There were phone calls, too, every half hour. People kept telling me what a saint my mother was, what an angel. The younger ones, students and protégés, had trouble getting the words out.

"You are her son?" one woman said. She was calling from some place far away; she sounded German.

"Yes."

"That is very luck for you."

"Thank you."

"Yes," she said. "Your mother is, there is a special word, someone touched by a higher good."

So there was this person out there, this giver of tremendous love and attention, whom I'd known as a child, but lost as an adult.

I let my father answer the phone most of the time. He spoke softly, in the reassuring tone I recognized as symptomatic of his fear. Late at night, I could hear him playing Caruso and I knew he was on his marriage bed, rocking back and forth.

I had assumed my father would want to come to the hospital with me, to run interference, keep the conversation flowing. But he told me he had errands to run, so I went alone. They had her on the third floor, in a room filled with bouquets. She was lying on a thin bed with high rails and her eyes were closed. I couldn't remember ever having seen her asleep. I thought she might be dead. She had a paper on her lap that she'd been marking up, entitled, "Maternal Slavery in the Lesser Antilles, 1880 to 1930."

I reached for the paper, but my mother opened her eyes just then.

"There he is," she said.

"Hey."

My mother has always been thin. But she looked frail now. I could see the outlines of her eye sockets and her breath smelled of carbolized fat. (It was a scent I remembered from Lina.) I kissed her on the cheek and she closed her eyes again, withstanding the gesture.

"You look good," I said.

"Nonsense."

"Considering."

"Please, Jonathon. Leave the snow to your father."

"Alright then," I said. "You look like death warmed over."

She smiled wanly.

"How do you feel?" I said.

"Eviscerated. These places are full of legitimized sadists. They slice you up, then poke drugs into your blood so you can't fight back."

"Would you prefer the alternative?"

"The medication makes me feel addled," she said. "I can't work."

"You're in the hospital, mom. You just had surgery. You're not supposed to work." It was tough between us. The air was full of this nervous vapor. I could see why my dad had ditched; it would have upset him too much to oversee so much tension.

My mother smoothed her gown. "Tell me about New York. Your father says you had a show. Somewhere in Chelsea. Did you sell any pieces?"

So I talked a little about that. But actually, my mind was unraveling a little. I was remembering the last time I'd been in a hospital with my mother. I must have been four or five years old. Lisa had come limping home from the park. Another kid had landed on her while they were playing dog pile. She showed me her ankle, swollen and purple, a horrible fruit. We both knew this was a bad situation, because Lisa was a dancer, a stone-cold natural, and the tryouts for junior ballet were two weeks off. Our mom wasn't some kind of awful stage mother. But she did take pride in Lisa's excellence, her possibilities. There was some love there, is what I mean. (She'd also told Lisa, in no uncertain terms, that she wasn't to play rough games in the park.)

"Are you going to tell her?" I said.

"No way," Lisa said. "And you better not either."

Lisa was probably nine years old. She was a tough kid. But I could see her wince each time she had to put weight on her leg. By dinner time, she could barely walk.

"What in God's name?" my mother said.

"I twisted my ankle," Lisa said softly.

They were standing across from one another, with the cutting board between them and a slab of London broil throwing up steam. A hard look was exchanged (the same look that would pass between Sunny and her daughter all those years later).

"How did this happen?" my mother said.

Lisa shrugged.

"Is that an answer?"

"Playing," Lisa said. "Just playing."

My mother shook her head. "Well, you better make a fast recovery. Take some aspirin, but not until there's something in your stomach."

After dinner, Lisa remained in her seat.

My mother watched her with some annoyance. "You need to walk on it," she said. "It's not going to get better unless you walk on it, honey."

It wasn't until much later that my mother took her to the emergency room. She was in a state of quiet rage by that time. "I hope you're happy," she said. I came too, because our dad was working late and there wasn't time to find a sitter. We had to wait an hour before anyone could see us. The waiting room was filled with people in pain. An older man was bleeding profusely from his nose, his handkerchief blooming red. My mother was visibly shaken. She loathed sickness.

Finally, a young female doctor showed up and asked Lisa to explain what had happened. Lisa tried to obscure the fact that she'd been playing dog pile, so the explanation came out kind of garbled.

"I'm sorry to waste your time," my mother said. "She does this sometimes."

The doctor smiled patiently. She rolled Lisa's sock down and immediately her expression changed. She touched at Lisa's ankle gingerly, as if it had suddenly acquired great value. Then she looked at my mother in a way that made me want to drag all of us away from that place.

"We're going to need to have this x-rayed immediately," she said.

My sister's ankle was broken in two places. The breaks were not severe, but they required that her leg be placed in a cast. I remember this cast, glowing white, almost incandescent. And also, the way my mother clung to Lisa as the doctor set her leg. She was nearly hysterical, whispering, "My baby, oh God, I didn't realize." Lisa was crying. We both were. We'd never seen our mother in such a state.

And now, nearly thirty years later, my mother was laid low in a hospital bed of her own, wrinkled as an old lunch bag, far too pale.

I asked her if she remembered this episode. I couldn't help myself. Something had risen up in me, a sudden need to pierce her defenses.

My mother looked at me blankly.

"You thought she was faking," I said.

"What in the world?"

"Then they put her leg in that big, white cast. You were both crying."

"Is this what you flew out here to do?" my mother said slowly. "Conduct a rehash of my maternal misdeeds?" Her hands were trembling a little.

"I was just remembering," I said.

"Don't play dumb with me, Johnny. It doesn't suit you." She squinted at me and the angles of her face (still lovely) took on a softer aspect. "I wasn't perfect," she said. "Is that what you want to hear?"

"I don't want to hear anything."

"But your sister," my mother said. She was trembling more noticeably now. "She had a knack for spoiling her own chances."

"I know," I said.

"Damn her," she murmured. "Goddamn that girl." My mother closed her eyes. She took a deep breath and slowly exhaled. Then she opened her eyes and stared directly at me and blue of her eyes sent a current of fear through me.

"I won't be treated this way," she said.

"I'm sorry," I said quickly. "I'm not trying to upset you."

"That's precisely what you're trying to do."

My mother let out a long sigh, a sigh of utter fatigue, which seemed to rattle inside her chest. I set my hand on her hand. It felt like a piece of driftwood. I could see what was happening. My mother was floating off toward death, slowly, inexorably. The thought had never occurred to me. I would be free of her someday. Was that what I was up to? Hurrying her along? Or was I trying to reach her, the soft inside, before it was too late. Was it possible I was doing both these things at once?

"Lots of people have been calling," I said. "Your various admirers."

My mother shook her head. She glanced at her nightstand, where she had laid her paper, atop a stack of books.

I didn't know what to say; the silence was crushing us. I couldn't think of a single thing to say. I should have had something at the ready, about Lisa, about the grief we shared, the need for mercy, but misfortune had torn our tongues out.

"I guess I can come back later."

She nodded.

I turned to leave, but she reached out and took hold of one of my fingers (it was all she could manage) and said my name so faintly it was only a disturbance of air.

"Yes mama," I said.

She closed her eyes and squeezed my finger a little. "Your father keeps bringing banana bread. Please tell him to stop."

There were a couple of visits after that. We did what we could to smooth things over. My father was onhand, to fill the gaps.

I suspect this story makes my mother sound monstrous. She was actually terribly frightened. She couldn't stand to see her daughter in pain, so she refused to see the pain. She despised weakness and humiliation because she knew their sting so intimately. It all traces back to her own childhood, the insane hopes her parents loaded onto her, and that she loaded onto Lisa. I expect some of this sounds familiar to you.

Having told you all this, two more confessions.

The first is that I've broken up with Maggie, for good and for always. Actually, I broke up with her about a month ago, on the night I (or actually, my cock) sent that wobbly missive. It was something I'd had in mind since the wedding, because I was tired of betraying her of course, but also because I had a hunch, a gut feeling, a dirty wish, after meeting you. So you should know that.

Which brings me, somewhat reluctantly, to my final confession, which is that I see hints of my mother in you and it scares me.

I realize how ugly and accusatory that sentence sounds,

but I'm going to let it stand, because it's really more a fear than anything else and because it's the rock bottom truth and that's what we've pledged to tell one another. I don't mean that you'll be the sort of wife or mother who allows their loved ones to hobble about on broken ankles. I just mean that I'm worried about that tough front you put on, that brutal insight. It's what drew me in at the wedding. I said to myself: Now here's a vital and dangerous woman, someone who might make me feel challenged as well as safe, who might, in the spirit of love, call me out on my own endless bullshit. And maybe this declaration is simply a part of that endless bullshit, my old friend Judgment rearing up to keep you at bay. I'm certainly aware of how presumptuous all this sounds. It's beyond presumption, into some new category. (Am I ruining things here?)

But you have to admit that there's something fundamentally phony about this arrangement. It plays to our raging egotism, our need to state the case as we like, avoid the tough questions, boss around our own history. The discourse of love, though, doesn't run on parallel tracks. It collides and makes a big mess. And I want that mess.

You asked in your last letter how much struggle I could bear. The answer is: As much as you're willing to provide. But you can't hold anything back, Jane, because I've suffered too many impervious types already, with underbellies I can never quite reach. And they keep dying on me, before I can offer them any comfort.

I've fallen for the woman in your letters not because of how sharp and funny and fast she is, but because of those tender moments when she feels vulnerable. Not Michael Hanrahan, with his black eyes and his mohawk, or Elton with his mushy ice cream, or sad angry Martha, but her, Jane, you.

I'm not sure how much of this will make sense. It's late. I

may be garbling things up, right at the end. (And here I was, hoping to seem so scrutable, so combobulated.) Here's what I keep telling myself: if this letter scares her off, it would have happened sooner or later anyway.

Are you the one? Am I the one?

Tell me the truth,

John

February 27

John,

What in the hell are you doing?
I remind you of your mother? I don't think
I'm anything like your mother. Indulge me in
a quick defense: she has aged well. I most likely will not. She
reads about Antilles slavery while in the hospital recovering
from death. I will only want bonbons and husky male pillow
plumpers. And I seriously doubt that anyone—foreign or
not—will ever accuse me of being touched by a higher good.
Plus, I can't get enough of banana bread. I don't say, Nonsense.
I'm inelegant and a little rude and blunt. For example: you
said about your mother and your sister *There was some love
there*, and, unlike your mother I would be able to admit that
there was more than some. I think your mother was swept up
in a overwhelming, consuming love for your sister, and that
it consumes her now, still and that maybe it wasn't a fear of
weakness that she suffered, but a fear of the giving into love
(which can be seen as a weakness). And If your mother could
admit to a consuming love for your sister, a devastating love,
couldn't she more readily admit that she loves you? Isn't that
what you're after? (Frankly, I'm not worried about reminding
you of your mother. I'm much too busy being terrified of reminding myself of my own mother. One mother at a time,
sweet Jesus.)

But what can I do if you think I've been invulnerable?

What can I do if you're worried about my tough front and
my brutal insights? Turn them off?

Listen, fine. How's this for calling you out on your endless
bullshit: Your Old Friend Judgement hasn't let you down. He's

rushed in and saved the day. Consider me officially kept at bay. That's easier, huh? That must be a relief. I have no idea how you expect me to react.

Jane

PS—Don't you know I've told you things that I've never told anyone, not even myself?

March 1

Jane—

You need to reread the end of my letter, Jane. I never said you remind me of my mother or that you're invulnerable. I was quite careful in how I said what I did, because I realized how loaded the words would sound. Your reaction has been to ignore what I actually wrote and focus, instead, on your own insecurities.

Love doesn't stand a snowflake's chance in hell if it's not cut with honesty. So fine. Take your marbles and go home.

It's what my mother would have done, too.

John

March 10

Jane—

Alright, look, I stepped over a certain line in my last note and I want to apologize. My intent wasn't to hurt your feelings. I said what I said in the interest of full disclosure. That's what I took to be the point of these letters. Not to play nice and flirt. Not to massage one another's egos. And not to go ballistic at the first sign of trouble.

I wasn't trying to attack you by bringing up my mother. I was trying to express my own anxiety. If I did so awkwardly, or hurtfully, I apologize. I don't want to fight with you, or engage in a battle of wills. (At least not yet. Let's wait the standard three months after sleeping together.)

The problem is, I've yet to receive a reply from you. I'm guessing that you popped one in the mail, then thought better of it and tried to retrieve it from your local postal carrier, in which case you are probably in La Tuna Federal Prison for Women right now, where you belong. But in case I'm wrong about this, and you haven't written me back: What the hell? Are you trying to punish me with silence? Is this how you do things, Jane? Really? Because if it is—if I don't hear from you again—I can only say that it would be terribly sad to squander what we might have shared over such benighted vanity. Then again, maybe we've been sharing a lot less than I believed.

John

March 23

Dear John,

Maybe I was punishing you, honestly. But here's my mind's rationalization for the delay. I was hoping that you'd be hanging out with some friends—passable translators of the female psyche—and you'd offhandedly mention the predicament: *Everything was going so well, and then I told her that she reminded me of my mother and she went off and stopped speaking to me.*

And one would friend would say, "You did what?"

And another would say, "You pushed the Mother Alarm?"

And a third would walk up and say, "What's going on?"

And the first two would say, "He pushed the Mother Alarm." And they'd shake their heads sadly in unison, all recalling their past traumas with the Mother Alarm.

And you'd say, "What's the Mother Alarm?" your voice keening with innocence.

And they'd say, "You don't know?" and they'd regard each other with a curious mix of awe and confusion. "He doesn't know? He really doesn't know?"

And they would explain to you that the Mother Alarm exists in every relationship—sometimes it's just a button on a watch, but other times it's a huge, red, wall-mounted bell behind glass, with a little mallet attached to it with a note that says: *Don't touch the fucking alarm.*

One friend would say, "You can polish the glass, you know, a little nervous habit, if she really, really does remind you of your mother, but not when she's around. When she's around, you've got to pretend the alarm doesn't exist."

(I can see now that these imaginings were all very *Seinfeld* diner, very *Friends* coffee shop, very—at the risk of dating my cultural signposts—St. Elmo's Fire—what was their bar called—My Place?)

One friend might go so far as to confess that the Mother Alarm in one old relationship was an air raid siren—it would just go off without warning and he'd run for a bomb shelter, his (now ex-) wife at his heels.

Now enlightened by your friends (played by excellent character actors), I hoped you'd write me a letter that put all of this mother-stuff aside—a way of promising, without saying it, that you'd replace the glass and put the mallet back in its rightful spot next to its *Don't touch the fucking alarm* sign.

But, okay, I get it. That's not what's going on here. That's the opposite of what's going on here. And so I'm saying—good enough. The alarm went off. I was disoriented for a bit. I come from stock that doesn't set off alarms much, and so alarms disorient me. It's genetic. I might be disOriental, in fact. But here I am, prepared to respond.

My previous defense doesn't matter. If you see me as being like your mother then I am—the perception being the reality. I'm willing to play it out. Don't read me wrong; I'm not interested in mothering you and you're not interested in me mothering you. But if, at some point in the distant future we find ourselves still together, I think that it will be, in part, because we each learned to return something to the other, something that's been ours all along—a love that we don't have to strive for, that isn't contingent on a set of rules, that is undeserved. And since I can't turn off the brutal insights, let me be optimistic; if you were drawn to me, in some way, because I made you want love from me because you want love from your mother, that's fine. That may even be good. Who am I to comment on such a thing at this point?

Am I the one for you? Are you the one for me? This is what you're asking. You want me to tell the truth. Here it is: I have been afraid of the endless versions of myself. But I think that when two people are right for each other and when they're really in love, there is the possibility to become a better, truer version of yourself. When I'm with you, will I be closer to the person I want to be? Is there a version of myself that I will love, that you will love, that will make me love you—when we're together?

I haven't been drawn in by your self-realizations or your hypotheses about why you do what you do. These are entertaining. Sure. They are odd looks into your hardworking rationality. Bizarre, sometimes, frankly.

What's drawn me in, you sweet jackass fuck-up, has been the way you see the world, because of what you choose to remember, and because you're willing to reveal it, to me, in this way. (Do I have to tell you that I felt the jolt too? I think I was pretty open about the jolt from the get-go. And I'm glad that you broke up with Maggie for the dirty wish of me—more than glad, more than flattered, more like . . . brimming?) I love the details that your mind has caressed over the years—the elusive quality of Jodi Dunne's orgasms, Billy Dunne, calling his father a fucking sailor out by the pool, and little Nicky Slocum's tubes of Ritalin, your father closing his eyes in the parking lot of an overpriced restaurant, your mother crying while the X-rays reveal two breaks in your sister's delicate ankle thirty years ago. I'm drawn in by your women—ever-loving Jodi, and Eve taking you home with her after the Spanish restaurant, and caramelized Sunny, and Lina calling you Thunder, and Maggie with her scarred lip. And there you are, not only among them, in the thick of it, the good mess, but you are these things you see, and smell—smell maybe most of all: the musty scent of

242   STEVE ALMOND AND JULIANNA BAGGOTT

your sister's sheets on the night of her funeral. You are made up of the details that your mind has chosen to keep.

Damn, see, what I'm saying is that you've explained to me a love life, and what I got isn't the story. I got your way of seeing, your way of remembering, your way of telling. I know more about you from that than anything you tried to put forth, than any possible factuality.

I assumed my tenderness would be apparent. Along with the raging egotism inside this stuffy confessional—I'm wearing lacy black; shoe size six and a half—is the tenderness. We both have an apparent desperation to be understood, by someone who might just understand, tenderly. We've been confessing here, and not to sound too old-fashioned, but I think what we want is reconciliation. Aren't we looking to be relieved of something? Aren't our souls—again, I apologize, but I don't have a better term—listing toward some kind of benediction and what better benediction than love? And not some generic version of love store-bought in cans like those novelty gifts of Florida sunshine, maybe not love at all but this understanding I just mentioned—which the world rations and hordes. You said in your last confession: What people want, in the end, is to be perceived. I hope by perceived you mean understood. I'm not afraid that I can't accept love. I'm not afraid that I can't give love, fully, doors swung wide open. I'm afraid that I will not be really and truly, deeply understood.

And that's as good a spot as any to talk about Mark Foreworth.

I was engaged to Mark Foreworth for fourteen days last spring. This isn't a pretty story.

First and foremost, my father was sick. He's had diabetes, well-managed, for years. But once my mother was gone, he let himself go. There was talk of blindness at one point, of losing a leg, and, beneath all of the doctors' medical terminology, the underlying message that we all die at some point of something, but that my father might die soon of something like this. And so I understand about your mother, about hospitals, that awful architecture of suffering. I spent a lot of time with my father, mostly watching him doze. I came to hate those rows of rooms, white and exact in their spare simplicity. His roommate only talked about killing Japs in World War II and how the blood darkens on wet ground. All of that grieving air! Everywhere someone in the process of dying. Giving life is labor, but death is labor too. And I imagined death being born from my father, this limp and sallow, shrunken version of himself.

It just so happened, however, that my parents needed a near-death experience. My mother moved back into the old house like a force of nature. She showed up and took over, scrubbing the rugs, floors, baseboards. It was clear she'd been poised. All of her energy had been spent trying to hold herself back, and so when she released herself, she sprang back into her old life. She quit Super Jack's Record Shack and sublet her condo—free of it all. She set up a makeshift bedroom in the living room where my father would recuperate, when the time came. Meanwhile, my mother slept beside his hospital bed in a chair.

There was one rule: don't talk about death. But death hung around us. I'd never realized how Death is so adoring, so constantly, unflappably amorous.

I hated all of this business. Most of all, the sudden preciousness of life. Life was precious! It wasn't meant to be wasted! My mother had said to me once in the airport before I left for France, "Don't waste." This time she'd taken it to heart. She started collecting things, adding to my father's overflowing attic and basement. She hunted through Goodwills and

Salvation Armies to find extras—fondue pots, Petula Clark albums, things we once had, but what if she'd thrown them away and now it was gone forever? Well, she would reclaim it. That's what. And so the house—not just my bedroom and the basement and attic, but the living room sofa, the dining room table became storage areas devoted to the past. "Life is precious!" When my mother wasn't singing it, she was embroidering it into little pillows.

Had I inherited the exorbitant pressures of want from my mother's side and sad need from my father's? I'd accumulated a life that wasn't standing up to any of my ideals about love. (I have grand ideals about love, as you might have noted above.) Thus, I decided to abandon my ideals. They were useless. My father was dying. My mother was watching him die. They'd had ideals too, once upon a time.

And why keep trying to unearth some perfect love when other folks, normal folks, were living quite happily without them—Kelly from Perth Amboy, for example, had a husband and a daughter in the Girl Scouts, according to a Christmas card with a picture of this quintessential, generic girl slipped inside of it.

I wanted Normal, and I was willing to accept the bargain that Normal demands. First, you hand over some basics— overwhelming joy, existential angst, a giving-in to desire, etc. And then you promise to withstand talking idly about the weather, to encourage cliché, to uphold the virtues of average. You hand over the need to be understood and are promised, in return, what? Some kind of security blanket? A kind of protection from the wilds? If you ask, Normal will hand you a bar of Normal soap. And you can wash in it and be daily reborn to a safe world of modest, enduring love or, at least, mild, well-mannered bonding.

Mark Foreworth and I met under a tent at some horse race amid lots of tents and boxy-hipped women in hats, their high heels wedging holes into the wet grass, and there were plenty of boxy-hipped men, too, for that matter. I'd gotten tickets from someone in the philosophy department. I'd secured a professorship; I had a clammy office with its office hours posted on the door. I took a girlfriend of mine who actually wanted to see the horse race, of all things. I wandered alone from tent to private tent—the Filipino American Club, The Junior League, Blue Ribbon Dog Showmen. Everyone was much too polite to stop me, the unusual effect of so many fancy hats. I ended up under the tent of a certain bank. I ate shrimp and drank wine, noticed someone was staring at me: Mark, seer-sucker suit, the tent filling up with wind, flapping. We made eyes at each other and then talked about the simplest, most obvious things: sun, tents, horse races, hats.

And what I could tell right off was that Mark belonged to the world of Normal. The beauty of his punctual tidiness, his way of talking with mock carelessness, his soft, scarless hands. Everything he said seemed to uphold the hunch that he'd been bottle-fed, but lovingly.

And all of the people around him liked him. (Mark worked at the bank. They all worked at the same bank. The tent belonged to the bank.) And I'm not really likable. For example: If someone tells me they're a dentist, I might bring up high-suicide rates among dentists. Mark wouldn't. He was smart, well-intentioned, jokey, decisive, only slightly immoral.

Mark wore Normal with such confidence that, without even knowing me, without knowing a thing about me, he seemed to be saying with every word and gesture, *Your father won't die. Nope. Not while I'm around. And, while I'm at it, you won't die alone. It just isn't possible. Everything's going to be okay!*

Look! And then he could provide a view of Normal that was filled with happy (or at least happy-ish) people.

And from the tent, we wandered hand in hand into a Normal relationship, and I was proud of myself for being so Normal. I wore Gap clothes, entire outfits, belts, khakis, button-downs, and wanted more. I said, "I wish the Gap sold winter shoes." And Mark understood.

We lazed around on Saturday mornings in sweats, ate bagels, drank coffee. He had a yellow Labrador retriever named Archie, after Mr. Bunker to whom, he admitted once, he had an unusually strong simpatico with as a kid. We washed our cars. We ate fried food in pubs. We walked around the park arm in arm with Archie straining at the leash and talked to other dog walkers about their dogs. I loved Mark's suit jackets, his glossy ties, his shoes polished publicly by immigrants while he sat in a row of men reading stock indexes. This was that world that my mother had always wanted and here it was sprawled out before me. It isn't hard to figure out why I found it all so appealing.

Once, early on, I told Mark a story—completely unrelated to any topic at hand, a kind of my-head-on-his-chest dreamy thought, spoke aloud—of how my parents took me to play croquet at some camping lodge, and the gnats swarmed and kept diving into my big eyes. My father would spit on a handkerchief, twist it, and dig the gnats out, over and over.

Mark said, "That's a strange story."

"Is it?"

"Why didn't you just leave?"

"I don't know."

"We vacation on a lake. There aren't any gnats there because of the breeze."

Of course there were no gnats for the Foreworths. I decided

then to tell fewer stories. (The gnat story hadn't seemed the least bit weird when lined up against most of my stories.) Mark wouldn't ever know much about my past, I told myself.

Mark took out a photo album from a closet and showed me sunny dock pictures. "You'll like the lake house."

See, Mark always included me in his world. He wanted me with him. He was good to me. When I came home from the visits at the hospital, I always drove back to Mark too slowly, too carefully, checking the seatbelt's click and hold, the rearview mirror's steady backward eye, the radio for its ardent promise of inclement weather. I was often shaken. I sometimes cried during sex and he'd stroke my hair and tell me everything was going to be alright—like that Beach Boys song, or was it Bob Marley? He comforted me, and I needed comforting. Maybe he needed something from me, too. Looking back, I remember he had a habit of sighing. I thought it was contentedness, but maybe it was relief that something had passed, a moment that had gone well, a stretch of time had elapsed without difficulty. And he had the habit of rubbing his hands together, as if saying, *Let's get to work*, or as if he were cold, but he did it even in summer when there was no work to get to, and so maybe it was a gesture of washing something away, some guilt or memory? Maybe he was simply nervous, maybe he was even a little terrified. At the time, this was the furthest notion from my mind.

In any case, I can say this without hesitation: he loved me, almost immediately and steadfastly, and I loved him. There were no dead animals hung on the walls or crazy women staggering around outside throwing rocks. Mark Foreworth wasn't married or insane or even French.

But, of course, Mark wasn't my whole existence. There was the world I'd created over time—this ghost-filled inner life studded, here and there, with the gorgeous, the grotesque. And I was this other woman, beneath all the khaki, who I'd always been, and I existed in this way—unrelenting, driving toward some ruin—in my small office in the Feminist Studies department, lodged like something hard to swallow, something that refuses digestion, in the basement of the college's oldest building. Here I knew that I could acknowledge that I wasn't really Normal, that I'd really only cut a shaky deal with Normal. Here, I thought about a bloody thumbless boy named Michael Hanrahan and a crazy guy named Elton Birch and the busted mouth of Pascal Lemir and the Paglias' greenhouse and my father's death and my mother's precious life. I wandered from my office to the classroom and back again. And, I think, because my past—good and bad—wasn't being released, it was building up, its images flew at me with great speed. How else can I say it? Here, in my basement office, I chewed on my heart.

We did things with his friends, exclusively. This was my choice as much as it was his. My friends were unpleasant to be around, always rolling their eyes. They knew we were doomed. But his coworkers, really, they were so damn convinced of us. They rallied around us like a good charity event—a polar bear dip in the ocean for special children. There was a long stretch there where Mark and I were a good promising stock that might just outperform the market. They had to concede that there was a risk factor: me. I was a little odd, not quite good enough, you know, in a well-rounded way, with a solid helping of extra-curriculars; they seemed to all know intuitively that Miss Flint had tried to talk me into yearbook staff, but I chose flashing on I-95. That notwithstanding, they invested. The market was prime for a rebound. I could smell the Pottery Barn future. Oh, the IKEA of it all! Vive Volvo!

We slept at Mark's place, because it was bigger, a more appropriate stepladder to some future we could have together. Also we could take care of the dog better here. The place was all set up for Archie, Mark told me, and changing houses might confuse him. Like all good couples, we felt sorry for dogs of divorce, and we were trying to enrich Archie's life by giving him the strong sense of a stable family.

One night, Archie sprawled out at the foot of the bed, breathing his big Labrador retriever breaths with his big Labrador retriever tongue hanging out, Mark said, "Why don't you come and work at the bank in PR? Didn't you used to do PR at that bookstore?"

This was true. Before I left Festoova's to take the full-time teaching gig, she had promoted me to community relations director of the bookstore because the authors depressed her. "I'm not sure," I said the Mark. "I mean, I'm a professor. I have a degree. It took a long time. I worked hard."

"I'm just saying," Mark said, "it's air conditioned and it doesn't smell like an ancient gym. You wouldn't have to grade papers and do work that, well, depresses you."

"Do you think it depresses me?"

"You always come back from that office looking gray and washed out. The bank would put pink in your cheeks!"

"It's air conditioned."

"Exactly!"

Mark seemed to know that I was another woman when in my basement office, and he was afraid of her. I was afraid of the chasm, the split inside myself. Maybe if I stopped being a professor, this other woman inside of myself would stop chewing, shrink away, and Normal would take over completely. While sitting in interminable department meetings where my co-workers chanted their mantra *I'm not angry, just disappointed,*

I wanted to be at the swanky bank, cool and odorless as a new fridge's vegetable crisper. The bank's office carpeting was vacuumed into rows of sailboats. This was very appealing. (Some days, still, when I feel too soft to utter statistics like the number one cause of death for pregnant women is murder, I miss the sailboats.)

Let me be clear: I'd gone a little crazy. Sometimes I would hold onto a simple object—a saltshaker, an aspirin bottle— and I'd envy how it knew its place, its role, its function. It's unbearable now looking back to think how impressed I could be by the pleasurable self-knowledge of a light switch.

I brought Mark to meet my parents at the hospital. They gazed at us as if they were peering up from a big hole.

My mother said, "Life is strange. Isn't it? Who would have ever thought . . ."

And my father said, "You can't predict how it's going to turn out."

For the first time, they seemed oddly contented.

Of course they liked him, but I was astonished that he liked them. I was floored. He thought that they had a certain purity. He said, "They're smart, in their own way. They've figured some things out." This made me take him more seriously. I decided maybe he fit into a greater scheme, maybe Mark would teach me to appreciate my parents. He said, "If you could listen, you might learn something from the people you least expect."

It was strange, suspicious one might say, that I hadn't met Mr. and Mrs. Foreworth, Jerome and Kit, earlier. They lived only an hour and a half away. Mark said that they said nice things about wanting to meet me, but it was never arranged. And there was that well worn question of whether he was ashamed of me or ashamed of them. I frittered over this at the time. But now looking back, I think he knew that it was simply a combination that wouldn't work.

They had a circular driveway and columns on either side of the front door. Archie came with us. He was usually a great bounding presence, but at the Foreworth's house, he slinked around and wagged his tail modestly and only when spoken to—I should have followed his lead.

Kit and Jerome met us in the pale foyer. They were a tall, knobby couple, who wore a lot of Irish wool. They spoke in unison, "So nice to meet you." It was accidental, unplanned unison, but disconcerting nonetheless. They were hand shakers, not huggers, but they loved Mark just the same.

They quickly started talking about a new pump they'd put in the basement—an exciting purchase for them. They complained about their mechanic and then the man who'd installed their windows.

Kit called Mark's younger brother, Todd, to join us. He was twenty-four and could never live up. He gave the family a little hope at being more real for me. He was back at home since a late graduation from college. "Just until he gets back on his feet," Mr. Foreworth explained loudly enough for Todd to overhear. Todd skulked the edges of the kitchen, the living room where we had drinks, the dining room. He wrestled Archie a little.

Mark called him Captain Jack, in a whisper. "He sits at home and masturbates like he thinks he found our dad in the swimming pool." And I looked at Mr. Foreworth, sitting absently at the head of the dining room table, picking lint off his navy blue sweater, a kind of bloated face on a thin neck. He looked like a drowned man to me, or at least fermented. This sounds harsh, I know. (Brutal?) But, see, I wasn't able to get at their humanness. They weren't wearing it sincerely or even ornamentally. They kept it hidden. I remember that Mrs.

Foreworth had a jagged cough and each time she coughed, she would look up at the rest of us around the dinner table, her eyes a little swimmy, and she would apologize, as if this were too much humanity to show.

His parents were economists. They understood the world as a giant flow of capital. But during dinner they tried to be intimate. They talked about beach vacations and Mark's old baseball games, but it was clear that they didn't have much aptitude for memory or story. One would say: Remember that old beach house? Yep. Yep. The end.

They did show some interest in me. Mr. Foreworth said, "Mark tells us you teach college."

"Yes, I do."

"What department?

"Feminist studies."

"Oh, you're a feminist!" Mr. Foreworth said, trying to act happily surprised.

"Well," Mrs. Foreworth added with a sweet smile, "you don't look like one, dear."

I said, "Actually, sometimes when I'm home alone, I wear gray cardigans and rubber-soled lace-up shoes." I lowered my voice. "Right now, I'm wearing extremely sensible underwear. I'm kind of a feminist cross-dresser."

Todd laughed hard. Mr. and Mrs. Foreworth smiled and quickly buttered extra rolls, and Mark rubbed his hands together sharply.

The Foreworths scared the hell out of me. They were a future that I didn't want to consider. And yet Mark walked like them; he talked like them. Halfway through dinner, I excused myself to go to the bathroom.

"Down the hall and to the left," Mr. Foreworth said. "You should go with her," he added to his wife. "Show her the way."

Mrs. Foreworth started to get up. This seemed strange, unnecessary.

"I'm fine," I said. "I'll find it." I wondered if they thought I was going to steal something.

"She's a big girl, all growed up," Todd said. "She'll be okay."

And so, with a certain amount of regret, Mrs. Foreworth said, "Yes, oh, right," as if remembering I was a feminist after all and wouldn't put up with any hand holding.

Actually, I have a terrible sense of direction. At the end of the hallway, I turned right not left. I opened a door to a dark windowless room with a twin bed bolted to the padded walls. There was a large, high handicapped toilet with the raised cushioned seat. There was nothing else in the room except for a helmet—again, white and hospital-regulation. The airless room smelled distantly of urine and sweat and cleanser. Mark hadn't ever mentioned any problems in his family. Who belonged in this room? Whose head fit in the helmet?

I closed the door quickly, went to the bathroom which was painted mint green and smelled of green apple soap, but I couldn't stop thinking about the room, and a retarded girl in I knew when I was younger. The girl's hands were curled, her jaw slack, her eyes oversized and heavy-lidded. The girl's mother took her to the swimming pool at the Y, and once we met them there. My mother told me to help out. "Take her for rides." I can remembered her slick weightless legs, the way she held me too tightly around the throat.

When I sat back down at the dining room table, the Foreworths were not the Foreworths. Mark and his mother and father—even Todd, too, a conspirator—were brittle, perched delicately on their chairs. They were so buttery in the chandelier light that they looked like they were melting. They seemed now to stab awkwardly at their food. They looked at each other and smiled. I thought of their abbreviated stories, how everything had to be abbreviated or they would tell more than they were allowed. The padded room belonged to one of theirs, someone who moaned and banged and seized, someone who'd been sent away on my account.

Before Jerome got our coats from the closet, Todd pulled me aside in the kitchen and he said, "Let me know what you need. Okay? Anything you need, you come to me." And I couldn't figure out if he was coming onto me, or if he was a drug dealer, or if he was just trying to be conspiratorial. Was he talking about the room? I'll say this about Todd, though, he seemed to actually like me. He'd laughed at my joke and once stuck his tongue out at me when his father said that Todd was really showing signs of progress. And the rest of the Foreworths—including Mark, from time to time—didn't seem to like me at all. He'd hated the cross-dressing joke. He still seemed a little steamed about it as we said our goodbyes and got in the car.

Driving home, Mark turned the heater on. It had just gotten chilly. Archie was stretched out in the backseat. The car smelled doggy.

"Do you know about my high school ethics teacher?"

"No," Mark said.

"I never told you about Mrs. Glee? You don't know too much about me, really."

"Of course I know things about you. What are you talking about?"

"I saw the room."

He looked at the sides of the dark road, back at Archie in the back seat. He touched the knob of the stick shift and then turned to me. "Why would you do that?"

"Why didn't you tell me? Whose room is it?"

"Why would you look in there? That is just like you."

"Why didn't you tell me?"

"Because it's not something I talk about."

"Why not?"

"There were three of us. But he was born with problems and he died young. My parents couldn't get rid of the room, I guess. They loved him. They weren't embarrassed by him."

Of course I took this unprovoked defense to mean that they were embarrassed by him. We were on back roads. We passed a church with a cemetery with a metal sign nailed to a wooden fence: Pray. God is listening. It was pocked by what looked like bee-bee bullet holes. "I didn't see him in the lake pictures," I said.

"He wasn't with us. He died."

The radio had turned to a raspy DJ with Hollywood updates. I turned it off. "I'm sorry," I said, meaning that his brother was dead, but Mark read me wrong.

"Well, I'm glad you're sorry. You shouldn't have gone in that room."

When we got home, Mark parked the car on the street. We got out. I was holding Archie's leash. He peed on a tree. It was cold and blustery, like it might snow. Mark rubbed his hands together. He sighed. He took my hands. He said, "I wasn't going to say this now, but I wanted you to meet my parents because I wanted them to know the woman I want to marry."

I still think about this moment. The wind that kicked up, the dark sky, the clouds passing in front of the moon, and the idea that Mark had chosen me. He was surrounded day in and out by appropriate women, but there was some longing in him for something else. At the time, I didn't think he longed at all for anything really. But now I see him as longing, quietly, constantly. (It's the kind of thing I'd like to tell him now, if I could, if that kind of thing were possible. I'd like to call him and tell him that I'd read him wrong.) In some ways, we weren't so different.

"Really?" I said. Archie bucked on the leash, off-setting my balance. I tipped to the side then straightened up. "Let me see if I'm reading you right. Are you asking me to marry you?"

"Yes, of course! What do you think I'm doing here?"

"I don't know."

"Well?"

I said, "Do you like me?"

"Like you? Of course I like you! I just asked you to marry me. I love you. What kind of question is that?"

"I don't know." I remembered reading a question out of one of Festoova's books on romance. (Festoova was a romantic. The self-help love section was mythic.) The question went something like: Would you rather be loved, purely loved, but not understood, or understood, but not really loved. At the time, it seemed like a stupid question. I wanted to be understood, because it seemed that being loved without understanding couldn't be true love. I didn't want to be loved falsely or blankly. But the question wasn't as simple as it seemed. Mark had loved me, really loved me, not blankly, not falsely, but not for the most essential reasons, not for the reasons essential to me. I'd specifically shelved my desire for understanding. Where had it gotten me anyway? Disasters. And my father was sick. I'd woken up for the past two years every morning and I'd chosen to be loved. I knew that Mark loved me, but did he understand me enough to like me? And what kind of a person proposes to someone they don't really like? There's the thing that Mark had going against him. In the end, though, it won't be enough. It won't outweigh my actions. But for now, let's cling to it. What kind of a goddamn person . . .

I wrapped my arms around him. I said, "Yes." Honestly, I loved Mark at that moment. I loved him enough to say yes and to mean it. But didn't love him too much. I never loved him too much, and I believe in loving someone too much.

A few days later, Mark called me in my office. I had the ring on by that point. It had gargantuan prongs and a fat diamonds. It caught on my sweaters, in my hair. It rose up and frightened me when I saw it out of the corner of my eye. It especially didn't fit in under the buzzing fluorescence of the department of Feminist Studies. I had my ear to the receiver, but I was staring at the ring.

Mark said, "Do me a favor. Todd wants to sit in on your class."

"Todd?"

"My brother, Todd. He's been thinking about grad school."

"In Feminist Studies?"

"I don't know. My father just called to tell me he's shown an interest in sitting in on your class and he wondered if that would be okay, and I said of course, sure. He doesn't need to get credit or anything. He just wants to observe."

"The semester's already in deep."

"He's shown interest. It's rare."

"Good. Okay then. Have him come."

I gave Mark the information for my afternoon class to pass on, and twenty minutes into my lecture, the back door opened up. Todd Foreworth shuffled into a seat in the back row. The two brothers looked nothing alike. Mark was well-shorn and always smiling, and Todd was rakish and shaggy. He looked beleaguered, but like he was beleaguered by sex. He had this affected just-rolled-off-her look.

In the middle of class, he borrowed a sheet of paper from one of my students and a pen from another, and he started writing. I wondered, Is he taking notes? It didn't seem plausible although he seemed to be listening. In fact, at one point, he asked an intelligent question. I don't remember the lecture, or the question or whether I answered it clearly. He watched me, carefully. He followed my gestures. He wasn't ogling so much as he was studying me.

After class was over and the students shrugged away, he walked up to the front of the room.

"Mr. Foreworth," I said.

"You're very articulate."

"You were late. You missed the best part."

"I'm sorry."

"I was surprised you showed up at all."

"I'm actually thinking of going to grad school, becoming a professor, the whole bit."

"Really."

"Look, I'm not crazy like they make me out to be. I was imported."

"What do you mean, imported?"

"Imported sounds more exotic than adopted. They wanted two children, but their second son isn't exactly what they expected, is he? So they did some recasting. I'm an understudy."

"Their second son *wasn't* what they expected, you mean."

"No, he still isn't what they expected. I don't know why everyone acts like he's dead."

"I thought he was."

"Oh, that old business. Did Mark tell you Jarvis is dead?"

"I don't want to get into it." See, I'd been going over it in my mind. Jarvis—now I knew his name—wasn't in the lake pictures because he'd already died, but the padded room's toilet was adult-sized, the helmet was large, and the room still held the strong undercurrent of sweat and urine.

"I wrote you a note, apologizing for my tardiness." He handed me a piece of paper.

Dear Professor, I'm in love with you. I find it hard to come to class on time because I get nervous and pace and loose track of time. Sincerely, Todd Foreworth.

Loose track of time? "Did you know Mark and I are engaged?"

He stuffed his hands in his pockets, shrugged and rocked on his heels. "It won't last."

"Why would you say something like that?" I shuffled papers in my briefcase.

"He doesn't get you. He doesn't know you're funny, for one. And you're very funny."

"We're in love," I said, glancing up at the clock on the wall.

"You should ask him to tell you the location of any specific freckle, any mole on your body. Ask him if he's got any of them memorized."

"That's a weird thing to say." It was what Mark would have said, an air-tight defense.

"Okay. Okay." Todd turned around to go. He paused, hanging in the doorway. "Aren't you going to correct my spelling?"

"I'm not a spelling teacher."

"Don't you think if time is on a track, it's fairly loose?"

Yes, I said in my head. Yes, of course. How had I been spending my days, but in the whir of memories. Just that moment there was my father, healthy and spry, waking me in the middle of the night. *Fishman's here.*

I said, "I'll mark it in red pen."

On the afternoon of day fourteen of the engagement, my mother called. She said, "Your father's going to pull through." We didn't talk about death, so we never talked about pulling through either because it nodded uncomfortably at an unacceptable alternative. "He isn't going to die." Of course I'd known death was a possibility, but it was at this point that I realized that my father had been truly close to dying. I started to cry. "What's wrong? I said he's going to live!" My mother kept at it. "He's been given a second chance!" But I stopped listening. I was being lifted up. My parents were both healed in some way. And so I had this overwhelming feeling of second chances, of things coming around, full circle, of some commonplace, ordinary grace spoken to me in simple words. This is where I was coming from—it's relevant to what happens next.

Mark and I were to meet at a restaurant that night. I showed up a little late. I told the maître d' that I was there to meet someone. The maître d' was the kind of maître d' who knows everything, who's bored by speaking. He didn't want any further information. "Of course," he said. "Follow me."

It was a large restaurant, a split-level with disorienting mirrors and a lot of private corners. He stopped at a table, pulled out a chair. I sat down and smiled. It wasn't Mark. It was someone else—a young man with nice shoulders, a smart striped tie a little loose at his neck. The maître d' disappeared. We sat there and looked at each other.

"Funny," the young man said. "I thought I ordered the smoked salmon." He looked drunk but also solid, practical—a little like a pilot, off-hours.

"Yeah," I said. "And you got a tart."

I looked up and I could see Mark across the skirted tables. He sipped his water, looked at the menu and I had an overwhelming feeling of close-enough, what's the difference really, this table or that? I was convinced at that moment that the world was filled with Mark Foreworths, like I'd been wandering around in a forest of Mark Foreworths, large, solid, swaying trees, like I'd tagged one, a keeper, to bring home at the holidays.

"What the hell? Stay," the pilot-type said.

Now Mark had spotted me. His expression said, *What are you doing? Who's that?* I told the pilot, "I'm supposed to be over there."

"Right. Right," the pilot-type said. "This was really nice. We should do it again sometime."

"Yeah," I said. And I knew I'd miss the pilot. In fact, I did miss him. There was this immediate little pang.

I walked over to Mark's table. I explained the mix-up. Mark said, "That could only happen to you. Why is that?"

"I don't know," I said, but I was a little put out. It was the same kind of tone of my mother had when I was younger, her refrain: *What's wrong with you?* I changed the subject to Norman Rockwell, some stuff I'd read in a magazine. (It was certainly no speech on Modigliani.) Norman Rockwell—good ole Norman famous for painting fishing holes and barber shops, for taking the world and scrubbing it behind the ears—got a divorce from his first wife Irene. She remarried and drown herself in a tub. Norman and his second wife, Mary, had children together, but she suffered depressions and when she died one day—the children were grown by then—it was assumed she'd killed herself because she'd been teetering for years, but they were wrong. She'd simply died. Years later, Norman married Molly, and she was fit and sturdy, and they biked through town. "And they were happy," I said to Mark. "I'm pretty sure they were happy. But I don't know anything, really, about love."

"I like his paintings. Small-town America and all of that, little pink houses for you and me," Mark said.

"But people can look very happy, very normal, very all-American and it isn't really true, is it? I mean take the Foreworths, for example."

Mark said, "What's that supposed to mean?"

"Tell me something about your childhood. Something true and awful," I said. Was this wrong? I wasn't trying to trick him. I wanted him to tell me about Jarvis. I wanted him to be honest. I was hoping he would break.

"Well, just the regular stuff. You know. We gave each other charley horses, a lot of charley horses. Is that what you want to hear?"

"No," I said. "Don't worry about it." But I felt nauseous. I didn't want to eat the rest of my food. I knew that he wasn't capable of telling me the truth. I was an outsider, and oddly, knowing this didn't make him less loveable. Actually, it made him more real, more human and therefore more loveable. But it also made it clear that I couldn't live with him for the rest of my life. It wasn't my job to teach Mark Foreworth how to be honest about himself. Is that selfish? Maybe that's selfish or lazy. Maybe it's my fault, but I knew my own weaknesses well enough to know I couldn't see it through.

I picked at my food and during dessert, I started to cry.

"What's wrong?" he asked, leaning across the table so close our head nearly touched.

I said, "I have a birthmark on my inner thigh. Did you know that? It isn't a mole really or a freckle. It's just this stain, like tea. Did you know that?"

"What's wrong with you tonight? Where did all of this come from?"

"My father's going to live!"

"Of course he is," Mark said. "He's doing well."

I wasn't being Normal. I'd given up. Normal can't protect you because it doesn't exist. The Foreworths weren't Normal, despite all of their inexhaustible efforts. Nothing can save us. This wasn't a comfort but it was a relief.

I put it simply. "I want to get out." I should pause here,

shouldn't I? I should dwell on this moment. I should allow myself to feel it, not just go rushing on, all tough-guy, onward. But, honestly, I wasn't really all that aware of myself at that moment. Maybe it was the first time in a long time when I wasn't so self-conscious. The words were there in my head and I said them out loud.

"Get out of what?" Mark asked, but as he said it he knew what I meant. This, in hindsight, is an indication of how fragile the engagement was. Maybe he was expecting this. He looked down at his plate. "What are you talking about? We've gone public. Other people are involved."

I didn't say anything. I was—what was I? I was breaking his heart. There's nothing pretty here. It was my own heart, the chewed one, rearing up. It was Todd Foreworth in my class, spouting the truth, the loose track of time, my moles, Jarvis. It was my father not dying. It was the pilot. But also it wasn't any of these specific things. What I mean is that if it hadn't been these things then it would have been other things. I didn't love Mark Foreworth, not enough.

He was shocked, exasperated. "Are you crazy?"

"Maybe," I said. "Yes." I slipped the ring off of my finger and laid it on the table.

"Stop it," he said. "Put it back on." He pushed the ring back at me. It snagged the cloth and pulled some of it along.

I put the ring back on. This was stupid. We picked at our desserts without really talking. I looked across the big room, the skirted tables, the people feeding themselves, groping for silverware, for each other, laughing, chirping. The waiters buzzed brightly, automated, robotic. They clipped in and out of swinging doors, like a Western, like gunslingers on coke. This was a fragile world. It tilted on an axis and now I could feel the axis, gravity, the pull and heft of the world, somewhere out there the ocean rolling around.

After dinner, we walked out of the restaurant. The night was warm and windy. He said, "Just, just think about it."

I nodded.

But then he squeezed his eyes shut. His face tightened up like he was playing the sax, and I felt sick. It was the first time I'd seen him weak, and honestly, he wore it beautifully. (And here, it's probably unwise to say it, but maybe I was wrong. Maybe he was capable, after all, of a real vulnerability. After all, hadn't he said that it was just like me to open the door that I shouldn't have. He was mad about it at the time, but it was just like me—and wasn't that something that he needed from me?) He let the tears roll down his face.

And so, why did I go on, here. Why did I have to push? I guess I needed to know. I felt lied to. I was closer to some truth—some real truth about Mark and I wanted to see if I could get to it. I said, "What about Jarvis? Where is he?"

He shook his head.

"He's still alive," I said.

"Who said that?"

"Todd told me."

"This is about us," Mark said, "not Todd or Jarvis or my family. It's about us."

"This is about us not knowing each other."

"Just think about it." He rubbed his hands together, letting them fold over each other. "No, you're done. I know you're done. I don't want to talk about it. No," he said, to himself more than to me, "we don't need to go over it."

And he turned and walked away from me down the street. What if he'd wanted to talk about? What if he'd been dying to go over it? Maybe things would have worked out differently . . . no, no, it would have only prolonged things. (This relationship hasn't been sorted out very thoroughly in my mind yet. I can feel myself waffling. I apologize for the waffling.) I was sure that it was the right thing to let him go, but in the same breath, I was sure it was the wrong thing. I was sure that I'd just sealed my odd, lonesome fate. I would never be part of one of those happy couples, all Americana, with sunny children in scout uniforms. I was sure that I'd turn into one of those people who believe that their cats really understand them. I would have to get a cat.

Really, I was lonesome without Mark, but I didn't go back. I found myself banging around my apartment with long stretches devoted to misery—but it was a strange misery, because the split inside of myself was stitching back together and that felt good. (This confessing feels good.)

It helped that Mark punished me. He told me that the fact that I'd broken up with him was a blow to the delicate psyches of middle management and the secretarial pool and what could have been my own nice-smelling coworkers in public relations, not to mention his parents and our poor Archie and his little brother, Todd, who had enough problems connecting to the world!

It was a relief to hear him angry at me. I said, "You're right. This is irresponsible on my part."

The fact that I could be so rational only further aggravated the situation. There was the flurry of heated phone calls, a meeting at his place where I picked up my things, returned the ring, and one awkward bumping-into on the street where he was walking with a group of buddies from the office. We acted chummy and jokey about the whole thing for the sake of morale. But it was over, abruptly.

Another time, walking at dusk, I ran into the lady who vacuumed the sailboats into the carpeting. I'd seen her a few times, propping the ladies' room door open with a gray supply cart.

She touched my arm. "Oh," she said, "it's you. That Mark Foreworth! You deserve better. You will do better for yourself!" (Who didn't know?) I wanted to agree with her, more than anything. My eyes welled up. She patted my shoulder and lugged her industrial vacuum cleaner inside.

About two months later, Mark's brother called on a Friday night. He said, "Hey, what's up. This is Todd."

"Hi," I said. Kit and Jerome had never liked me, but they'd taken the engagement to heart, and I'm sure that had taken a good bit of effort. It didn't matter why he was calling. I didn't even question it. I wanted to apologize. "Look, I'm sorry about what happened. Tell your parents that I'm so sorry for putting everyone through all of this . . ."

"Mark wanted me to come over and pick up some of his stuff, but he didn't want to see you, you know, particularly."

"Okay. That's fine . . ."

"Can I just come over and pick it up? That's all."

"Sure."

He hung up. I gathered up a couple of CDs, a baseball cap. There wasn't much. I had a drink or two—three tops. Todd buzzed, and I let him up, opened the door. He was taller than Mark, but he'd never seemed taller before. He glanced around the living room, his hands in his pockets. He looked at me. "Nice place."

"It isn't really that nice." It still isn't. I have this old red velvet couch that I love and packed bookshelves and a coffee table that one of my artist friends made out of a surfboard. It isn't a look.

"It's better than living with your parents. Kit and Jerome have this dismal vibe."

"You want a beer?"

"Sure, thanks."

I walked to the kitchen. "Mark's stuff is in a box on the coffee table."

When I came back in, he was sifting through. I handed him the beer. "I don't give a shit about his stuff," he said. "Mark doesn't know I'm here." He stood up and stepped over the coffee table. He said, "I should go."

It didn't seem plausible in retrospect that he'd send Todd to pick up a few lousy things that didn't even fill a cardboard box. "Why did you come here then?"

Todd downed his beer. He put the can down on the lip of a bookshelf. He smiled softly. "I wanted to tell you that you did the right thing. And I was so fucking psyched. You made me really happy."

"I'm glad I made somebody happy."

"Mmmhmm. You're happy too, though." He leaned in closer. "Because he's Mark and he'll always be Mark, and everything will always go well for him. But this. But you. He failed you."

"I think I failed him." And I did.

"I'm not hung up on the details." He moved closer to me. "He didn't deserve you."

"Look, I'm old enough to be your mother."

"If you'd had me at what? Six? That's not possible."

"I'm old enough to be your babysitter."

"I'd like that."

This kind of thing went on and on. It was unrelenting. And I let Todd get really close to me, so close that I could smell his sporty deodorant, his toothpaste, even something that was purely him, and—this is another rocky part of the confession—I let him kiss me, too. It was a great kiss, soft and long. I can't think of a fucking rationalization that would make this okay.

I think that the truth was that even though I broke things off with Mark, I resented his superiority, in a way, because, I guess, life was easier for him than it was for me. This seems unfair to say. How can you judge someone else's burdens? He was longing. I can see that now. But still it seemed to me that Mark fit in more comfortably with the larger world. And I don't, not really. Neither does Todd. (And neither do you.) I agreed with Todd that Mark had failed me, in a way. And I knew that Mark would be just fine. He'd be better off in the end without me. He'd find a more graceful companion, one more adored, and they'd waltz through life. And I wasn't so sure about my own future.

And Todd. Sweet, mussy Todd. He was deserving, because he knew that there was more to me to be understood. He was pulled to me for more essential reasons. He was a good soul, struggling along as best he could. He was fucking happy, in his own way. He was fucking enjoying things. He was fucking admirable, fucking oddly chivalrous.

But I think you'll be relieved to know that we didn't have grudging sex. No unbuckling, unzipping, no stripping down, just enough—like a guilty life insurance salesman and his secretary up against a filing cabinet. It was just this slow kiss.

Did Mark ever find out? Was Todd compelled to tell him? Will he hold off until one Thanksgiving twenty years from now when something comes up about money or where they're kids are going to college or the larger affairs of the heart? *I kissed Jane after she broke off the engagement.* Who's Jane? one wife will ask or both, the future Mrs. Foreworths. And the original Mr. and Mrs. Foreworth, old now, careening around in their cardigans and boat shoes will register the long-forgotten name. (And where's Jarvis now? Is he in the padded room? Is he in an institution?) But then a kid will run in from the other room to announce a touchdown, and the dishes will be cleared. Maybe it'll just be a small family secret in a family that has much bigger secrets to keep.

It turns out that my family has a secret too. My parents loved each other all along. They were just idiots about it. Desperate idiots, flailing at love, needing it too much, despairing. And now they're finally generous. Even if their supplies of love are finite, they've figured out that life is too, and they're no longer rationing. My mother doesn't stare, dreamily, out the window. She doesn't wear her denim vest. And my father doesn't spend his days in the basement pondering the intricate mechanisms of clocks or brooding over his boxed-up versions of the past. They're still dreamy and brooding in their own ways, but they're pink now. Death swooped in, and they braced for it. They withstood. And now freshly doused by the grimmest reality of life—dying—they march on, heartily, heartful.

Your friend Curt is married to my great-aunt's brother-in-law's sister's daughter, Elaine. (That took excruciating mental configuring.) My parents couldn't make it, what with my father's condition. I was supposed to go to represent the joy of the family. I didn't bring Mark, as had been the plan when the invites arrived. I went without a date, and I met you by the not-dead cat. And here we are and what will become of us?

I can't remember your face. Were you thin in your ribs? Were your shoulders square? I heard somewhere that a man went blind and slowly he forgot what he looked like, completely, and it made him feel like he was no longer a body, but a soul. You're a soul. Should I even let you stuff yourself back into a body? Should I become myself again for you? How will we fit inside those skins?

You still have questions: Am I impervious? Will I refuse

to expose my underbelly? Will I die on you? Yep, if we last long enough, there will be times when I'm impervious, when I refuse to expose my underbelly, when I will die on you.

And what will you do? Will you leave? Will you comfort me? Will I comfort you?

Let me give it to you straight: I'm no peach. If you've read this last confession and if I'm just too much, me with my chewed-up heart and my restless ghosts, the bizarre adornments of my soul, my dogged memory and reckless ways, then that's alright. That's okay. These are confessions after all. And I'll just say this: You're going to be alright, John. In the end, you're going to be fine. And, though I've got no power to say so, not really any at all, everything is forgiven. Lisa would be proud. You are not one of those men.

The truth is that I don't regret stripping down with you in the coat closet even if nothing comes of the two of us. Because it seems to me that the greatest most ordinary sin is the act of passing people by. Yesterday I was walking home in the rain and I watched how we scurry around each other, how we ignore our humanity. There was a woman tugging her child along by the wrist, there was an old man taking shallow breaths under an awning, there was an Asian woman wrapping flowers in cellophane. I stopped and I looked into their faces, and I saw something like love, maybe love itself. I don't think that this would have happened without you and your stark honesty.

And, here, out of a fear that, for one reason or another, this will be the end of us, that we won't ever meet up again face to face, I want to admit that I love you. It isn't the kind of love you'd imagine or that I'd have suspected I'd ever feel. It's the kind of love that you're supposed to have for everyone, every stranger you pass by. But it's a love that I've never been capable of and it's come from knowing you, like this, and it has bled out into the world. And although this isn't clear, I can't explain it any better than that.

You and I, we didn't pass by, and we didn't let go, and even if this is all we have gotten—confessions, a kind of forgiveness, the frail kind that one human being can hand over to another—then that is good enough.

But just in case . . .

I live in Philadelphia. You live in New York. Equidistant is the unsuspecting town of Hopewell, New Jersey. Not that I'm trying to make any puns on Hoping well. I can't muster such cuteness at this point. It's just a nice little town on the train line. Little happens there. But I suppose it could bear two near-strangers showing up. It could handle them meeting at a hotel lobby bar, under a movie marquis, in a certain restaurant. Or, no, in the train station where people bustle and stall and get turned around, where people feel lost and unmoored, clutching their earthly possessions, their coats, searching for giant grillwork clocks. It seems fitting. (Or is this all overdone, overblown?)

Let's me say that this coming Saturday, I will be at the train station in Hopewell, New Jersey at four o'clock. I'll mill around. If you show up, you show up. If not, I'll understand.

But, if you do, I can't help but think, at some point, it seems like a giant conspiracy of unwitting strangers—Jodi and Michael, Eve and Elton, Lina and Pascal, Sunny and the Paglias, Maggie and the Foreworth brothers—who've arranged to create a train station scene, based on a series of our prolonged idiocy and grave errors and endless miscalculations? (Haven't we been sinning toward each other?) Maybe they'll haul us to the town of Hopewell where, if we get together a quorum and state our feeble case, the good people will confer unanimously, for better or for worse: *Oh, but these two deserve each other.* When has the small town of Hopewell last witnessed two more perfectly suited fuck-ups, two just-so unparalleled jackasses?

Perhaps never.

In fact, look the world over.

> With utmost, foremost, tendermost
> affection, and thump and zing,
> Jane (and Her Various Addictions)

CODA

April 4

The day starts well enough, anyway, one of those early April gifts: gold flashes off the Chrysler Building, the fangs of ice on the fire escapes melting, the handball players back at their meaty smacking, the farmers' market in Union Square teeming with fruit peddlers in knit caps. Only the cabbies are pissed, because the fine weather has people walking. A breeze sweeps down Broadway and across my cheeks, which are properly shaved (for once), and I'm properly dressed, too, hopped up on a jigger of cafecito and striding north toward Penn.

I tell the woman at the Amtrak counter I want a roundtrip to Hopewell, New Jersey. This is one of the benefits of living in New York City: you never worry about whether you can get to a particular place, because New York reaches everywhere. I'm busy checking myself in the glass partition between us, examining the angles of maximum sexiness, and in particular the articulation of my jaw muscles, when the woman glances up from her terminal. "No stop there," she says.

"Excuse me?"

"No Hopewell station."

I smile and tell her this must be a mistake, I have it on very good authority that there is a train station in Hopewell, which, by the way, is roughly equidistant from New York and Philadelphia. I then repeat the name: Hopewell.

The woman shifts in her seat. She is heavy-lidded, on the downside of fifty, plump and surly, perhaps professionally so. "Heard you the first time, bright eyes." She hands me a train schedule and smiles, utterly delighted to be able to puncture my bonhomie.

She is right, of course. You can stop in Newark and Princeton and Kendall Park. But you can't stop in Hopewell, because there is no Hopewell.

A series of thoughts occur to me, roughly in this sequence:

1) I've been had. There is no Jane. This entire sequence of letters has been a prank, rather an elaborate prank, and if I turn very slowly I will find an entire film crew assembled behind me, ready to capture my reaction for the inaugural episode of the Fox TV reality series Duped By Love.

2) I misread the letter. It didn't say Hopewell. It said Hopeville. Or Hopeshire. Or Hope-on-the-Hudson.

3) Jane is testing me.

4) Jane has made a mistake.

I rule out one—no film crew—and two doesn't seem possible. I admit to three as a slim and frankly annoying possibility, and conclude that four is most likely, given that Jane's attention to details is precise but idiosyncratic. (I see her as someone who might, unwittingly and with honest regret, allow a pet too die.) None of which bears on the question at hand: what am I supposed to do?

I could attempt to contact Jane. This would require a call to my friend Curt, whose number I do not have, a long potentially indicting explanation—Remember that chick at your wedding?

Tight dress, big green eyes, we almost fucked in the coat check,
yeah, her—along with the ability to reconstruct her familial connection to the wedding (something involving a great-aunt and
a cousin named Elise) and might also entail a discussion with
Penny, Curt's wife, who still holds me responsible (unfairly) for
the mermaid tattoo on his left buttock.

A small line has now formed behind and it's all suddenly
quite humiliating, because I can now see how much hope I've
piled onto this visit, how desperate I must look in my new sweater
and khakis and shiny, scented cheeks. Who is Jane, after all?
Some sexy sass merchant from the soggy side of Jersey, the
kind of woman who breaks off an engagement fourteen days
in, then French kisses her ex's kid brother for good measure. A
real catch. What I need to do is settle down, come to my senses,
at the very least head home to regroup.

And I'm just about to do that when Miss Amtrak looks up at
me. Her face has, inexplicably, softened.

"Used to be a stop in Hopewell," she mutters. "Few years
back. Station's still there. Fixed up pretty nice." She lifts her hand
from her dingy keyboard and beckons me closer. "Not hard to
get there, if you've got a good reason to. Just get off in Trenton
and take a cab." Before I can thank her, she turns back to her
terminal and her face goes blank again with the ancient reflex
of disinterest.

So, okay, now I'm figuring: what's the worst that can happen?
A film crew from Fox TV is waiting for me in Hopewell and I'm
reduced to a laughingstock on national TV. It was bound to
happen sooner or later.

Only it's a little more complicated than that, because the
cab driver in Trenton tells me he don't got permission to take a
fare to Hopewell, so I have to take a shuttle to the next town
over, Pennington, then walk through the slush to the taxi stand,

where the driver is happy to take me to Hopewell, but can't find the place. And because I've gotten a late start, and because I refuse, on principle, to buy food on trains, I'm starving, so that when I finally arrive my mood is lurching toward homicide.

The station in Hopewell is just as fucking quaint as billed, a red brick Victorian with a gilt railing and a widow's walk of new slate. And Jane is there, standing in a slant of light, against one of the tall windows, and my heart does this loopy little dance as I step from the cab because she really does look striking in her dark pea coat, a bit taller than I remember, with her hair pinned up around her neck and her big green eyes, and her beauty makes me want to forgive her instantly, which makes me feel entirely helpless (as I did at the wedding) and this, in turn, somehow makes me angrier, so that I don't know whether to ball her out or throw myself at her feet, a question she neatly elides by leaping toward me and losing her footing.

This is not a dainty little tumble, either, but a true, tailbone-crunching fall. "Wow," she says.

I hurry over to help her up. "Are you okay?"

She clambers to her feet, blushing and wincing at once. "Oh fine. Just a little ritual I perform before meeting potential soul-mates in obscure central Jersey townships."

"Seriously," I say, but she waves away my concern.

"Hey, I'm just happy you made it! Because the train, well, I guess you figured it out by now, there's no stop here. My friend Pete promised me there was a stop, he's such a goddamn flake, and of course so am I, because I didn't even check the schedule until this morning and then it was too late to call you, and I couldn't figure out how to reach you. I spent the morning trying to track your friend Curt down and I don't think he was very happy to talk with me, and by the time I got your number you must have already left. There are a couple of messages from me on your machine—ignore them, I was out of my mind—and anyway, after I'd left those it was too late to catch the train, so I just drove up." She glances at me, wrings her gloves a bit. "But you made it, anyway! Here you are. In the flesh. You look so handsome. Hey, do I even get a hug, you big lug?"

I give her hug, but something in the breathy rush of her words unsettles me.

"You're mad, aren't you?" she says.

"A little frustrated," I say. "I was sort of expecting an apology."

"Of course I'm sorry. Didn't I say that?"

"Not really."

Jane takes a step back. "Well, obviously I'm sorry. This is what I do when I'm nervous, I steamroll a little. But I'm very happy you're here. Are you going to be able to forgive me?"

I nod.

"Is that a real yes, or a yes-under-duress?

"No, It's real," I say. "I should have checked the schedule myself. I'm just grumpy because I haven't eaten."

"Oh," Jane says, "that we can fix. Low blood sugar is a curable disease. They've made real advances in the past decade."

So we set off down Hopewell's one street toward a restaurant called Soup De Jour where, despite my expectations, I am served a delicious bowl of red lentil and buttered bread. Jane has a Shirley Temple—shaken not stirred—and watches me eat. She's wearing a loose V-neck sweater that shows the pale skin at the base of her throat. Her lips leave delicate prints on the rim of her glass.

When she's sure I've had enough, she says, "Now listen, I'm not trying to be impervious, but this whole Hopewell mess was my idea, so I've cased the joint and here's what we could do: a quick stop at the Hopewell Museum, drinks and dinner at the Hopewell Valley Bistro, then maybe a play. There's a little theater where they pass around dessert at intermission. It sounds dangerously folksy, I know, but the options are limited. Then I deliver you wherever you might want to get delivered. How does that sound?"

"Good," I say. "I mean, we can alter the itinerary for photo ops and so forth "

"Of course," she says. "This is just so the paparazzi have a ballpark idea of our movements."

Jane sets down a twenty and smacks my hand when I try to give it back to her. "I may want to take advantage of you later," she says, loud enough that the little pothead behind the counter actually smirks. I watch her pass through the doorway. Her jeans are old and faded, snug across the bum, and I can see, as we head back into the dusk, that's she's limping a bit.

"You're hurt," I say.

"Not really. Maybe a little bit."

"Where?"

"Just about where you'd think."

"You should take some aspirin."

"When it comes to soft tissue contusions, I'm strictly a Valium gal," she says.

The museum turns out to be closed, so we head back down Hopewell's main (and only) drag, which is, I kid you not, 90 percent antique shops. I ask Jane if she wants to browse, but she shakes her head. "Gifts from the dead. Family's should hang on to their heirlooms."

"You sound like your father," I say.

"Oh God, do I? But that's not what I mean. My dad doesn't know crud from an heirloom. To him, a ball of yarn and a pearl brooch are equals. I just mean there's something ghoulish about raiding the family crypt for sellable possessions."

"I'm not sure anybody's really raiding any crypts."

"You know what I mean. Antiques are always marked by this shadow of the previous life."

I'm not really sure I do know what she means, and I can tell that Jane knows this and is a little annoyed and I'm annoyed at her annoyance, actually, but rather than get into all that I ask her how her father is doing, though the moment this question comes out of my mouth I can hear how phony it sounds.

She tells me he's doing fine and asks how my mother is and I say fine and we walk another block in silence. She's back to wringing her gloves. We make a few more stabs at banter. But we can both feel the strain. There's no liquor to rescue us this time, no sexy cloak of anonymity, and we can't revise ourselves (or idealize each other from a distance) and we know far too much about each other and not nearly enough. So we're stuck dragging our bodies through the dusk.

Jane sets her hand on my arm and I stop and turn to face her.

"This is harder than I thought it would be," she says.

"Yeah. I was noticing that."

"Too much pressure."

"Way too much pressure."

"I feel like a mail-order bride or something."

"Precisely."

"Or like I'm walking into an arctic wind, buck naked, with a huge sack of history digging into my spine." She lets out an exasperated sigh, blows a strand of hair out of her eyes. "Maybe we should just pass notes back and forth."

"Look," I say. "Let's just take a mulligan."

"What's a mulligan?"

"Like in golf."

"You play golf?"

"No, it's just a term, like a do-over. We need to just start this over from the beginning. Sort of lower the heat a little. And we need some wine. Not a lot. Just enough to stop judging our-selves. So, I mean, what do you think?"

"Do I have to fall on my ass again?"

"No," I say. "But we should do another hug. Can we do another hug?"

Yes. Yes we can, a nice long hug that conveys the rough contours of our bodies through all the wool and cotton, and the smell of her hair (peach), and her perfume (closer to cinnamon) and a glancing kiss that's pure seventh grade.

"I thought we were supposed to lower the heat," she says.

"I misspoke," I say, and my mouth moves to the cuff of her ear.

The bar at the Hopewell Valley Bistro is attractively dim, a little smoky, the kind of place where the landed gentry might come for an extramarital martini or five. We stick with wine (red) and olives (black) and Jane tells me all about the Lindbergh baby kidnapping, which is the town's lone claim to infamy. She has written about the case, as one of the earliest examples of media frenzy.

She is, by the way, no fan of Lindbergh, whom she refers to as a Nazi sympathizer. ("He was big on racial purity. How's that for high-flying heroism?") The subject brings a high color to her cheeks, which I am suddenly tempted to lick. The wine may be a contributing factor.

She is particularly fascinated by the photo of the child's body, which was found three months after his abduction. "They forced Lindbergh to come and identify the kid. I don't know how he did that. There was quite a bit of decomposition, no face to speak of, no skin, no soft tissue. Various animals had gotten at the body. Can you imagine?"

I shake my head and Jane smiles, almost shyly. "I'm being macabre again, aren't I? I'm a bit focused on the macabre."

"Michael Hanrahan's thumb did seem to come up a lot."

"That was my leitmotif," she says.

"Very sexy," I say. "Very digital age."

Jane pours the last of our first bottle and takes a long sip and gazes at me. "I never told you about Jennifer Song, did I?"

"No," I say.

"Wow. I probably should have told you about her. I mean, I'm not sure how much it will explain. It doesn't really fall within the rubric of romantic misdeeds."

"Who's Jennifer Song? Does she wind up with Hanrahan's thumb? Is that where this is headed?"

Jane reaches beneath the table and sets her hand on my thigh and her hand is very soft and sure of itself there, so that, for a moment, I feel certain we've reached the point of sexual initiation. Then she pinches my thigh, hard. "This is serious."

"Okay," I say. "Tell me."

She takes a deep breath. "Actually, I'm not sure I should get into all this."

"Oh no you don't. You can't just say that then not tell me the story."

(Did I mention that we've already drunk one bottle of wine?)

"Alright," Jane says. "Fine. Here's goes. Jennifer Song was a girl in my sixth grade class. We sat next to each other. Her father was Asian. He was distantly related to the family who ran the Chinoiserie on the corner. Her mom was white, vaguely Irish I guess, a volunteer in the school library. Jennifer had long black hair, all the way down to her waist, and a slight stammer. She must have been twelve. One Tuesday, after school, she walked her bike to the gas station to fill her tire with air. I was supposed to go with her. That was the plan. But my mom sent a note through the school nurse that I was to head directly home, which is something my mother, as you could probably guess by now, did a lot. You know why she needed me home, John?

You know what the emergency was? She needed help canning tomatoes. That was the emergency."

The water arrives with another dish of olives and Jane fumbles at them with her fingertips and wipes at the napkin in her lap.

"Jennifer Song didn't make it to the gas station. Her bike was found in a dumpster two days later. By then, they'd mimeographed her picture and tacked it up all over town. It was her school picture. I had a small version of it in my wallet. Because we were about to become good friends. We were just on that threshold. I'd been over to her house to play just two days earlier. And if I'd gone with her to the gas station—because, you know, she had this plan that we'd ride our bikes all the way down to the main library. She talked about it all Sunday. She was going to show me how to use the micro fiche machines." She lets out a soft laugh. "I wasn't much of a library girl, to be honest."

"What happened?" I say.

Jane looks at me and for a second I feel quite stupid and male, because no woman would ever ask such a question, because they would know what happens in such stories.

"I don't even remember my mother telling me that Jennifer was missing or how I got the news. I'm sure my lurid little imagination cooked up all sorts of images: the silt from the riverbed streaking her body, her mouth and eyes open wide, the solemn expression she wore in chorus, all that kind of thing. What I remember, though, is how everything continued on. We filed past her empty desk every day. We stood in front of the mirrors teasing our hair. Her mother disappeared from the library. And my mother: she felt she'd saved my life. Over and over again, she told me, I don't even like to think about what could have happened to you. But sometimes it seemed like that was all she ever thought about."

Jane's pretty face has gone queerly still. It's nothing I've seen before. At the wedding she was all velocity, a restless prowler at the edge of things, a graceful dervish, fast talking and fast moving. But now, alone with her in the crepuscular gloom of this bistro, she's frozen.

"Are you alright?"

She nods. "I don't even know why I got into all this."

"It's important," I say. "It sounds important."

"Yeah?" she says. "How so? I mean, what do you make of that story, John?"

"You really want to know what I think?"

"That's why I asked."

I look at the wine bottle, which is empty now, a little contrite looking, and listen to the bustle of the Saturday night crowd around us, a polite, monied bustle, as one might expect in a place called Hopewell. "I think you wanted to escape your mother, the limitations of her world, and she knew this and so she constructed some fantasy that she could protect you. And I think you helped her out with that, throwing yourself at all those dangerous characters, because you felt guilty for wanting to leave her. And you're still helping her out, by fixing your mind on all the perils of the world. You should be able to see that. I mean, you've got *my* mother nailed. What you wrote, about her fear of love that was totally on the money. You have a right to leave the nest, you know. Being strong doesn't make you heartless."

Jane stares at me, tired, maybe a little skeptical, but she doesn't say anything.

"Anyway, that's what I think. Maybe I said too much, or it's some kind of horseshit psycho-babble. But you asked for my opinion."

We sit in silence for several long moments, waiting to see which way the mood will turn. Jane shakes her head. Her hair has started to come loose around her shoulders. "You really are an earnest little shit, aren't you? How do you do it? Don't you ever get tired of all the scrutiny?"

"I take it you're mad at me."

Jane shakes her head and grins. "No, you lummox. I'm trying to pay you a compliment."

"So that was a compliment. Are your insults that ambiguous?"

"Afraid not."

"Anyway, I'm sorry. I didn't mean to get all intense."

"No," Jane says sharply. "Don't do that. You don't have to apologize. I was the one who got us on the subject."

"Okay," I say. "I just mean I'm sorry if this conversation is, whatever, too intense, or upsetting."

"Now listen, John: you don't need to worry about me so much. That's one thing I need to tell you: stop being so damn careful. Don't treat me like china. Because, frankly, I find it a little condescending. And I'm not saying this in anger, believe me. I just mean that you can let it rip with me. I'm not like your mom, in that way at least. I'm not a big grudge holder. I promise you. I'm something of a pushover deep down. You should know that by now. So you can just tell me what you're thinking." She runs her hand over the table and looks at me. "Understood?"

"Okay," I say. "If that's the case, I'd like to talk about Mark Foreworth."

We're both struggling not to be snippy, defensive, all the old feints. But as I say this, I can feel a suspiciously pleasant pang of righteousness in my gut.

"What about Mark?"

"Well, frankly, I found that relationship very strange and troubling, and given that it's your most recent one, I mean, it's hardly a cause for hope."

Jane regards her empty wine glass. "I was trying to be honest, not inspirational."

"Because, I mean, I get that he was wrong for you. And he was avoidant and he didn't understand the full depth of your dark world of bullshit and all that. But you were so cruel to him. Really, Jane. The guy doesn't want to talk about his brother, it's obviously more than he can bear, and you treat it like a personal betrayal. And then you dump the guy. And you know who you were really angry with: yourself. Because you were the one who got yourself into that situation. Okay? Okay?" My voice has gotten a little louder for the venue—the couple next to us may be glancing over—and my eyes are sort of jumping around. "So that's what I think."

"Okay," Jane says. She is gazing steadily at me.

"Because you asked."

"I did."

I sit back in my chair, try to sort of settle myself down, or brace myself or something.

"Are you through? Because now I'd like to say something."

"Of course," I say.

"Here's what I'd like to say: you're right. I was angry at myself for making such a lousy bargain, choosing comfort over the deeper forms of understanding I claim to want. And nothing undoes the basic facts. I broke his heart, and I shouldn't have accepted it in the first place. I behaved badly. Honestly, I wanted to love him more. I wish I didn't have a darker world of bullshit. I often wish I were a better person. So you're right about Mark. So thank you. And also, your eyebrows do this wonderful dip thing when you're angry, and they make you look sexy. So that got me a little turned on, which is definitely perverse, but there you have it."

Jane smiles and my cheeks flush instantly. She leans forward and her sweater brushes the table and I wonder if we're going to kiss again.

"There's something else," she says.

"Of course," I say. My voice is all breathy and hopeful, because I'm thinking about that kiss, the wet warmth of her mouth, the softness of her lips, parted just slightly now. *Kiss me*, I think. I'm so ready for that, ready to close my eyes and make a wish.

"I've been thinking about your relationship with Maggie," Jane says. "I know I'm supposed to be happy you ended things with her, but it makes me sad. Partly, I suspect, because Maggie's rougher beginnings remind me of my own. But mostly because I can see that old superiority complex of yours still humming away and the thought of having to battle that makes me tired, physically tired." Jane sighs softly. "I'm not perfect, John. I'm never going to be perfect. I'm going to screw up in ways yet unforeseen, perhaps on a daily basis. And I don't mind if you hold my feet to the fire. I realize—the world realizes—that you're an insightful guy. But you can't use that insight as a weapon. It's not enough to be right, not in love. You also have to be forgiving. So that's my little lecture. Any questions?"

"We're not going to kiss now, are we?"

"No, not right now we're not."

"Is this stuff going to be on the final?"

"Come on, now. Be serious. This is serious."

"Alright," I say. "Look, I can't argue with you. Don't get me wrong, I'd like to be able to argue with you. But the evidence is in: I can be a real snob. What can I tell you? It's something I'm working on."

"Okay," Jane says. "That's all I'm asking. You work. I work. We keep each other honest. So listen: I have to go to the bathroom now, not because I'm upset or want to put on more lipstick or anything like that, but because the wine has made its way through my system. So you stay right here and I'll be back in a second. Then we can eat."

Actually, though, I have to pee as well (does this count as work?) so I head to the bathroom and when I arrive back at the table the wine glasses have been cleared, and I stand there for a second, alone, sure that Jane has ditched me. Then I hear her voice rising above the muted clinks of the main room. She's seated at a corner table, beaming, a candle lighting her cheeks in the manner of a De La Tour.

I sit down across from her and pretend to read the menu. I know we're supposed to move back to the flirty stuff, the wooing, but my mind has been sort of churning. "Can I say one other thing, Jane? It's about Jarvis, though I might as well be saying this about Hanrahan or Elton or Jennifer Song. And I know this isn't going to sound very profound, but I think it's important. There's no need to go looking for danger, because, I mean, it's unavoidable. It's the price of living. And love is its own form of danger, but it's also a form of bravery. And that's all I have to say except that you look really pretty right now and I'm sorry for being such a grump before and I'd like another bottle of wine and I'm going to order something with garlic, for which I apologize in advance."

Before any more plangency can ensue the waiter arrives and we get ourselves another bottle of wine and the conversation over dinner is light and easy. Jane tells me about this meathead football player she taught a couple of years ago, who thought misogyny was a form of yoga. But I can tell from her tone that she loves her students, especially the meatheads. She's one of those teachers (like good old Mr. Park) a little self-indulgent and theatrical, but hoping, always, with every gesture and sentence, to light the flame of learning. I tell her about the opening I attended last week and how the artist, a woman called Bone, who paid homage to Karen Finley (I think) by performing an indecent act with a giant Hershey's Kiss.

The food arrives. It is glorious to watch Jane eat. She plows through the green figs stuffed with gorgonzola, moves on to the risotto with shaved parmesan, and eats half the grilled eggplant on orzo. I don't mean that she's indelicate. The word that comes to mind is concerted. Or better still, enthused. She does a lot of appreciative moaning. We move steadily, judiciously, through the second bottle of wine, and when the waiter asks if we want to see the dessert menu Jane says, "I thought you'd never ask."

"Aren't we going to get dessert at the play?"

"Oh, that's right."

We are (I guess I should make this clear) a little drunker than I've been letting on.

"Give us a minute," she says to the waiter. "Here's the thing about the play."

"Yeah?"

"Well, first things first, it's "The Taming of the Shrew," which, I mean, let's not even start in on that. But the main thing, well, two things. First, the guy playing Petruchio has a lisp. That's the first thing. *For I am wough and woo not wike a babe!* I'm having trouble feeling his biscuit. And the second thing, the woman playing Kate is about twenty years too old for the part, a real community theater Blanche DuBois."

"How do you know all this?"

"I got the lowdown from the guy at the Mobil station. He's the understudy for Lucentio. He might just be bitter. He sounded a little bitter. But, I mean, even if we look past those things, it would still be one of those experiences, you know, the little play that could, the hand-painted sets, the hammy deliveries, the soggy pound cake and plastic forks, and we'd sit there either snarking at these folks, which is wrong, or bearing it all in hopeful seriousness, which, I'm sorry, I don't think I can quite manage right now."

"That's fine with me," I say. "I can live without the Bard tonight. But we should make a plan."

"Oh, I've got a plan," she says.

The plan begins with mocha pudding and two spoons and an aperitif (cognac) and proceeds, rather sloppily, to a second aperitif and some light necking across the table. I insist on paying and Jane insists on leaving the tip, which includes her hair clip. "It's sadistic, tyrannical," she says, "a little Napoleon of a hair clip."

We stumble into our coats and proceed into the night, where a light snow is falling, dusting the new brick of the non-train station. The cognac is sitting rather nicely, a small flame beneath the ribs. Further up the road, older couples in cashmere coats and mink mufflers are heading off to the play. Jane grabs my hand and swings me toward the parking lot behind the station. There, sitting ominously alone, is what I can only describe as a large, automotive vessel. It is canary yellow.

"That isn't yours," I say.

"Oh, you poor Californian. You really don't know anything about Jersey, do you? We don't drive imports in these parts. May I introduce you to the granddaddy of all muscle cars, the 1967 Gran Turismo Omologato?" She bounds over to the car and runs her hand along the trim, game-show style. "Under this expansive hood, you will find an eight-cylinder, 400-cubic-inch monster, with fuel injection, a wazoo Richmond 6-speed and dual exhaust. Zero to sixty in the mid sixes."

"But the car you had at the wedding "

"A rental. This is my official vehicle. The engine is so powerful in this beast they were almost recalled. That's American engineering for you: all juice, no suspension."

"And you're going to drive this thing? Right now?"

"Actually," she says, "you're going to drive it."

"Funny," I say.

But Jane is not kidding. She throws me the keys and hops in the passenger seat. "Come on," she says, slapping the window. "Get your ass in the vehicle. I'm freezing." Something of the primordial Asbury Park has risen up inside her. She rolls down the window and makes her face into a lurid pout. "Haven't you ever wanted to drive down a dark road with the wind in your hair? Come on, Thunder! Live a little."

"Now listen," I say, "We've both had a fair bit to drink. I don't know any of the roads around here. It's snowing. And you're asking me to drive a car with the propulsive capabilities of a rocket. I ask you: Is this a wise decision?"

"Oh, please. What are you going to hit, an antique bidet?"

She really does look adorable in her massive bucket seat. "Alright," I say. "But only if you promise to hang out the window half naked."

"Alright. But only if you promise to come in your own mouth later."

"Deal," I say.

I slip into the driver's seat and examine the various devices (the speedometer tops out at 180 mph) and start the engine. The accelerator is ridiculously responsive. I practically fishtail pulling out of the parking space. The denizens of Broad Street look up in alarm as the car rumbles past.

"You see," Jane says. "Hopeville loves us! The whole town."

"Hopewell."

"Doesn't it feel good?" Jane cuddles up next to me. "All that power!"

"It feels great," I say, which is actually true. "But I'd feel better if you put on your seat belt."

"Sure, sure. But let's get on the highway first."

"Where's that?"

"It's around here somewhere."

Yes, somewhere. For the moment, we're winding through Hopewell, which is not quite a town anymore, but a series of estates, manor houses, faux Victorians, with driveways like long black tongues and barren shade trees and vast lawns.

"This must be the other half," I say.

"More like three-quarters," Jane says. "Welcome to the central Jersey of my mother's dreams: the land of tax shelters and conservation easements and undetectable accents. But can you imagine living in one of these atrocities, with the Doric columns and the butler pantry and the stables out back? God, wealth bores me. It's such a primitive scoreboard. Where the hell is that highway, John?"

The snow is falling harder now and the heating vents are pumping the smell of burned rubber into the car and I have no idea where we are. Finally, we come to a larger road and Jane claps.

"Yes! This is it! Route 51. Good old route 51!" She's screaming now, because she's rolled her window down again and despite the cold I can see her shrugging out of her coat, reaching around to fiddle with something on her back.

"What are you doing over there?"

"Just keep your eyes on the road, buster."

She's got about half her torso over the edge of the sill, a posture I recognize from my surfing days as a double back. The dark, manicured farmlands of Central Jersey are whipping past, neat rows of corn stubs and a lone cow that registers as a faint shape against the snow-covered pastures.

"Faster," Jane shouts. "Open this thing up, John."

I feel lighthearted, intoxicated by the bulky power of the vehicle. Out of the corner of my eye, I can see Jane slip her bra from one of the sleeves of her sweater and toss it onto the floorboard. "I promised you, didn't I?" she yells. Then there's a sudden flash of fabric and I glance over for a second and there she is, her sweater pulled up around her neck, her hair flying around her shoulders and her breasts in the biting wind.

They're just as goddamn sexy as hell, those tits of her, the wobbly swerve of them and the goosebumps and flecks of snow sticking. And it occurs to me, in that pale half-second of seeing her, that I will never meet another woman quite like this, by which I don't just mean a college professor capable of baring herself on a winter highway (though this is, in and of itself, a pretty rare order) but a woman as eager to throw herself at the world, as ecstatic for the grand mischief of life, as alive. And I suppose it's this realization that causes me to tap the accelerator, give it a little extra gas, a kind of gesture of celebration or exorbitance that causes the car to wobble. Jane starts to howl. I start to howl. "Faster," she yells. "Come on, Thunder! It's a straightaway!"

I can see, also, that Jane is testing me (duh) that she must have done the same thing all those years ago with poor soon-to-be-thumbless Michael Hanrahan, steering him onto those empty highways, tearing past the shore in her naked skin, ravenous for a way out. Yes, I get it. Her sense of power has gotten all mixed up with reckless male behavior. Surely, the sensible thing is to slow down and let the back end stabilize. But of course, I am a male, underneath all my skirts of caution, and something reveals itself in me just then, a kind of answering pride, or maybe simply the desire to scare her into self-recognition, whatever it is, I give the gas another tamp and the car bolts ahead, seeming actually a little smoother than before, though still terribly loud, and then, rather suddenly, I spot something in the headlights, a small creature in the road, a white, animate lump, and I hit the brakes and the car starts to shudder again and then—I'm not sure how this happens—but we're in some kind of a skid. Jane is thrown back against her seat. The back end carries us across the divider, into the other lane, off the road then back again, both of us screaming in terror now, the car only vaguely under my command, zigzagging, ready to fling into a full and permanent disaster. I can hear Mr. Chopra, my driver's ed instructor, urging me to turn into the skid and I suppose that's what I do, though my hands feel pointless on the wheel, at the mercy of some larger force, and time has slowed down, a kind of lazy tumult during which the world snaps into sharp focus, as we lip onto the shoulder, toward the snow bank and the trees beyond, and I think: Lisa. Of course, my sister, my beautiful ghost, are you there waiting for me?

My foot is still on the brake and the tires are bouncing on the frozen pebbles of the shoulder, zooming toward the tree line, and Jane's hands are clutching at my body and then they're gone and I miss them terribly and there's a loud screech, a burst of yellow, a soft, metallic crunch, and we're thrown forward hard enough to slam our forearms into the dash. Only Jane, for some reason, is curled around facing me and I look down and see her hand—it's wrapped around the emergency brake, which she has somehow yanked nearly vertical.

We say, in the ensuing silence, all the things we're supposed to. Oh my God. Jesus. Are you okay? Are you? We examine our limbs, the miracle of our bones unbroken, our faces unsmashed, and the snow falls and radiator is throwing steam from the hood. Jane is shivering, breathing in gulps. "Fuck," she says. "Oh, fuck. That was so fucking stupid. Jesus, John."

"It's okay," I say. "We're okay. You saved us."

I want to hug her, but her face has taken on that same queer stillness, the blood all drained away, and her hand remains on the brake, clenched and trembling, while her other hand pulls her sweater down taut. She is, I think, a little in shock. I get out of the car and stand stiffly. I can't be sure, but I may have sprained my wrist. I look up, through the snow, and it's clear what we've hit: the bottom of a sign reading: *Shoulder Ends.* And below that, 20 mph.

Jane emerges from the car and joins me and stares up at the sign and suddenly she's burrowing into me. "We would have died," she whispers.

"But we didn't die," I say.

"But we would have! And it would have been my fault! My fucking fault!"

"No," I say. "You saved us. You kept us from crashing."

"You don't understand!"

"What? What don't I understand?"

"I knew, John! I knew! I knew!"

And then she begins sobbing, and clings to me with a kind of hysterical fervor, so that all I can do is hold her and say, "It's okay. We're alive. It's over."

After a few minutes, a car pulls up and the light pools around us. I turn, fearing a siren. But it's some overgrown SUV. A deep voice from the driver's side says, "You okay there, son? You need me to call the police?"

"Just a little spin out," I say. "The car's okay, I'm pretty sure."

Jane is still attached to my torso. "We need to get back in the car," I say. "Okay, honey?"

I'm a little stunned at my own poise. I feel tired, but oddly buoyant. The key is still in the ignition. I turn it and the engine squeals disconcertingly, then dies. The prospect of the cops, given our circumstance (not to mention our blood alcohol level) is not exactly welcoming. I remove the key and pump the accelerator, an old trick from Mr. Chopra, and this time the engine turns over. The SUV flashes his lights. I give him a honk of thanks and watch him pull back onto 51. It takes every ounce of strength in both my arms to release the emergency brake.

Last call at the Hopewell Valley Bistro is 11:00 p.m. We beat it by five minutes and seat ourselves in the darkest booth. We had hoped to find a non-alcoholic option, some empty diner reminiscent of Hopper, but this being Hopewell, only the Bistro is still serving. Our drive back to town was virtually silent, not unpleasant, but quiet and bruised, and now we're sitting next to one another, our faces bathed in a steam of apple cinnamon tea.

Jane's hair is loose and wild; think Kim Novak after her weekend with the Wild Ones. I can see a few strands of gray threading the light brown waves. She lets a golden band of honey spiral into her tea.

"I don't know what got into me," she says. "Some stupid juvenile energy. It's been a while since I've been this worked up, I guess."

"You didn't force me. I was the one driving."

"But I started it," she says. "I baited you."

"And I took the bait."

We sip our tea and gaze at the bartender, who is shooting us somber little daggers of please finish and leave.

"What was that thing in the road?" I say. "That animal."

"A cat," Jane says.

"No. It couldn't have been a cat. A raccoon, maybe. Or a opossum."

"It was a cat," Jane says. "We passed it on the way back."

"You're bullshitting me."

"No," Jane says quietly. "I'm serious. I saw it on the way back, just sitting by the side of the road, calm as you please."

"Why didn't you say something?"

"Shock, I guess." She shakes her head and takes another sip and her hand slips into mine, smooth and warm. "I just need to say, let me just say sorry again. Okay?"

"It takes two to tango," I say. "Besides, you were the one

bailed us out. If you hadn't cranked the emergency brake, well, I don't want to quote your mother "

"No," Jane says. "Please don't."

"But I still don't know how you managed to get that thing all the way up."

"Abject panic is a great motivator." Down below the table, Jane runs a finger along my palm. "I'm glad you're not mad."

"We're alive. We're safe now, more or less. The GTO is relatively intact. And we are not, despite your long history of public nudity, under arrest."

"No," she says. "There's that."

We're both silent for another minute, sipping our tea.

"There's just one thing I'm wondering about," I say. "What did you mean back there, when you said, 'I knew'?"

Jane's hand goes limp and she looks away for a second and when she looks back her eyes are wet. She says a single word, but so softly I can't make it out. "What?" There's a long pause. "Lisa," she whispers finally.

"What?"

"Lisa. I knew that she died in a crash. Oh God. I'm going to start crying again, dammit."

And she does start weeping, much more tenderly this time, and I reach to hold her again, but Jane places her hands on my chest, so she can face me.

"No," she says. "Let me say this. I've been wanting to say this for the last two months, how sorry I am for your loss. Because Lisa, she really was your first love, wasn't she? And I knew that, before all the others, she was there, and then she left you and then she died in that horrible accident. I'm so sorry, John. That must make you so frightened, to lose someone you loved so much."

Jane stares up at me with her red nose.

And I know she's right. The ache of that loss isn't something I can undo. But there are things I can do: I dry Jane's cheeks with cuff of my sweater and kiss her, lightly, on the crown of her forehead.

"I probably am frightened. I won't be forever, though."

"Why not?"

"Because she's gone," I say slowly. "And we're still here."

We finish our tea and head outside again, onto Broad Street, past the theater, where the crowd is just letting out, older couples arm in arm, looking a little defeated by the play, a little revived by the cool air.

"What's a combless cock?" one of the men demands of his wife, and a woman behind them says, "You mean you comb yours, Bob?" and they all crack up.

"Cock," Jane says.

"Cock cock," I say.

"Cock cock cock."

Agreed.

A little farther out, there's a park with stately oaks and maples and walking trails and a gazebo in the middle. We wander onto one of the trails, trying to find a good rhythm, not saying much of anything.

The heart can only bear so many words. That's what Jane tells me, when, at last, we stop on the steps the gazebo. She's one higher than me, which brings us to the same height and her huge green eyes bear into mine.

"What do we do now?" I say.

"Kiss."

"Oh yeah."

Our lips slowly meet and open and our hands slip inside one another's coats, burrowing for warmth. The snow is still falling, lightly, as if the moon were emptying itself of ashes and there's no sound but our joined breath and no smell but perfume and wet wool and no taste but apples and honey on her tongue.

"Do you want to sit," I say. "There's a bench."

She shakes her head. "I'm still a bit sore."

"From the crash?"

"No, from before. The fall."

"Where's it hurt?"

"My bum."

"Do you suppose there's any swelling?"

"You might want to check on that."

I slip my hand below the lip of her panties. "Here?"

"Lower."

"Here?"

"Yeah."

"Is it tender?"

She nods.

"So smooth."

"Not swollen?" she murmurs.

"Not too bad."

She reaches around and slips her hand beneath my boxers and we stand, leaning into one another, touching.

I start to ask her about what comes next, where we go, whether alone or together, the great hovering future of hours and days.

And that's when she says it, tells me to shut up in the kindest possible way: the heart can only bear so many words.

"I'm just worried about the time," I whisper.

Jane sets her fingers to my lips and kisses my neck. An owl hoots. The snow falls. The wind draws us closer. All around, the ghosts of our lovers are there, dancing, stubbornly alive, mad with envy and hope, waiting to see what comes next.

"We have time," Jane says. She lets her head loll to one side and shuts her eyes and smiles. "Trust me, loverboy." Her lips reach forward to kiss me again. "We do."